THE REPARTEE BEFORE THE STORM

The wolf, the man who claimed to be Ambrose Bierce, had no trouble finding me, and he pulled up a stool next to mine at the bar. Again I noticed his eyes, as black as a witch's cat and every bit as curious.

"I prefer you without a mustache," I said when he failed to speak. "I don't feel like I'm looking into the face of a walrus. And it's easy to tell when you're smiling."

Ambrose caressed his clean-shaven chin. "There is a school of thought which holds that after forty a man's responsible for the face he has."

"Hm. Your face is completely unlined." I pointed out gently. "I think the theory must therefore be flawed. If you're really Ambrose Bierce, of course."

"I sleep the sleep of the just these days." He smiled slightly and gestured to the bartender. A shot glass of whisky came skating down the polished smoothness of the bar.

"There's a similar saying about women's faces," I remarked, taking a sip. "After forty, you'd better give your face to Estée Lauder or you get what you deserve."

Other books by Melanie Jackson:

MELANIE JACKSON

DIVINE FANTASY

LOVE SPELL

NEW YORK CITY

LOVE SPELL®

February 2009

Published by

Dorchester Publishing Co., Inc.
200 Madison Avenue
New York, NY 10016

ISBN 10: 0-505-52803-7
ISBN 13: 978-0-505-52803-2
E-ISBN: 1-4285-0604-7

The name "Love Spell" and its logo are trademarks of Dorchester Publishing Co., Inc.

Printed in the United States of America.

10 9 8 7 6 5 4 3 2 1

Visit us on the web at www.dorchesterpub.com.

For my friend, Susan Squires, who also knows about the world of big, bad wolves and the things that go bump in the night.

DIVINE FANTASY

Prologue

Call a code!

Where's the crash cart! Damn it—she's just a kid! Where are the parents?

Light her up!

All around me I heard the panicked voices. I didn't know what they meant, except that I was in trouble. Again.

I was four. I didn't call for my mommy. I didn't call for anyone. Because I knew that no one would come.

Man, *n*. An animal so lost in rapturous contemplation of what he thinks he is as to overlook what he indubitably ought to be. His chief occupation is extermination of other animals and his own species, which, however, multiplies with such insistent rapidity as to infest the whole habitable earth and Canada.

—Ambrose Bierce, *The Devil's Dictionary*

Chapter One

I want to tell you a story about a rather repressed girl who ran a long, long way from home. In fact, she ran so long and so hard that she made it all the way to the far side of the planet from where she began. There she stopped to catch her breath because she was tired, and also because she was about as far away from home as she could get. And it was in Fiji, on the little rocky islet called Dolphin Island, that this story of danger and romance really begins.

Now, I'll admit straight off that running away from home isn't the mature way to handle most problems; in fact, it is in many cases an idiotic and cowardly thing to do. Sadly, this wasn't the first time that I had run away, or done something idiotic and cowardly. But I have found that running is generally a fast solution, and in some circumstances it is effective, such as when there is no chance of winning a battle if you stay and fight. And since every cloud has a silver lining, I can say that past experience always helps when doing stupid things, so I am confident that I will somehow survive my latest misstep . . . though bookies would probably rate me as a long shot. It's also doubtful that any insurance company would let me take out a policy.

Why did I run away from a job and a nice apartment with an excellent seasonal view of the chorus of the Bavarian Nutcracker ballet carried out in the streets and open-air markets? Let me respond to this as Socrates might, by answering a question with a question. Have you ever spent a Christmas in Bavaria? Or Switzerland or Denmark? Or any place in the icy north that is desperately picturesque but also desperately cold and dark, especially when you are all alone? Well, I have—and too damn many of them. First in Vermont at a boarding school I detested, and then in Munich. In the beginning with a lover, and then without.

Truth to be told, I've never enjoyed Christmas anyway. I know that will make some of you sad, and I would like to tell you that things were different in happier times like childhood, but there were no happier holiday times. Not in *my* childhood. I grew up unwanted, almost an orphan—though without an orphan's hope that some other family would fall in love with me and take me home. I spent Decembers feeling like a young Ebenezer

Scrooge ditched at boarding school while every-one else got to have presents and turkey and, above all, time with a loving family. It's always been envy of others' seasonal happiness, pure and simple, that makes me hate the holidays. An ugly sin, envy, but I think understandable in the circum-stances. Maybe.

In recent years, I'd thought that I'd evolved emotionally and reached a sort of peace with the holiday, that a form of détente was at last achieved and I was provisionally safe being happy—or at least unafraid—in December. I foolishly believed that this state of affairs could last even without Max in my life. But last year, three days before Christmas, as I wandered the winter bazaar in Mu-nich referred to by the locals as the Nikolausmarkt, nibbling at some marzipan, an attempted force-feeding of holiday spirit to bolster my frozen smile even though my heart was standing steadfast against the snowy tide and wouldn't be bribed with sweets, I saw what is actually a very common sight at that time of year: a little girl and her mother shopping at a toy-maker's stall for some miniature wooden animals to add to the family manger. I had just bit-ten into a fat marzipan pig with a friendly but stu-pid face and discovered that, gulp as I would, the gooey pink mess just wouldn't go down with my gorge on the rise.

There is nothing intrinsically horrible about this custom of adding wooden animals to a manger, nothing to cause the average person to gag and flee. It is, in fact, rather touching and delightful—so *familial* and *loving,* so *marshmallow fluffy* and *sweet* that it gave me a dizzying case of contact diabetes, followed immediately by the thrust of my old envy honed to lethal sharpness as it cut my heart in two. I stood there outside the stall, my feet slowly freezing in the slush that had leaked into my boots, and heard myself making a noise that sounded almost like a woman in labor. Only it wasn't life that was leaving my body. It was long-delayed grief. Thank goodness the nearby carolers were so loud or someone would have called for an ambulance.

Gagging, I spat out the almond mess and threw the rest of the suddenly loathsome sweet into the snow. It stuck fast, pink rump thrust helplessly in the air. I took it as a sign to get my own ass unstuck pronto. Sometimes retreat really is the better part of valor.

I had put off mourning my loss for months, denied it, refused to acknowledge it, but something inside of me looked at that mother and daughter and broke like a ruptured piñata, albeit one overstuffed with baked apples and roasted almonds. Maybe in my quest to find some Christmas spirit for filling the void in my heart I'd had too many grilled sausages, or too much spicy gingerbread washed down with too many mugs of the mulled glühwein. Maybe I just saw one too many crèches at the Krippenmuseum, the Nativity Museum packed with cheery British and French tourist families, or perhaps I had been pressured to buy one too many Nutcrackers or other wooden toys by one too many jolly vendors who assumed that I had children who would want them. Whatever it was, my brain cracked open its defensive barrier and dumped all my fake cheer, and into the breach rushed all those icons: painful glowing candles and twinkle lights and cheery carols and hand-carved crèches and worse, thousands of hand-holding lovers and families with cuddly kids and cuddlier dogs, none of which I have. Not anymore.

No, I didn't have any of it. My parents were dead, Max Ober and I had called it quits a day after the miscarriage severed the last thing we had in common, and since I had no one to answer to, not even a dog, I took my aching spirits in hand and ran away from home in the early hours of Christmas Eve, renouncing not only the bad relationship but also the hopeless sad-sack identity I had been wearing like a hair shirt since the split with Max. I was going somewhere no one knew me and I could reinvent myself as anyone I wanted to be.

I'd have left sooner, but I had to pack and there were no tickets available that snowy Saturday, not at any price. I would have had to murder someone at the airport to get a seat to anywhere. The idea had merit, but I wasn't quite—*quite*—that desperate. Instead I waited until the tears had unclogged from my throat; then I picked up the phone and called my—well, really Max's—travel agent. Normally, I don't call Max's floozies when I want something, but Gretchen, the part-time astrologer and full-time man-stealer, was the only agent I could find still in the office. And, to give the devil her due, she was efficient, even if she was a big-breasted Bavarian hussy.

We talked politely about anything except Max while she typed with her polished acrylic talons and I rummaged through my dresser drawers in a vain search for a bathing suit and periodically glared out the window at the twin onion domes of the Frauenkirche that were topped off with postcard-perfect dollops of new-fallen snow. As Gretchen blithered on about the approaching holiday and seeing her family, I tried not to recall the last argument I'd had with Max. Which had been about Gretchen, actually. It started with English words like *self-absorbed egotist* and *faithless hound* and ended with German words like *hessliche Schwanz* and *schmutzige Arschloch.* (Don't ask. They're really bad and colloquialisms. If you look them up online, the dictionary will just say: *keine Übersetzung gefunden.* Meaning: *There's no translation.*) My command of that language isn't good enough for phrases like *penis-driven he-slut,* and I ended up calling him creative things like a *toilet-dweller* and a *hole-in-the-ground* and anything that came close to what I wanted to say. Poor Max must have thought I was speaking in tongues—and I was. I had sailed right past rage and entered a zone of complete berserk insanity. Max was shocked. Absolutely nothing in our previous relationship had suggested that I was anything other than reserved, well-mannered and sane. I didn't even talk dirty in bed. He called me Miss Modesty and probably felt justified in seeking out someone for more adventuresome sex. Like Gretchen.

I must say that even limited German is an excellent language for ending relationships. It has the proper gutturals for expressing deep rage. Max, the hound dog and *hessliche Schwanz*, packed his bags and left that night and hasn't spoken another syllable to me since. His final words to me were that I should see an exorcist.

In the normal course of events, there should have been an angry phone call or two, since he left some things behind, and who really vents all their stored-up spleen in one argument? But maybe he found his forgotten CD collection in the shrubs under my small balcony, off which I had thrown them, along with a few odds and ends of clothing and all our couple photographs. And maybe he just couldn't take any more of my daily accusations because they cut a little too close to the bone. I did hold him responsible for the miscarriage and had made no secret of it. He hadn't really wanted the baby, you see.

And neither had I—until I lost her. That day, in the cold sterility of a hospital emergency room, I got a look at myself and was repulsed by what I saw. I was as selfish as my parents, and probably as unfit to have the care of another as they ever were. And, worse still, the child had spontaneously aborted because she had a severely malformed heart. A genetic mutation. Like mine, only she was more damaged. I guess it's the sins of the fathers and all that. But that wasn't something I could accept about myself at that point—that my genes had killed a child I hadn't realized I wanted until it was too late. It was far easier to blame Max and his philandering for breaking us up. And outwardly, that's what I did. But on the inside my self-loathing grew until I knew that I had to forgive myself or die.

Once I decided to bolt from Bavaria, I wasn't fussy about where I was going. The only instruction I left with Gretchen, before I hung up the phone on her muttering about Mercury being in retrograde and messing up her computer, was that I wanted somewhere warm. As soon as possible, and damn the cost. I didn't add that I was tired of Max's memory. He loved Christmas, and I knew that he was probably off reveling somewhere without me while his presence was hanging about my apartment like Banquo's ghost, pitying me all the while, though that specter was at least half of what had me in full retreat from the festive season. That bastard Indian-giver! Making me sort of feel safe about being happy at Christmas and then taking it all away again! I hated him for so many things, even the ones that weren't really his fault. It was reflexive.

Realizing that I was spiraling into rage again, I forced myself to stop. Max lived by a lot of rules and sayings I didn't agree with, but he had one axiom I liked. Translated, it went something like: *Never rent out your brain to assholes because they're hard to evict.* That Max was just such an anatomical object didn't negate this advice. It was time I ejected the jerk from my thoughts.

Gretchen finally found what I wanted, in spite of her gremlin-ridden computer. She had a last-minute cancellation of a friend of a friend who'd broken a leg in a skiing accident and who would be spending the holiday in traction instead of basking on a beach. I was very fortunate, she informed me. It was after the full moon, and therefore a cabin was available. The island never allowed guests the week of the full moon, which had ended on the twenty-third, Gretchen said. *Sind Sie jetzt frei?*

I answered rather impatiently, *Natürlich.* I wanted it yesterday even, and gave her my Visa number.

And that's how, nine thousand dollars and thirty-two grueling hours later, I ended up on Dolphin Island in Fiji on the day after Christmas. The dreaded holiday had come and gone unnoticed while I passed through a great many time zones and three longish layovers in London, Sydney and Nadi, and then a last leg in a seaplane, a single-engine floatplane that was too small for comfort. And maybe for safety, though that wasn't foremost in my brain at that point. If I had been in my right mind I would have worried about going to an island accessible only by seaplane, where there was no law, no government, no health care or building codes, a place so obscure that even cruise ships that plied their trade in the islands didn't stop by. But I was punch-drunk with exhaustion and grief and just wanted to be done traveling even if it meant death by drowning.

Things were looking up, though. The resort was

beautiful, the weather fine, and there wasn't a Nut-cracker or child in sight. I'd had the hotel pack me a picnic lunch—lobster in lemongrass with some slices of mango—and hiked out to Sylph's Hole where I was assured of seeing some giant green turtles (and by the way, I discovered it's the turtles that are green, not their shells). This wasn't a life-long ambition or anything, but it seemed as good a way to spend the first day of vacation as any other. And it was there, by the gurgling waters, which had as yet to deliver up any living creature to my newly purchased digital camera, that my unhappy life took a turn for the . . . bizarre.

I lolled in the sun, feeling about as capable of sustaining heavy thought as a helium balloon, but it did briefly cross my mind that I was very, very alone in the world and that, except for Gretchen, not a soul knew where I was. This, I decided, was a good thing. Alone didn't have to mean being lonely. Alone could mean safe and peaceful and unpressured. And I'd had a lot of practice at it. Be-lieve it or not, there is an upside to being orphaned at eighteen, if you are born to parents with bigger bank accounts than hearts and to whom you were at best nothing more than an accidental tax write-off. Their deaths in a plane crash on—you guessed it—Christmas a decade ago had left me alone, but no more lonely than I had been while they were off living their terribly glamorous lives and I was stuck at a school I disliked. And I was considerably bet-ter off financially. Perhaps not living on Easy Street with the beautiful people like Bill Gates and

Oprah, but situated on Easy Cul-de-sac, which wasn't terrible even if it wasn't very good for a stifled spirit that wanted to travel beyond the borders of its self-made cage.

Fortunately, I was allowed vacations from time to time and was able to see how the normal people lived. That is more than many people have. So though I had no family, no lover, no baby, I did have a new wardrobe, purchased mainly at airport gift shops, but nice gift shops. I justified the added cost of the holiday buys by telling myself—mostly truthfully—that two years in Munich, passing myself off as a biographer documenting the life of Max's ancestor, the exceedingly dull Graf von Faber-Castell (founder of the first pencil factory in 1761, though not the inventor of the device, which honor belonged to a Frenchman named Nicholas Jacques Conté) had left my closet devoid of any frivolous clothes appropriate for a tropical paradise.

Running my hand over the vivid orange and turquoise pareu I had wrapped around my pale hips, I was certain that I had been right. A puritanical wool skirt would have struck a ridiculous note.

Since I am only a semiresponsible adult and answerable to no one, I have eccentric eating habits. Frankly, I'm addicted to a certain kind of green olive from Di Bruno Brothers—they're stuffed with garlic and peppers and you can order them at *http://www.dibruno.com/Detail.bok?no=611.* The hotel kitchen didn't stock them, but fortunately I am pretty much fond of all olives, and any brand will get me a fix when I'm desperate, so I had a jar of Forest Floor Olives that I was devouring with the open enjoyment of the unobserved snacker who doesn't have to fear being labeled a glutton by censorious dieters. Olives weren't as good as, say, twelve hours of sleep, but with a few under my belt I was feeling less defeated. I noshed my way through most of the jar as I waited for the appearance of the elusive turtles, and tried to soak those warming rays of sun into my bones and frozen soul.

There were no turtles on the horizon, but the view was breathtaking. The ocean is vast and by its enormity managed to make the small yet beautiful island feel terribly significant, even miraculous. It caused me to think about God for the first time in years.

The islet's main claim to fame is being the site where the eight semipornographic *Lover's Lagoon* films were made. It is also unusual in that it has only twelve cottages—*bures*—and there are never more than twenty-four guests there at any given time. One can even rent the entire island, though my mania for quiet, crowd-free beaches hadn't reached this stage. It is also quite expensive. Too expensive, even for me. Gretchen had also been correct. The small engraved card on the dresser said that the island was closed for one week every month while maintenance and restocking was done. No mention of moon cycles was made, so I was inclined to lay that bit of misinformation off on Gretchen's astrological fixation.

Though I had asked no questions before leaving on this trip, it seemed that the island offered a number of diversions I had never tried. The same card mentioned that there was scuba diving, deep-sea fishing, sailing and of course biking, and hiking through the mangrove swamps on the other side of the island. This would not be arduous because of the raised boardwalk the island's owner had thoughtfully provided to keep us out of the muck and water on the southeast (wet) side of the island, which was everywhere on account of the island receiving over one hundred inches of rain every year. To get to the swamps I would either have to hike over the mountain that divided the island or walk the perimeter. I decided to put this pleasure off for another day when I was feeling more ambitious.

I had also brought my portable computer, in case guilt drove me to work before the new year. At that moment it seemed unlikely that anything would motivate me to write about Max's boring ancestor before I was faced with the last drop-dead deadline.

I mentioned that I am a biographer. Trust me, you haven't read any of my books. Really. Ever heard of Audrey Atheneum? No. See, I told you so. But I'm there on Amazon if you really want to know about Beethoven's valet or the man who invented buggy whips.

By the way, Audrey isn't my real name but it's my pen name and the name I was using on the island, so I hope you can tolerate it. I chose it long ago because it was the name of my grammar school best friend's dog, which I actually liked way better than that human friend, with whom I sometimes spent weekends. What can I say? I was a user, a selfish child who wanted a dog that neither the boarding school nor her parents would allow, and got one the only way she could. For a space of five years, Audrey was the only thing or being I loved and was willing to share my dreams with.

Unlike my more successful contemporaries, I don't write biographies about obviously famous people. Instead I write about quirky people that Fame—or Infamy—overlooked. I can do that because of the trust fund that prevents my starvation, and because I had found a niche publisher who treats his business as a tax write-off and therefore doesn't care if he turns a profit, so long as he produces "quality" books. It was to this man, Harold Webster, that I owed a final three chapters on the life and wild times of Graf von Faber-Castell.

And he'd get it, no matter how angry I was with Max, I promised silently, fishing the last olive out of the jar and then flopping onto my back with a contented sigh. Eventually. A more conscientious writer would have felt guilty for taking an unscheduled holiday with a deadline looming, but I was not feeling conscientious. I was, in fact, wallowing in glorious irresponsibility. This was exactly what I had been needing: a reason not to slit my wrists for New Year's.

It was then that a human-sized shadow fell over

me. Reluctantly, but with no real alarm, I opened my eyes and found myself looking up into the backlit face of a man who looked vaguely familiar. His body was lean, shirtless, unusually pale and efficient-looking. I choose that last descriptor because though he obviously had some muscles under that eerily white skin, he did not bulge with them. This man was more feline than canine in orientation; a cheetah, not a bulldog.

He was also admiring my own rather pale but shapely body. It would be disingenuous to pretend that I didn't see this immediately and make note of it. But since he wasn't leering or doing anything that felt in any way threatening or disrespectful, I found myself smiling up at him instead of following my usual impulse to ask him to go away.

It was only at that moment, as my cheeks twinged slightly, that I realized those particular facial muscles had fallen into disuse over the last few days.

"Doctor Livingstone, I presume," I murmured before thinking.

"Close," he answered. His voice was pleasant, West Coast American. His smile was likewise charming, and as open as a toothpaste ad. "Actually, it's Ambrose Bierce. And you must be the biographer, Audrey Atheneum. May I join you?"

He stepped closer. The hair on my arm raised itself, and for a moment I was alarmed. Then I recalled that I had booked under my pen name, since I was thinking it might be possible to write this trip off on taxes as a research expense. It would mean writing about an islet in Fiji that had never been visited by anyone historically famous, but I figured Harold might go for it since they had green turtles, which I had discovered were howlingly rare and on an endangered species list. This stranger's knowledge of my name was momentarily surprising but not unexplainable. This was a very small island, and it was entirely possible that other guests could talk to the staff and would know who was visiting.

Of course, that didn't explain how he knew I was a biographer. I did not for one minute think that he was one of the five hundred people who had purchased my last book about Beethoven's valet and somehow remembered me from my rather dreadful author photo.

"Please," I said, sitting up and pulling my pareu over my legs in a belated gesture of modesty. I also smoothed a hand down my arm, if to little effect. My pale hairs remained on end. "I must say, Mister Bierce, that you are looking remarkably well for a man of your age."

"Aren't I, though? I was one hundred and sixty-five last June. You might say that I'm well nigh immortal."

I couldn't tell for sure at the time, because of the sun behind him, but I thought his dark eyes were twinkling. Perhaps this wasn't the first time that someone had recognized his name was the same as a late great American storyteller.

"Literally and literarily, it seems." One might also say he was crazy, if they were impolite. I was not. At least, not usually. When you are a little bit weird yourself it is best, or at least less hypocritical, if you pursue a "live and let live" policy with the other oddballs. And if my name were Ambrose Bierce, I might run with it too.

Unlike many people, I actually knew a bit about the first Ambrose Bierce. He'd been born June twenty-fourth in eighteen-forty-two. I didn't know this exact date because of eidetic memory or anything so impressive, but he happened to share a birth date with Henry Ward Beecher and Norman Cousins, two men that also interested me in my professional capacity, and I found this coincidence to be remarkable.

I recalled from my college reading that Bierce had been involved in a horrible marriage with a socialite named Mary Ellen Day, that he had two sons who died young and a daughter who lived to adulthood. She was the last person to hear from Bierce before he apparently fell off the face of the earth, was kidnapped by Martians, or, more likely, was shot by Pancho Villa, though both men were trying to overthrow Victoriano Huerta at the time and should have been allies. "Bitter Bierce" had a knack for really pissing people off. He and William Randolph Hearst were steadfast enemies, though their publishing relationship spanned more than two decades. Apparently Pancho Villa hadn't liked Bierce much, either, and hadn't been blessed with geographical distance from him when their tempers flared.

One of Bierce's brothers blamed Ambrose's ill

temper on a fragmenting bullet he took to the head during the Civil War. His wife said he was simply born with a nasty, paranoid personality that made him a brilliant writer and a lousy husband. Both may have been correct. Perhaps I'm wrong, but I doubt a bullet could confer acerbic literary genius where none existed. However, it could make him cranky if the fragments were moving around and pressing on nerves and causing headaches.

Other than that, I knew Bierce was an ardent abolitionist and in nineteen hundred he was the literary king of San Francisco, a friend of H. L. Mencken, and probably the most famous writer west of the Rockies—though there are those who can make a good case for why both Mark Twain and Jack London deserve the title. I still stand by Bierce, though, because he wrote my favorite book: *The Devil's Dictionary*. I keep a copy of it right next to the *King James Bible* on my writing desk. Both are valuable literary references, though *The Devil's Dictionary* is miles more fun.

His disappearance was also one of the most dramatic in literary history. No one knew for sure how he'd met his end.

"A lot of people have been wondering what happened to you," I said, playing along. What the hell. It was a bit loony, but I was on vacation and determined to have a good time.

"I know. But it would have ruined the fun if I told them the truth . . . *then*," he answered, sinking gracefully into a cross-legged squat that was called Indian-style before the political-correctness

Nazis ran amok and neutered the language. His increased proximity amplified the number and size of goose bumps on my arms. "Now would be another matter. I've been thinking that perhaps people would like to hear about what actually happened. And it should be safe enough with all my nearest and dearest finally dead."

I stared at him for a moment. "You were right about keeping quiet, I think. People adore a good mystery. And just disappearing was so much more appropriate literarily, given your choice of material. High school kids that might otherwise have forgotten you keep reading your stories as they look for clues about what happened." I didn't say anything about wanting to hear the true story of Bierce's disappearance, since he knew I was a biographer and I wasn't certain I wanted a possibly crazy person, however attractive, attaching themselves to me while they tried to convince me to write about them.

Those flexible features arranged themselves into a grin, though the lips were slower to move than the eyes. I had the feeling that his mouth was also unused to the exercise of smiling. Maybe he'd had a bad year, too.

"I've always thought so. The past casts shadows and, worse, it leaves stains and relics to clutter up our memories—especially when we love," he agreed. This last observation seemed a bit insane, but in the delightful way that is captured so well by British literary playwrights. "One may pack up and move the body on its way, but all those stains and emotional shadows move along with us."

I nodded, still bemused. The image of Ambrose Bierce preserved in old photographs had always sported a luxurious mustache that I found a bit repulsive. Fortunately, of this soup-sieve today there was no sign. Otherwise, this man really did look a great deal like Bitter Bierce. I wondered if he was an actor. I had a friend who made a good living touring in a one-man show about Mark Twain.

"What stains are you seeing this morning?" I asked politely.

"The smell and taste of bitter coffee sweetened with condensed milk. It goes oddly with green olives."

The answer was surprising. I looked down at my jar as he added: "I shared a pot of it every morning in the winter of nineteen-thirty and 'thirty-one with a woman who called herself Amorosa."

"What happened to her?"

"The same thing that happens to nearly everyone." Ambrose shook his head. "I'd have married her, but she was already dying of what they used to call consumption. I told her I could save her, but she refused me—for my own good, she said." He smiled wryly, and I found myself fascinated with the mobility of his features. He also reminded me a bit of the actor, Jim Carrey.

"Have you ever noticed," he asked, "that when someone tries to do you a kindness, it is only rarely actually kind?"

"Yes." I naturally thought of Max, unwillingly opening the memory of his most recent "kindness" of throwing everything out from the nursery while I was still in the hospital so I wouldn't have to "deal" with it when I came home. Was the spot too tender, too bruised to endure exploration with a stranger? I decided that it was not. Sometime in the last few days that hurt had healed. The change in geography had given me mental as well as physical distance. That was good. Experience had shown me that sometimes seemingly unrelated things are actually like plants in a garden: separate entities above, but underneath the roots have all grown together in a solid mat. Try to pull out a dandelion and you get a daffodil as well. Which is a poetic way of saying that for a long time I couldn't think about losing Max without thinking about losing our baby. It had been impossible to look at one without thinking of the other. But the roots of that relationship had died and withered into nothing, and I could now extract Max's memory and not pull out anything else painful with it.

This meant I didn't have to stop talking with this rather strange man so that I could run and have a long hard cry in my cottage. That made me happy.

"Are you my neighbor?" I asked him, not commenting on the death of Amorosa by what they used to call consumption in 1931. Nor did I volunteer any thoughts about my own so-called stains. As a loner, if you lose an arm, a leg, an eye, people notice. Even losing a baby or a boyfriend, someone—if only your doctor or the nosy women down the hall—will comment. But lose yourself—your spirit, your will, your soul—and there is a good chance that no one will ever know. Maybe not even you. People form an opinion, an impression of what you are, and it becomes hermetically sealed in memory, resisting revision or updating, especially when we refuse to see ourselves for the flawed creatures we actually are. That was convenient. I didn't need anyone seeing me as vulnerable until I got my psyche sorted out.

"After a fashion," he said. "I own the island. Or, my corporation does. Once in a while I come to visit. Normally I'd be gone by now, but I saw that you were coming in today and decided to stay on for a bit."

"That's nice," I said sincerely, pulling my thoughts back to the conversation at hand. "I think I'd like to own an island. And be an eccentric millionaire." Technically, I *was* a millionaire, but nowhere near his league of eccentricity or wealth, assuming he was telling the truth. I think that I might best be described as a pragmatic upper-middle-class loner.

"Yes, it is very nice. Convenient even," he agreed, though not specifying whether he referred to owning the island or being rich. "You like these olives? They are a new product for us. Most of our produce is grown locally, but we've had no luck with olive trees."

"I like all olives," I said. "In that, I am not entirely particular. But these are exceptionally good."

He nodded. "I'll be sure to see that we get more on the next supply ship. They go well with yellowfin tuna, which is on the menu tonight. I can tell the kitchen to send some to the table if you like."

This was a weird but thoughtful gesture. Still, I declined. It was too soon for him to be doing me favors.

"That's okay. Let's not upset the chef with special requests on the first day. I also try to limit myself to one jar per diem. Too much sodium in them," I added. "It's bad for my blood pressure."

He nodded again, and then hesitated an instant before speaking. Perhaps he was out of practice making small talk. When he did speak, I had the feeling that he had decided not to share whatever was really on his mind.

"Well, I will leave you to your olives and to the turtles. I want to visit the mangroves this morning and make sure that last storm didn't do any damage. A lot of endangered species nest over there. You should bring your camera when you come. There's lots to photograph."

"Have the turtles finally made it?" I asked, rolling onto my left side out of his shadow and propping myself up on an elbow. I squinted at the Sylph's Hole. For a moment it seemed that shadows in the water danced away from my view. Were they mostly nocturnal creatures, afraid of observation from the enormous land animal that had staked out their space?

"Yes. They are here." And he was right. I could finally see some nickel-sized emerald turtles with grayish shells paddling about in the frothy water.

"They're cute!" I exclaimed, sticking a finger

in the water and waggling it at them. "Not giants at all."

"We aim to please. Have fun on Cannibal Island, and perhaps I'll see you at dinner." There was a hint of smile in his voice.

"Cannibal . . . ," I began, and then recalled that this was the old name for Fiji. I had read about this on the airplane. Thanks to the onboard magazine, I also knew that the country consisted of three hundred and twenty-two islands, and over one hundred of them were inhabited. Also it is smack-dab in the middle of the ocean, midway between Australia and Tahiti and due north of New Zealand. This is the long way of saying that it's one hell of distance from anything.

I turned back to look at my companion but he, like the real Ambrose Bierce, had disappeared into thin air, leaving not so much as a track in the sand, unless the deep gouge in the silky white beach some eight feet away could be considered a footprint. He might have been a hallucination for all the sign he left of his visit.

"Weirder and weirder."

I rolled back to the turtles and picked up my camera, trying to recall how to make the zoom lens work.

I didn't believe that this stranger was really Ambrose Bierce, I assured myself. Of course not. Nevertheless, he was very plausible and pleasant, and I began to think idly about the commercial possibilities of a supposed biography about Ambrose Bierce in the years after Mexico. They do things like that now. It's called speculative fiction. Two years ago there was a biography about Santa Claus released by some millionaire who claimed to be an elf, and it had made quite a stir. I'd write under a suitable pen name, of course, so Harold would never know that I had sold out and produced something popular for the masses. Maybe I would begin with Ambrose's love affair with Amorosa who put condensed milk in her coffee . . . .

Woman, *n.* An animal usually living in the vicinity of Man, and having a rudimentary susceptibility to domestication. . . . This species is the most widely distributed of all beasts of prey. . . . The popular name (wolf-man) is incorrect, for the creature is of the cat kind.

Spooker, *n.* A writer whose imagination concerns itself with supernatural phenomena, especially the doing of spooks.
—Ambrose Bierce, *The Devil's Dictionary*

Chapter Two

Dinner that night was in turns wonderful, lonely and then fascinating. Wonder came at what the chef could do with tuna and chutney, loneliness developed at watching the other couples cuddle and talk in intimate whispers, and fascination began with the man who called himself Ambrose Bierce.

Sometimes, if a person is sufficiently interesting at first glance, I like to know things about them—even when it's none of my business. Especially when it's none of my business. Ambrose was one of these people. My nascent curiosity would not be thwarted.

Nobody else called him Ambrose. I questioned the staff and one of the guests, a rather vapid if excellently Botoxed creature called Pamela, who had two impressive piles of strategically placed silicone on her chest and a blank look in her eyes. When they say that absence makes the heart grow fonder, I don't think they mean an absence of expression. Of course, she was also wearing expensive cruise couture and seemed happy in a vague way, so I didn't know if I should feel pity or envy for her. Pamela seemed to be under the impression that his name was Caleb Harris and that he was a multimillionaire property developer who vacationed frequently on the island. He never brought any women along with him, had never made a pass at her, and she thought he might be gay.

I attempted to subtly question Pamela about Caleb's other hobbies as she knocked back some pink blended drink, but it didn't work. My delicately worded questions flew over her head. Or, since this wasn't a particularly elevated conversation and she had a lot of airspace up there, the observations might have sailed right through. I thought about quizzing her husband—or whatever he was—when he rejoined those gathered for cocktails before dinner, but the man—Greg? Garth? I can't remember much about him except that he was beef-faced, specifically a medium-rare chateaubriand, which suggested he'd been getting too much sun—seemed intent on nothing except getting his hairy hands inside Pamela's gold sarong.

The one other eyesore in the otherwise beautiful setting weighed in at about two hundred and forty pounds and talked all the time, even with his mouth full of prawn cocktail. He wore a sort of poet's shirt that must have been made of Kevlar and laced with piano wire, as it functioned as a sort of corset. Perhaps he was an opera star. Even braced with this modern marvel of engineering, his growing paunch was evident. I would have forgiven the affectation if I thought he was doing it to please the woman he was with, but I got the feeling that he was more interested in showing off for everyone else. He was also loud. Very loud. He was apparently quite a catch, too, and willing to offer endless anecdotal evidence to support this claim, in case anyone was interested. I had to marvel and even feel a pang of annoyance. Even this boor had a girlfriend who looked at him admiringly. What the hell was wrong with me?

To add injury to insult, he wore some kind of cologne that crept through the room like a chemical fogger. I prayed that no plants or animals had died to produce such an abominable smell.

Feeling emotionally apart from this mini Noah's ark of lovers, I escaped Pamela and then chose a chair at the end of the bar, half hidden by an elephant-sized ficus, and told myself it was a good thing that I had been inoculated with the loneliness antivirus and no longer envied people who weren't reserved and distrustful—you know, people whose parents and significant others actually wanted them.

I sipped cautiously at my margarita. It was my concession to paradise-appropriate drinking, but I had it on the rocks and without salt. I had also eschewed the paper umbrella. The ripe lime was refreshing, but I found myself wishing for a whisky. Smoke and ash were better matches for the bitter taste in my mouth.

The bartender smiled at me and let his eyes flick over my body. This cheered me up. I was pleased with how I looked, even if I was hiding in the shrubbery. As I'd started dressing for the evening I'd suddenly realized that the one thing I really missed since the breakup—and I was fully aware that it wasn't specific to Max—was getting ready for an evening and picking out something to wear that is attractive. For someone special and not just for myself. I hadn't dressed for someone else for a long while.

At the time I was fleeing, I'd questioned the wisdom of packing my one teeny, tiny, backless, strapless black dress with the barest excuse of a rhinestone strap that draped over my right shoulder, but now I was glad that I had. I hadn't told myself that I was zipping into my favorite cocktail frock for Ambrose, but I was. He might be a bit weird, even a lot weird, but I was pretty sure I liked him and wouldn't mind if he noticed that I was gorgeous.

Also, I look good in black when I am my usual shade of winter pale.

As though guessing where my thoughts trended, Ambrose/Caleb made an appearance. He was dressed casually in linen slacks and a cotton shirt of finest Liberty lawn. The shirt sported palm trees; the slacks had been tailor-made.

The clothes were casual, but some men have a certain male gravitas that overcomes even silly attire. They wear their clothes rather than letting the clothes wear them. Perhaps it was just the role he'd been playing for me since I arrived, but I kept seeing him as a serious man of upright posture in a dark wool suit and white linen shirt that was stiff with too much starch, and I had the feeling that no amount of Jimmy Buffett casual wear was going to change that. The sober wolf had been spotted hiding under his eclectic sheep's clothing. That he was hiding at all was very interesting.

The wolf had no trouble finding me among the ficus leaves, and pulled up a stool beside me without asking. Again I noticed his eyes, as black as a witch's cat and every bit as curious.

"I prefer you without a mustache," I said when he failed to speak. "I don't feel like I'm looking into the face of a walrus. And it's easy to tell when you're smiling."

Ambrose caressed his chin, a gesture Max had often made after he shaved his winter beard, and it made me wonder if Ambrose had been sporting chin fur in the recent past.

"There is a school of thought which holds that after forty a man's responsible for the face he has."

"Hm. Your face is completely unlined." I pointed out gently, "I think the theory must therefore be flawed. If you're really Ambrose Bierce, of course."

"I sleep the sleep of the just these days." He smiled slightly and gestured to the bartender. A moment later a shot glass of whisky came skating

31

down the polished smoothness of the bar. He intercepted the speeding alcohol and set the glass in front of me without spilling a drop. "Go ahead. Any woman who loves green olives as much as you isn't going to enjoy sweet drinks. You don't have to pretend in front of me."

He gestured again and a second shot glass came skating our way. The bartender was grinning. I think he enjoyed showing off. Ambrose captured this one as well.

"There's a similar saying about women's faces," I remarked, taking a sip of whisky. It wasn't a brand I recognized but I liked the smoky smoothness as I swallowed.

"Yes?"

"After forty, you'd better give your face to Estée Lauder or you get what you deserve."

Ambrose nodded. "Will you have dinner with me?" he asked.

"Of course." He wasn't being coy, and I decided not to be either. Ambrose was interested in me, but not because of my little black dress. Or not *solely* because of the dress. That left me feeling more pleased than piqued.

He picked up his whisky and stood. I followed suit, though I was more careful getting off the stool, since I had a longer drop, higher heels and a short skirt.

Ambrose led the way out an unnoticed side door and to a small round table set up on a rug laid over a clear patch of sand. There was a definite breeze and the smell of rain in the air, and the shifting currents made the tiny flames inside their glass bowls dance wildly.

I had thought that the in-room guidebook was perhaps indulging in hyperbole when it called this restaurant a culinary paradise, but for once the praise was insufficient. The food cost about as much as God's eyeteeth and smelled like something they'd eat at a heavenly barbecue where everything was cooked by cherubim. Guests understood this and spoke in a reverential hush. All except Mr. Loud, who drew a frown from Ambrose as he bellowed an off-color joke and slurped his wine. I saw Ambrose's right eye twitch, and a moment later there was a pained exclamation and someone said: "David, did you back into a candle?"

Ambrose smiled at this, a not-very-nice grin that held a certain mischief. Suddenly slightly on edge, in a good way, I crossed my legs, enjoying the whisper of silk on silk as my stockings rubbed together. I felt ready to play any game.

Ambrose's head turned my way and he stared at my legs as though he, too, could hear my hosiery's murmurs. His smile changed and I thought that there was actually a chance that he might eventually charm me out of my garter belt.

"What do you think of my island?" he asked, raising his eyes before the gaze could go on long enough to be rude. I was a lady and I expected men to treat me that way. Ambrose understood this, or at least understood that I expected to be treated politely. "Lady" would have carried a slightly different definition in his day.

"I think that I should have come years ago."

It was no idle comment. Everything on the island was green and lush and usually wet. If I don't mention this in every other paragraph it is because I don't like to be redundant, but feel free to mentally insert any of these adjectives. The island was beautiful—*is* beautiful. To call it paradise would be understatement. Which only goes to show that even paradise can have its problems if you bring them with you. Still, any shadows hanging over me that night were my own doing and not the fault of the geography.

I touched the linens as I settled into my seat. The damask was heavy and, though I couldn't be sure, felt old. One can still buy linens with five-hundred-thread count, but they tend to be quite stiff. The tablecloth draped beautifully.

There was a bowl of flowers on the table, a kind of bloom I didn't recognize. I bent over the blossoms and breathed warily. At first sniff, I recoiled a bit. The scent was a mishmash of dirt, feral moss, marsh gas, and the bittersweet of the crushed peel of pomegranate that reminded me of childhood Christmases. But on second smelling, I noticed that there was also the barest hint of lemon. I wouldn't wear it as a perfume, but oddly enough, the smell managed to stimulate my appetite.

"The local name for the flower is *The Hunger Plant*."

I looked at my companion and again marveled at his resemblance to Ambrose Bierce. Except the eyes, I reminded myself. Ambrose Bierce hadn't had such dark eyes. No one I knew had eyes like this. They were a bit spooky.

A stray breeze blew a strand of hair across my face. My hair has never been well-mannered and I am always plucking it out of my eyes and mouth. As I pushed the offending lock aside, I caught a whiff of something unpleasant that raised the small hairs on the back of my neck. I can't describe the smell exactly, but it made me think of a sly winter wind in the hour before dawn, creeping through empty beer gardens near my apartment, licking up the spilled lager in the cracks between the stones and biting at the abandoned picnic tables with sharp, gnawing teeth that could eventually splinter wood. It wasn't an odor that belonged on the island.

"You smell it?" he asked me, eyes narrowing.

"Yes. What is it?"

"I don't know. But the wind has shifted around to a new direction. I've never seen it blow northeast to southwest at this season."

"Could it mean a storm?" I asked uneasily, recalling some of the recent weather disasters in the area that had carried high body counts.

"No," he said slowly. "I would know if there was a storm coming. At least if it were coming tonight."

"How?" I asked, half expecting him to lick his finger and stick it in the air and then come up with some fey folk wisdom like *red sky at morning, sailor take warning*.

"Satellite hookup," he said prosaically. For one

moment, I actually thought he was—for reasons I couldn't even begin to guess—lying. Then he added: "We don't do TV, phones or Internet in the cottages since it ruins the whole primitive paradise experience, but as a matter of safety we do get regular weather reports and have contact with the big island in case of emergencies."

"Oh. Good," I said, feeling a bit stupid for having been so imaginative.

A waiter appeared, bearing a large platter adorned with a number of goodies, including the tuna I had requested on the dining card turned in at the front desk earlier that day. True to his word, Ambrose had also arranged for some olives, but these were gigantic and stuffed with something I couldn't at first identify.

"Blanched horseradish," he said, guessing what I was thinking as I chewed my way through the first of the green globes piled in the small teak bowl.

"I'm going to have to go on blood-pressure meds if I keep this up," I said as I swallowed and then licked the brine from my lips. "These are delicious though."

"I'm glad that I could so easily please you."

"Good whisky, good olives—I'm easy."

"Somehow, I really doubt that."

"What gave me away?" I asked, just playing at conversation. I liked his voice. Swiveling sideways, I crossed one leg over the other. There is more than one way to flirt.

"Seamed stockings." Ambrose smiled apprecia-tively. "I haven't seen them in half a century. Only a particularly adventuresome kind of woman would wear them."

I found myself smiling back. *Adventuresome woman?* I liked that. A new me couldn't do better than to be adventuresome.

Seamed stockings—Cuban style, they are some-times called—are a pain to get on. It takes forever to get the seam running up the back of the leg per-fectly straight. It generally requires two mirrors. Then you have to attach your garters just so, or the stockings begin to spiral inward and the seams get crooked. Straight seams are very controlled and sexy, even a bit dominatrix-styled; crooked seams make you look way too *la dolce vita*. And, finally, you can't carry the look off in anything under a three-inch heel. Four is even better. Very few women wear actual stockings anymore, let alone with four-inch heels. They prefer to risk yeast infections in pantyhose and avoid the orthopedist. I think they have their priorities confused.

"What's it like here on New Year's Eve?" I asked.

"Quiet. We aren't like some of the resorts that do saturnalian orgies to welcome in the New Year."

"I've never been to an orgy," I replied.

"They're overrated."

I was about to ask if he knew this from firsthand experience when he spoke again.

"Do you feel it?" he asked suddenly, leaning

37

forward. The table was small. With a little leaning on my part I could bring my lips within kissing distance.

Instead, I froze while I did a quick check of my senses. I could see nothing alarming, the odd scent was gone, and all I could hear was soft water easing up on the sand.

"Um . . . no." Jumpy. I was feeling very jumpy and couldn't think why. Again I smoothed my arms, trying to rid them of the feeling of tiny stings and shocks that danced over the skin.

"Ah." He sat back a bit. "A pity."

"What is it?" I nearly whispered.

"It's the sound of a plot thickening." His eyes were very warm as they looked into mine, which I know widened for an instant.

Pretending to be annoyed, I reached out with my foot and kicked his leg. Not hard, but with enough force that his leg should have moved. It didn't. I might as well have nudged a tree.

"You knew Mark Twain, didn't you?" I asked, changing the subject. I did not hide my legs away, though. My skirt had inched up just enough for the edge of my garters to show. Ambrose didn't stare but I was betting he could see them with his peripheral vision.

"Yes. I liked Twain. We knew each other quite well. And Bret Harte was my editor at *Overland*. He published my first story, 'The Haunted Valley.' "

"You were also friends with H. L. Mencken. But you hated Oscar Wilde. I have never read a more comprehensive excoriation of a fellow writer. What did he do to annoy you?"

Ambrose appeared both surprised and pleased that I would know this.

"It's true. I detested him with the blazing hot passion of a million suns. The bastard was arrogant, a genius but contemptuous of everyone . . . and he reminded me of *me*. Except he always wore that infernal carnation in his buttonhole, along with that damned floppy necktie. He was a fop, a disgrace to the Irish race. And he got paid five thousand dollars for that speaking tour. Worst of all, he had the nerve to invade the sanctity of the Bohemian Club, which was where I reigned as the literary genius!" He grinned. "I used to care about things like that."

"But not anymore?"

"No. I no longer need the praise of outsiders to make me feel whole. In fact, I find the scrutiny of strangers to be dangerous and annoying. Still, I think it may be time for my story to be told. At least part of it."

Ah-ha! I had been right. He was not after me solely for my long legs. That was a bit of a letdown.

"Why not do it yourself?" I asked. "An autobiography would get a lot of attention."

"Too much attention, at least in the wrong quarters." He shook his head. "I am sincere about wanting to avoid celebrity. I need someone intelligent, low-key, and competent. And someone who would be willing to shade the truth in my favor this time."

Well, I was definitely low-key. One could stretch a point and claim I was competent. But intelligent, or willing to shade? This I was less sure of.

"You used to avoid a lot of other things, too," I pointed out. And maybe I was digging. "Women among them. Why look to a female biographer for help?"

His response was heated. "That's an out-and-out lie, perpetrated by my wife and the critics. I didn't avoid women. I just avoided marriage after my first and greatest mistake. It's not the same thing at all. I assure you that I like women very much. Always have." The wrong look could have made this exchange a bit too pointed, but his dark eyes never dipped from my face.

"I never talk business over dinner," I said at last. It suddenly occurred to me that I would very much like writing this biography, but I also knew it might be the whisky and candlelight doing the thinking.

"Very wise," he answered, relaxing. "Now, do try the tuna. My chef is a master at his craft."

I nodded and forked up a small morsel of the delicate fish. He was absolutely correct; his chef was a master. I had never tasted better.

Prepared to enjoy both the meal and the company, I leaned back in my chair and encouraged Ambrose to talk about his supposed work on the Panama Canal. He was very attractive and I knew that he also fancied me, but I also knew that absolutely nothing would happen that night. Unlike most men, in terms of morality Ambrose had more fiber than a granola bar and understood the art of delayed gratification. I could put off deciding whether I wanted to have a vacation fling with a madman.

Ghoul, *n*. A demon addicted to the reprehensible habit of devouring the dead.

Rational, *adj*. Devoid of all delusions save those of observation, experience and reflection.
— Ambrose Bierce, *The Devil's Dictionary*

Chapter Three

The next morning I decided to try snorkeling in the sea. I had only ever used a snorkel in a swimming pool, but I was feeling brave. I wasn't sure I would like it, since I have always found the oceans I've known to be rather big and scary. But life is full of surprises and I figured that statistically I should like one of them. A call to room service, the only place the telephone could reach, brought a young man—his name was Emori—with a mask, snorkel tube and flippers, and a lovely basket of scones and jam, and a small pot of coffee.

I ate all of it. That was foolish, since I was planning to go into the water alone, but the beach was so tranquil and the azure sky so calm that it seemed impossible to even imagine that anything bad could happen out there. Besides, I was famished, more hungry than I could ever remember being.

I did have a small bit of help with my meal. The island had a mascot, a small calico cat whose beaded collar said ASHANTI. There were no mice on the island, so she wasn't required to earn her kibble by the sweat of her brow. Or paws—or whatever cats sweat from when they engage in honest toil. She wasn't all that interested in my scones or jam, but she obligingly shared the small pitcher of cream intended for my coffee.

The ocean was indeed big and scary as I waded into it a half an hour later, flippers flopping gracelessly as I splashed myself with surf and sand, but it was beautiful too. Even now I can say that and mean it, though I am not sure I'll ever go in again. I waded out perhaps ten feet into the blood-warm water and then let the gentle waves take me out to where the hotel brochure said the reef would be.

To say that the reef is a rainbow of color is to do it an injustice. No rainbow has ever been made with such intense hues and shades. The colors in that clear water were so bright they almost caused the eye pain. There were corals in gold and violet. There were vivid red sea fans where equally red crabs went about some urgent crustacean business that involved a lot of antennae waving.

Keeping near the safety of the surface and the shore, I could still see a carpet of what I later learned were zoanthids, a kind of wormy coral whose flowery white tentacles looked like a field of African daisies caught in a stiffish breeze. I saw a giant clam that was too large to be anything but frightening, but there were also tiny gobies, scalefins and a variety of pastel anemone fish. I thought for a while that I was being followed by an octopus

43

but it turned out that he was after a royal blue ribbon-eel. The octopus was fast, but the eel even faster.

There were also gray reef sharks, but they were small, no more than eighteen inches long, and they seemed indifferent to me, so I decided not to waste energy being panicked by them when they swam by beneath me.

That was a mistake. Without realizing it, I allowed myself to be lured farther from shore than I intended. I was frog-kicking along, engrossed in the view, when all of a sudden, the reef just disappeared and I was over barren white sand that sloped away from the island at a precipitous angle and disappeared into utter darkness.

I pulled back abruptly, fanning my hands as I treaded water and resisted the small waves that wanted to bump me farther from the shore. I don't know why deep water is so very frightening, when anything over three inches can drown us just as effectively, but for some reason it just is. However, though I was unnerved at the sudden drop-off, I didn't turn back immediately. There was something wonderful and awe-inspiringly awful about staring into the gray-blue twilight; something mesmerizing. So, I just hung there, aware that the waves were rougher beyond the reef and the water colder, but unwilling to turn back and admit that I was more frightened than fascinated by the vast nothingness.

My bravery lasted maybe thirty seconds and then a great many small silver specks began rushing toward me. In an instant they were on me and then over me, a horde of baby green turtles like the ones in Sylph's Hole. Right on their green heels—or flippers—came an uncomfortably large number of gray reef sharks. These were bigger, maybe three to four feet long. They seemed to be chasing the turtles along the surface instead of clinging to the sandy bottom.

I was suddenly cold on the inside. It wasn't fear and it wasn't shock or anything else internal, of that I am sure. Not at first. But something from the outside had reached inside me and put a chill on my heart. The expression, I believe, is feeling that someone has walked on your grave. I was in the presence of some kind of evil, and it was only then that true fear awoke in me.

I did an about-face and began swimming hard for the shore, clawing at the waves as I tried to pull myself to safety. But I stopped when all the thrashing sharks had overtaken me and I could feel myself to be alone again. Not sure why, I turned around and stuffed my face back in the water and looked back into the blue void.

And that was when I saw it: the impossibility, the sanity-stripper.

Know this about me. I don't—didn't—hang around in weird neighborhoods. I never saw a ghost or Loch Ness monster, and never expected to be kidnapped by a UFO. Nevertheless, I have an adequate imagination and an open mind, and I like to think that I can stroll the spooky side of the street with the best of them. But this abomination was beyond anything I had ever imagined, or had the capacity to envision or even hallucinate. I can describe it now, but at the time my eyes didn't understand what they were seeing. That might be why I was more shocked than terrified in those first instants.

It looked like a man. A naked, drowned man that was a few shark bites shy of an entire skin. The wounds didn't bleed, they just flapped like flexing gray gills as the currents pulled them open and shut at irregular intervals. Everything was magnified underwater and I could see that he wore a leather belt with an Oakland Raiders buckle on it, and a pair of dark pyramidal charms about eight inches in length that could only be weights. He had the remains of dark canvas deck shoes on his feet. His skin was wrinkled and prunelike and hung down around his belly and ankles like it was trying to slide off his bones.

This would have been bad enough, but the thing's eyes were open and he was walking—*walking*—up the slope that led to the reef and then the island. The eyes—eye, really, the one that didn't have an eel in it—paused on me, who was floating up there on the surface, and it opened its mouth. The lower jaw fell all the way to its chest and I could see things moving inside.

I turned and fled, swimming for shore like I was being chased by a walking corpse with an eel in its eye. I fled right into the cloud of thrashing sharks and never paused, though I could feel their hard bodies all around me as they whipped back and forth in the water. It's a wonder I wasn't bitten repeatedly. But all of us were united in our desire to escape the horror, none wasting time on petty squabbles.

I finally reached a place where I could touch bottom. I ran forward in slow motion and finally stumbled up onto the sand, stripping off my mask and flippers with shaking hands, and began staggering for my cottage with some notion of calling room service and demanding help. I was, if not blinded by terror, certainly limited to severe tunnel vision and unable to catch my breath as I staggered toward the phone and what felt like my only hope of salvation. My head swiveled back toward the water frothing with fish that were as panicked as I, and I was not watching where I was going, so it is fortunate that the first thing I ran into was Ambrose.

"Whoa there! What's wrong?" he demanded when my head whipped to the front and he got a look at my face.

"M-m-monster," I stuttered, gasping for air that didn't seem to be reaching my body.

"Was it a shark?" he asked, hands still on my dripping shoulders. They were very hot hands, and I was grateful because fear had frozen me to the marrow of my shaking bones. "A crocodile?"

"No. *Monster,*" I said again, and then my brain chose a very interesting word. "Zombie."

Most men would have questioned this statement, but not Bierce. It may have helped my cause that the thing chose that moment to stagger out onto the beach. In the sun it looked even more bloated and horrible than it had in the water, especially when the eel wiggled out of the eye-socket and dropped back into the surf.

Expecting that Ambrose would now grab my hand and we'd both run for it, I was shocked when he released me, took a leap forward, bounding into the air at an impossible height and speed and somehow managed to travel the impossible distance necessary to get behind the shambling horror and land without stumbling in the turbulent surf.

Then he did something so terrible that, even months later, my hands are shaking as I type this. Without one second of hesitation, he wrapped an arm around the bloated thing's throat and one around the top of its head. I was certain that he was going to break the creature's neck—and maybe that was his plan, but the corpse had simply rotted too much to have anything in the way of connective tissues left. In any event, he didn't just break the thing's neck; he tore the entire head off, leaving a bit of ragged vertebrae sticking out of the top of the torso.

There was no blood as the head came off, just a small gush of sludgy brown gore that dribbled down the trunk of the body.

I have no words to describe what this event sounded like—deboning a raw chicken, maybe. I could take a stab at describing the smell, but you don't need these things creeping around in your memory and haunting your dreams.

The head went sailing and landed about ten feet away in a stand of some kind of stiff aquatic grass with feathery white tassels. The head had red hair and a small tattoo under its left eye. I might have noticed more, but Ambrose wasn't done mutilating the still-thrashing body, and though I didn't want to see anything else bloody or horrible or impossible, my eyes refused to look away as he shoved the headless body to the ground and punched a fist through the ribs and into the thing's heart. After that, it quit moving.

I realized that I had been rescued. It had been done violently and with maximum gore, but I was no longer afraid of being chased by a bloated corpse. My brain took a stab at trying to decide if I needed to be afraid of Ambrose, but was too frozen with shock to make any decision except to evacuate my stomach of my breakfast.

Ambrose got to his feet and looked back to see what I was doing. Which was nothing once I was done retching. I was staying as still as a corpse. Stiller, actually. The headless body continued giving an occasional twitch and wheeze through its headless windpipe, whereas I was as quiet as even the strictest librarian could wish.

I made an unsuccessful effort to speak. After two ineffective tries I managed to gasp: "What is it?"

"A zombie, like you said. Good guess. Few people outside of Haiti—apart from horror movie fanatics—could have pegged it."

Apparently satisfied that I wasn't hurt or on the brink of hysteria, Ambrose bent down and, with a casual strength that wasn't human—nothing about him seemed human in that moment—he picked up the body by the belt around its waist and then walked over to the head, which he picked up by the hair. He began hiking east along the beach. I swear by anything you like that the intact eyeball was still looking around as the head swung back and forth at the end of Ambrose's long, pendulous arms.

"Let's go," he called back over his shoulder.

Not sure what else to do, I followed. My footsteps were clumsy and I was weaving like a drunk. My world was still dark around the edges and I wasn't far from fainting. Hands down, this was the most insanely dangerous situation I had ever been in, but still I staggered along behind him instead of heading for my cottage and my heart medication.

"Where are we going?" I asked as my heart and breathing calmed a fraction and I could see again. My voice was barely more than a whisper, but he heard me.

"The barbecue pit where we roast pigs. It should have kindling in it."

My stomach rolled over at this, and the periphery of my vision began to go dark for a second time. "Why?" My voice was faint.

"The body has to be burned. It's . . . possibly contagious. A monster roast seems wise." I had known he was going to say something like that, but it didn't stop my dismay and horror—and sheer bewilderment—at his answer.

"He . . . he has a disease?" I reviewed every disease I had ever heard of but drew a blank on symptoms that included being able to walk underwater. And hadn't he agreed that this thing was a zombie?

I tried to keep up with Ambrose, but my feet were heavy and awkward. I was glad when Ambrose stopped at a ring of stacked stones and dropped the body onto the sand. Again using strength that wasn't normal, he hauled a heavy grate away from what proved to be a pit that was about five feet in diameter and three feet deep. It was full of dry sea grass and driftwood. The wind changed directions abruptly and flung a new smell into my face. The barbecue pit held the scent of charcoal, dried tinder and a pinch of chimney dust where too many resinous pinecones have burned. It was a melancholy winter scent, poignant and nostalgic, that had no place in the present circumstances or location. I noted that I seemed to be having a number of olfactory hallucinations. Perhaps my brain wasn't getting enough oxygen.

"Well, he's dead and walking around. So he's probably diseased and may be contagious. And we need to burn him before anyone else sees or touches him. And before he manages to heal his wounds and start walking around again."

"Heal decapitation?" I asked.

"You have a point. This one is probably not getting up again. It just takes a while for the body to get the message."

"Does this happen often?" I asked stupidly, sinking into sand that was blessedly burning hot on my too-cold skin.

"No. Not around here. Last one I saw was in Mexico more than half a century ago. I thought they were all killed by the army at the end of the war."

I focused my eyes on my bare feet and not upon whatever Ambrose was doing in the fire pit. I tried to control my shivering. I told myself that my chest didn't really hurt, that I was just cold from being in the water and there was nothing wrong with my heart.

"Mexico?" I didn't actually know what I was saying. I was just hoping that if I kept asking questions he would eventually say something I would understand and all this would be explained.

"Yes. Pancho Villa was using them in his army—much to the dismay of his human soldiers. I tried to explain why this was bad, but in those days tact was a second—actually third—language, and I was far from fluent. Villa didn't agree me."

Pancho Villa. Ambrose had mentioned him before, but this time I believed he had really met him.

"You're really Ambrose Bierce, aren't you?" I was surprised when this came out of my mouth.

"Yes, I really am." He tossed the zombie's body and then head into the pit. Then he peeled off his spattered shirt and added it. I didn't see him strike a match but there was a flash of light that looked a bit like lightning, and suddenly there was smoke rising from the ring of stone. I was glad to be upwind. "And I'm very sorry about this, Audrey."

"Why? You didn't know he was there." I paused. "Did you?"

He met my gaze. "No. And I find his presence to be disconcerting. Mysterious. I might even say ominous."

"Ominous. Yes. I'm trying hard to think of an explanation for . . . it . . . but so far nothing has suggested itself." I admitted, "Maybe I'm just not up on my tropical diseases. We don't have many zombies in Bavaria."

"They don't like the cold much. They have no internal system to produce body heat, and freeze fairly quickly if they're outside."

"Oh. Well, that explains everything."

"You always try to put the best possible interpretation on things, don't you?" he asked, turning back to the pit.

"Not lately," I said, thinking about my recent deplorable behavior with Max. I wasn't used to tithing at the Church of Eternal Guilt, but I really did owe him an apology. Someday. "But usually . . . yes. I am as optimistic as a reasonable IQ will allow."

"I'm not." His smile was charming. Perfectly square and white teeth, full sensual lips. The expression was inappropriate under the present circumstances, but very attractive.

After a moment I said, "I know. I studied you in school. Did you know that they call you Bitter Bierce?"

"Yes. And the name was earned." Ambrose got up and walked down to the water where he spent a moment washing his hands and arms. His actions were casual and unhurried. "I applaud your optimism, my dear, but you will have noticed that

53

these are not reasonable circumstances. I suggest that caution and a degree of discretion might be in order for the next little while."

Caution and discretion. Translation: *Don't go off babbling hysterically about seeing zombies.* Like I needed to be told this.

"You're not worried about disease?" I asked as he came back to sit beside me. The water sparkled on his blindingly white chest. Paleness usually suggested ill health, but not in his case. He looked more like an alabaster god.

"No. I've already had it already. In Mexico. I'm immune."

"You've had . . . zombie-ism?"

"A strain of it. And it isn't so much a disease as a condition brought about by . . . ritual. Usually."

"Do you think maybe you could tell me what's going on?" I asked finally. My voice was meek, not at all its normal demanding self.

"I can take a stab at it. Part of it is guesswork, of course."

"The zombie part?"

"No. That I know about. The only question is what a zombie is doing in Fiji, on my island."

"Maybe that's *your* only question, but I have tons!" I growled. "This is *not* normal for me, so you're going to have to cut me some slack." My verbal defense mechanisms were kicking in. I needed to shield my brain with something and words were all I had. They were all I'd ever had.

"I'm certain you do have questions, and I assure you that these are far from normal circumstances for me, either. Not these days at any rate." Those eyes studied me. For the first time I noticed that they were truly black. I could see no pupil in the black of the iris. There was also a strange gold tracery of what looked like scars across his chest. I hadn't noticed them before and couldn't imagine what caused them.

He continued, "I'm just not certain how to begin answering them. It's all going to sound more than a bit strange and improbable, you know."

"Just start at the beginning," I urged, forcing my eyes back to his face. "And keep talking until I stop you."

Ambrose nodded.

"I was very ill when I left for Mexico," he began. "The doctors told me I had only weeks left to live and I decided that if I was going to die, I preferred it be in a good cause, so I went into Mexico to join the revolution. It was there, in Pancho Villa's camp, that I met a Dark Man, a brujo—a witch doctor— who haunted the battlefields, gathering up the wounded and even the recently dead. I found out later that his name—one of his names—was Johann Dippel." He paused somewhat expectantly, and I felt an itch begin deep in my brain. I couldn't identify it yet because my mind was still rather taken up with the walking corpse thing and disinclined to be distracted by a search for historical trivia.

"Dippel. Should I know this name?" I asked, unable to let it go completely.

"Not necessarily." He shrugged. "Perhaps you

would have read about him under the name of Doctor Xavier Bichat. Anyhow, once he found out who I was, he offered to cure me—to rid my body of all disease if I helped General Villa. I was agreeable since that was what I had planned to do anyway. And dying people will grasp at straws of hope, however unlikely or tenuous. Besides, if the procedure killed me, it would only be depriving me of a few pain-filled days. What did I have to lose? Nothing, I thought."

"I see. And it worked?"

"Oh yes. It worked and then some."

I closed my eyes and lay down in the hot sand, not caring that it was getting in my hair. I wriggled until it was comfortable and the heat began to seep into my back.

"I woke up after the drugs and electrocution in Saint Elmo's fire—"

I cracked open an eye and squinted at Ambrose. "Electrocution? Wait, wait, wait. Johann *Dippel*. I remember now. He was the real Doctor Frankenstein, wasn't he? The one who was killed by the peasants and whose castle was burned? I've read about him. I thought about writing on him for a term paper but there wasn't enough material. And Bichat—wasn't he the one experimenting with animating corpses taken from the guillotine during the French Revolution? They executed him, didn't they?"

"That's the one. Only Dippel wasn't killed quite dead enough at the time—either time. The destruction of his body, his monsters and his castle was incomplete and he was able to find his way to his lab and patch himself back together." Ambrose looked over at the fire pit. His face was hard. "That's the trouble with leaving this job to amateurs. They don't destroy the bodies."

"It . . . it figures though that he survived. Pure evil wouldn't just die without a fight." I had to say something and this was all I came up with. I did not look at the fire pit. The thing would have to burn for a long time before it would improve in appearance—in other words, become ash. I didn't doubt that it would, though. Ambrose seemed to know what he was doing.

"Not usually. Evil often lives on long after good has given up and quit the battlefield." I could feel him staring at me again, perhaps gauging my level of repressed hysteria. I think my response puzzled him, but I had learned long ago to moderate my emotions or risk blacking out. My heart could not pump an adequate supply of oxygenated blood to fuel full hysteria.

"Go on," I urged, now reluctantly caught up in this improbable, but I suspected entirely true, story. "You woke up from electrocution."

"Yes, and this Dark Man told me that I had become immortal, that he had improved on his process over the years and I was now virtually indestructible. Though I was lying there with the mark of the lightning that should have killed me—*did* kill me—etched on my chest in a golden ceraunograph, I didn't believe him." He shook his head. "Once the first instants of pain passed I felt better, fabulous even . . . but immortal? I laughed at him as he talked to me about my new state, and then got dressed and left the plateau where he had chained me down for the procedure. The Dark Man said nothing else, just returned to camp, packed his bag and went away with a small platoon of . . . zombies. Though, at the time I thought of them only as wounded soldiers who had had miraculous recoveries." Ambrose shook his head. "He was smiling when he left, enjoying a great joke. That damned grin has haunted me ever since. It pleased him that he had told the truth and I failed to believe him."

"Obviously he was right about you, though."

"Yes. I continued to deny it all through the war, but evidence began to pile up. There were severe injuries that healed too quickly when they shouldn't have healed at all. I never got sick, though I passed through cities where there were epidemics of contagious disease. Pancho Villa eventually shot me when we argued about using zombies—one had bitten me and I broke its neck in a fit of rage—and he dumped my apparently dead body in a shallow grave and left me. But I didn't die, though that was the end of our uneasy association. Never say I can't take a hint when it's delivered with a bullet." He smiled fleetingly.

"One day, after waking up on a beach after a shipwreck, somehow alive though everyone else on the boat had drowned, I realized that I had exceeded every law of probability and even luck. I could no longer pretend that my good fortune in matters of health was mere coincidence. The Dark Man's treatment had done more than rid me of disease. I wasn't aging and I had become something akin to immortal." He paused. "Obviously new plans had to be made for a postresurrection life. I understood that I couldn't return to my family and friends and I would have to become someone else."

Immortal. Resurrection. He really meant it. As a supposed Christian I was trained to believe in resurrection to an eternal life. But it was meant spiritually, metaphorically. The modern-day Christian isn't like an ancient Inca or Egyptian. We don't believe in literal resurrection. So we don't do anything like make travel arrangements to the next life. We try to be good enough that our souls aren't turned away at the Pearly Gates, and of course our relatives dress us nicely for the last hurrah with the candles and flowers—but that's it. Immortality, the kind Ambrose was speaking about, wasn't something we were raised to accept. In fact, as someone born in the late twentieth century I had an obligation to deny what he was saying. Only, I couldn't. There was a walking corpse twitching on the barbecue and a man more than a century old sitting beside me that contradicted my beliefs about the laws ruling the physical world.

"What did you do then?" I asked.

"I decided to put his theory to the test, of course."

"How?" I asked, opening both eyes.

"I killed myself again." He grinned once more.

I pestered him for a more complete answer, but he refused to say anything else about it.

He said instead, "I'm stronger now than I ever was. Faster. Much faster. And I get faster and stronger each time I resurrect in the lightning. All my senses have been heightened—especially hearing," he remarked. "I can stand outside the kitchens and hear a bottle break and I can tell you if it was made of clear glass, or green, or brown. I know it sounds crazy, but colored glass makes a different noise when it cracks. Regular glass breaks at about three thousand miles per hour. The colored glass is slower." He looked at me. "I can hear your heart too. It's broken. You have a flaw in one of the valves, don't you?"

This bit of knowing, after all the rest, shouldn't have disturbed me. But it did. I didn't want anyone to know of my flaw, my literal and metaphorical broken heart that had caused my parents to reject me.

Nature designed the human heart with four chambers in order to regulate our blood pressure so we don't blow out the delicate veins and arteries in our lungs when the blood drops around for oxygenation. Put another way, my heart was only about eighty-five percent efficient at controlling that pressure—as long as I didn't have one of those inconvenient episodes of ventricular tachycardia, which hardly ever happened now that I was an adult and carried Vasopressin. (Ah, better living through chemicals indeed. Did you know that Vasopressin causes pairing and mating in voles and pigs? I have yet to run into a lonely vole or hog, but have always thought that it might be rather embarrassing for everyone present, and thus have avoided petting zoos.)

Day in and day out, going to the market, picking up the dry cleaning, reading research material at the library, this flaw didn't matter much. I had a feeling it might matter now, though. This knowledge frightened me a bit and made me feel defensive and angry about my limitations.

"I have a minor prolapsus of the mitral valve," I admitted, proud that to my ears my voice showed none of my annoyance. Not that it mattered; he could probably hear annoyance anyway.

"But you're feeling better now? Less faint?" he asked, and I realized that I was. The feeling of pricks and tingles in my arms was gone too.

"Yes. . . . Sorry, I don't mean to belabor this, but just to be clear, you're saying that you are immortal? Johann Dippel did something to you with electricity, you died, were reborn, and you can't be killed?"

He hesitated.

"As good as immortal," he finally answered. "Maybe if I stood right on top of an atomic bomb or an erupting volcano, or dropped myself in a tree shredder—though I'd hate to try that and find out it didn't work. . . . I thought I'd found a way out after I was bitten by a . . . a werewolf, let's call her. It happened down in Panama in 'thirty-two after Amorosa passed on. There were rather a lot of them around then, though they have pretty much died out now with all the other wild species in the region. I may be the last of their kind."

A way out. A werewolf. I didn't like the sound of either of those things, and decided to put off any questions about his state of mind until another day. If he was still suicidal, I didn't want to know it. There might be other zombies that needed killing. Since he'd done so well with the first, I wanted him in fighting shape.

Still, I had to ask.

"Lycanthropy was a way out?" I was proud that I knew the proper term for the disease associated with werewolves.

He raised a brow but nodded. "I thought all I would need to do is get someone to shoot me with a silver bullet when I was in animal form."

So, he was definitely suicidal. And possibly delusional, though I had just seen a walking corpse, so I was reserving judgment about the werewolf thing for the time being.

"But it didn't work, obviously."

"No. And it hurt like hell for weeks after. It didn't even cure me of being a . . . werewolf." He obviously didn't like the word. "Apparently I can regenerate the lycanthropy virus as well as flesh and bone." He frowned slightly and fell silent.

"But on the bright side, as monsters go, you are rather attractive," I finally said, closing my eyes again. I'd decided I didn't want any more questions answered. It was too freaky. One impossibility at a time. Okay, two: I believed in walking corpses and that this man was Ambrose Bierce. Acceptance of the werewolf part would have to wait until some of the other shock wore off.

"Yes. And I still have an absolutely superhuman knack for chicanery. And for spotting it in others.

It's like . . . psychic pattern recognition of my enemies' thoughts and plans. Or maybe it's precogni-
tion. Which is why this zombie is disturbing."

"Is *that* why the zombie is disturbing?" I asked.
"And I thought it was that a dead body was walking around trying to kill us. Uh . . . it was trying to
kill us?"

"Oh, yes." He chuckled, and I wondered if I was
ever going to see what amused him. After a moment he stopped laughing. When he spoke, his voice
was serious."No one except you knows I own this
island. I have a new identity and it was purchased
by a shell company owned by a series of blind corporations. And I was willing to swear no one knew
about the lycanthropy either. That attack happened
in a small village where everyone human was killed
a week later. It's why I've felt safe exiling myself
here during the full moon."

"So you . . . ?" I searched for a way to phrase
the question.

"I go furry," he said. "I shape-shift. I'm not completely out of control as a werewolf, but let's say
my inhibitions are lowered to dangerous levels and
it isn't safe for me or anyone around me. I have to
hide myself away from people who seem like little
more than things to play with."

Inhibitions. I usually think of this word in connection with sex, but he might have meant the
other inhibitions. The ones that keep us from being cannibals and eating each other when we start
feeling peckish.

"I see. And the zombies?" I sat up and began

brushing off sand. It was a futile gesture. It had dried on me in a gritty powder that refused to be dislodged. "They're the voodoo ritual kind, not *Night of the Living Dead* disease kind?"

"I think so. I hope so. They're bloodhounds of a sort. The man who makes them now—he's the Dark Man's son, actually. You've heard of him, too. He's the philanthropist, Saint Germain. I know it's him doing it because I am ninety-nine percent sure that Dippel is dead. Finally. He died at Christmas three years ago, and even Dippel doesn't have that long of a reach. Zombies don't last long in hot climates. They're rotting, walking flesh bags, and other diseases and parasites feed on them. Any creature Dippel made would be gone now."

Ambrose didn't wait for me to comment, which was a good thing because I was speechless. Saint Germain? Santa Claus to the poor and sick of the third world, recently nominated for some peace prize, was making zombies? "He sent that thing after me," Ambrose said. "Deliberately and with malice aforethought—just as he has his father's other . . . patients. That means Saint Germain knows I am alive and that I come to this island during the full moon. And since a zombie would have rotted or been eaten by something if it walked all the way from Mexico, that means Saint Germain is somewhere nearby, raising the dead and searching for me."

"Why?" I asked baldly. "Why would he care about you?"

"That is the question of the hour. A zombie is a

rather hostile calling card, don't you think? Not as bad as a ghoul, but unpleasant enough. Especially if they travel in packs."

I didn't want to ask—I didn't! I already had more than an enough on my terrified mind. But my mouth formed the words anyway: "A ghoul?"

"Yes. An eater of the dead. The very newly dead. In fact, they usually like to kill their prey—humans—and eat them on the spot if there are no protesting witnesses. They are much faster, much meaner and much smarter than the slower zombies, who prefer to eat the living. It saves time when you don't kill your food first. They are a sort of uber-zombie, often made of animal and human parts. They're Saint Germain's version of a Frankenstein monster."

"How fortunate for us that we were only attacked by a zombie," I said.

"Indeed. And I must say, you've taken this all rather well." His voice was approving. "A lesser woman would be screaming for a seaplane and the American consulate. And perhaps for the men in white coats to come and take me away."

"I haven't taken it *that* well. On the inside I'm having hysterics. They'll probably come out when I catch my breath. Though not in front of any consulate employees, because I'd be declared insane instead of you, wouldn't I?" This wasn't entirely true, though. I mean about having hysterics. The rest was. Any government employee would definitely declare me bug-munching mad if I appeared in their office and started babbling about zombies.

But blind panic had left me some moments before. I was freaked out, but beginning to be fascinated by the sheer weird horror of the situation. Maybe it was the writer in me, the historian who wants to know the truth and is willing to accept unpleasant things if it means getting to the bottom of a story. Or maybe I was even less normal than I ever realized. Did chronic alienation from the rest of the world enable a person to accept nontraditional beliefs?

"On the inside, eh? It's the best place to have them. They are less annoying to others that way." Ambrose rose easily and offered me a hand. It was long-fingered and, I recalled, very strong. There should have been some hesitation after what I had witnessed him doing, but I reached out immediately and let him pull me to my feet. As our hands clasped, I felt a jolt of what might have been electricity travel up my arm and reach into my chest. Some of my pain went away as my heart returned to a steady beat. I've been defibrillated before, when my heartbeat has become erratic, and this was something similar though far less painful.

"Let's get you back to your cottage so you can have a hot shower. And some olives. You've earned them."

I nodded in agreement. I also kept holding his hand. I don't normally follow meekly when men decide to lead, but I still didn't know if I was coming or going, and I was just as happy not to loiter on the beach alone.

I glanced back once, feeling odd about walking

off with a body burning in the barbecue pit. There was surprisingly little smoke now. It seemed to mainly be steam that was rolling out of the pit and toward the water. Deep down, in the part of my brain that likes things neatly classified, I did hear a small voice asking if what had just happened was murder. But the rest of my brain answered back with a resounding *no*. The creature Ambrose had cooked was already dead. I was absolutely sure of that. The worst thing we could be accused of was destroying a body. That wasn't good, but it wasn't murder.

"Ambrose?" I asked reluctantly.

"Yes?"

"How do you know it was just one zombie headed here? That it wasn't part of a pack?"

"I was rather hoping that you wouldn't ask me that. Once I've stashed you in the shower, I'm going for a swim."

"Absolutely not," I said, stopping. Or, rather, pausing. I may have stopped moving my feet, but Ambrose didn't, and he was stronger than I. It was walk or get dragged. "What if something happens to you? I'll be here all alone with the zombies."

This was a slight exaggeration. There were a half-dozen employees and at least a dozen guests. But I wasn't willing to bet that any one of them knew how to deal with zombies as effectively as he did. I wasn't so out of the mainstream of human life that I didn't know that zombie hunting was unusual. "You may be immortal, but I'm not."

"What do you suggest?" he asked. "I really can't

recommend getting back in the water. You were lucky to get away from it, you know. They're very strong, and they don't need air."

I swallowed. "I know. I mean, I know I was lucky. The sharks gave me some warning but it was still too close a thing."

"The sharks?"

"Yes, a bunch of gray reef sharks came blasting out on the void like Moby Dick with Ahab on his tail. At first I thought they were chasing after the baby turtles, but I could see that they were swimming right past. I figured if that thing could scare sharks away, then I would be dumb to linger."

That wasn't exactly what had happened, but it made me seem less cowardly and more logical, and I found that I wanted Ambrose's respect.

"I don't like the sound of this. There could be more than one if the sharks are being driven shoreward in any numbers."

"All the more reason for me to keep watch," I said. "From shore. Do you have a gun?"

"Yes," he said slowly, and then changed directions abruptly, cutting into the narrow belt of palm trees that separated the cottages from the main office and dining room. Since my feet were bare, I was grateful that the sand was smooth and free of shell fragments. "We'll go to my cottage first. You do know how to use a gun?"

"Yes." And I did. Not well, but I had once gone shooting with my father and the day had rather branded itself into my memory.

"Okay. Be careful not to shoot anyone except zombies," he instructed.

"For sure."

"And if you have to shoot a zombie, you'll need to do it twice. Once in the head and once in the heart. Anything else just annoys them."

"Okay," I said, though things were far, far from being okay. "How many people are on the island now?" I asked. Translation: *How many people might I accidentally shoot?*

"Only six cottages are rented, but the other guests will be leaving tomorrow. Everyone wants to be home for New Year's Eve. It seems that it's all right to avoid your family on Christmas, but not your friends on New Year's."

I shrugged. I didn't feel judgmental.

"How many staff?"

"Emori, Jope, Manasa . . . Um, six. I can send them away tomorrow as well. If need be."

Translation: *If the island is about to be overrun with zombies.* It was amazing how much information we were conveying to each other without actually saying much of anything.

"But you're staying?" I asked him.

"Yes. Some fights you can't back away from."

"But some you can," I insisted as we walked up to a small cottage set away from the others. The small windows were shuttered.

"I agree. But first I need to know what kind of fight this is. If I have to make a stand, I want it to be somewhere that innocent bystanders won't be involved. Anyway, if he's found me once, he'll find me again. At least this time, thanks to you, I have some warning and a home-field advantage."

I sighed. "You're a complicated man."

Translation: *You're an idiot, but very brave and I like your weird dark eyes.*

"Only on the outside," he answered, opening the cottage door. I noticed at once that this cottage was different from mine. For one thing, the walls were a foot thick, the door was made of some kind of metal, and there were iron shutters on the inside of the windows and not just those cute bamboo ones on the outside. There were also no light fixtures, just an oil lamp on a small table. This seemed appropriate since Ambrose had been born before the days of neon and fluorescents and other man-made glares.

"Early Norman-invasion style," I muttered. And unappealing in every way except one. Unfortunately, at that moment, thick walls and an iron door were what mattered most to me. I was ready to move in.

There was also almost no furniture. The effect was not some sort of restful Japanese simplicity, but reminded me more of a penitent's cell. There was some support of this notion when I saw a small plaster statue resting on the window sill next to a burned-down candlestick. The inscription read: Lazaro.

Lazarus, patron saint of lepers and other outcasts. This item seemed strange to me at first. Ambrose Bierce had believed in God but had not been a religious man. It would have taken something life-altering to drive him into the bosom of Catholic mysticism. But wasn't that exactly what had happened? I'm theologically neutral and am not usually bothered by religious icons of other people's faith, but this statue was disconcerting because it made things feel very real and very immediate, and all about good and evil. Ambrose Bierce required strength from a higher power. Wouldn't I, a mere mortal, require help too? And if I did, would it be forthcoming? I don't usually pray to any of the pantheon of Moral Absolutes of the ultimate gated community: saints, angels, Jesus, God himself. I guess I never had any faith that they would help little ol' flawed me who was neither particularly moral nor absolute.

I forced myself to look away from the statue. If I needed anything else to confirm his story of being a werewolf, there were deep gouges in the concrete floor, suggestive marks that looked an awful lot like they were made by giant claws. I also saw what looked like a wisp of animal hair caught in the rough wood around the door. The golden brown fur was at shoulder height. There might also have been smudges of blood. Obviously housekeeping hadn't been in to clean for a few days.

"Bad weekend?" I asked, staring at the fuzz and then the torn floor.

Ambrose paused, looking at the fur in the jamb for a moment before brushing it away. "Same old, same old. Like you, I hate the holidays. It seems that no matter what I do, I always end up with coal in my stocking and blood on my floor," he answered, disappearing into another room. I heard a drawer open. It screeched like a rusted file cabinet. Ambrose reappeared a minute later with a nine-millimeter handgun and a shotgun. He was also wearing a T-shirt that said: ANY DAY ABOVE THE GROUND IS A GOOD ONE. I concurred with the sentiment.

He handed me the pistol. It was a Colt Peacemaker. I recognized it both because it was the gun I had shot on that memorable occasion when I had my one father-daughter bonding experience, but also because of the lecture I got along with the lesson on how to shoot this rather heavy pistol without injuring myself.

For those of you who don't know the Colt, it had an illustrious history—and by that I mean it has a long and bloody history. It was the handgun of choice at the OK Corral, for instance. It's shot a lot of soldiers and a lot of "injuns." Unlike its sleeker, modern brethren that shoot high-velocity, steel-cased, narrow-caliber shells that leave neat little holes in targets—and bodies, I assume—the Colt shoots large, unjacketed, soft-nosed bullets that mushroom on impact, ripping large messy holes in targets. And bodies, again presumably. My father told me that if I was stupid enough to shoot myself in the foot with it, I would no longer have a foot. I had handled the gun with great care. As I still valued my feet, I handled this one with great care as well.

"Don't worry. It's already loaded. You just have to point and shoot."

"Okay," I said, again at a loss for words. Miss Manners's etiquette guide just didn't cover a situation like this.

I kept the gun pointed well away from my feet, though my finger was nowhere near the trigger. I know, it's dumb, but the whole "if I shot myself in the foot I wouldn't have a foot" thing has always stuck in my mind.

"Ready?"

Well, not really. But I nodded and we went back outside. In the few moments we had been indoors, the weather had changed. Clouds had roiled in from the west and blocked out the sun. The smell of ozone was strong in the air.

"So, shower and olives first?" Ambrose asked. "Or do we head right for the beach?"

Olives! Pick olives! My cowardly side sniveled. But I said: "The beach. We need to find out what's going on."

I sounded so brave I almost fooled myself. I could never have faked it if I hadn't known that Ambrose really wasn't afraid, and confident that he could handle anything we might face. I was strictly a second-string benchwarmer.

"Or at least if there are any more zombies," Ambrose muttered. I don't have supersensitive ears, but my hearing is rather good and I was listening carefully, so I caught this.

Ambrose and I were walking differently as we stalked over the sand. Weapons do that to a person. They make one move with deliberation and purpose. Also, one's balance is different when one is holding a handgun out to the side so it doesn't point at one's feet.

We didn't speak, though it was unlikely that we could have heard anything over the sound of waves shushing across the beach and the increasing screech of the wind as it whipped its way through the thrashing palms and up the side of the mountain that divided the island in two.

"A storm's coming. That's odd, because there wasn't anything in the long-range forecast about one." Ambrose sounded a bit grim.

"Great," I muttered, thinking of all the horror movies I'd seen where people got trapped on islands because of terrible storms. For a moment, I thought Ambrose was going to say something more, but he decided to keep his counsel for the time being.

All too soon we reached the edge of the water. I stopped a foot away from the waterline, reluctant to get my feet wet with water that had also touched a zombie.

"I'm going to put you up on the rocks. You'll have a better vantage point," Ambrose said, taking me by the waist and tossing me and the Colt on top of a flat-topped, shoulder-high boulder that was damp but not slimy. The casual use of his unusual strength was still disconcerting, though I had no fear of him turning that strength upon me. "You're sure you're okay?"

I nodded, being tired of saying so. Particularly since I was increasingly less okay every time he asked.

"Keep this for now," he said, handing me the

shotgun, which I laid on the rock beside me. It was probably more accurate than the Colt, but I'd never used one before and I didn't think this was the day to begin lessons. Ambrose's dark eyes considered me as I straightened. "I'd prefer you not shoot me, but if I come out of the water with anything attached, feel free to let fly. I don't like getting shot, but even less do I like getting bitten by zombies."

I looked at the deadly Colt in my hand and remembered how it kicked and how loud the percussion was. Then I thought about the zombie and what it might look like fastened to Ambrose's neck. Injury by bullets or teeth, neither option appealed to me, but his preferences had been clearly stated. I would honor them.

"I'll try to keep away from your face," I said, which was a grim sort of truth, but for some reason it made him laugh.

"Please do. That Colt will drop a charging bull at fifty yards. I'd be hours picking up pieces of my head."

Before I could say anything else, he peeled off his khaki shorts and T-shirt and began walking naked toward the water. I thought about asking him what the hell he was doing, but decided that I didn't want him to turn around and talk to me while he wasn't wearing clothes. One naked body a day was enough, even though Ambrose's body was a much more pleasant form to look at.

In a distressingly short period of time he had disappeared under the water. I saw him break the surface once when he was out beyond the waves. He traveled the distance in half the time it had taken me.

It began to rain the moment I was alone. Big fat stinging drops, which I hated both because it decreased visibility and also because it was surprisingly cold after a while. Or maybe it was fear whose cold hands ran themselves over my body and lingered at my heart.

"Shit. Why me?" I asked the heavens. "I'm not good at stressful situations, and this situation would turn John Wayne into a bed wetter." In answer, the rain began falling hard enough to hit the rocks and then bounce back into the air. The drops that hit me bounced back, too, but only after they had bruised my flesh. Also—and I tried hard to tell myself it was only my overwrought imagination—I thought I could smell traces of rot and sulfur in the air. That wasn't normal. I didn't know if I should be looking for more zombies creeping up behind me from the beach, or watching for the cone of what might be a reawakening volcano.

All around me the wind jeered and bushes whispered slyly. I could have shouted back, but the wind would have shredded my voice as it did all other sound.

I recalled a particularly horrid story that had haunted me all my days at boarding school. It was about the Jólasveinar or Yulemen. They were sneaky goblins who showed up around Christmas time and lingered until Twelfth Night. These are the thirteen progeny of Grýla and Leppalúði, an Icelandic troll couple opposed to family planning who, additionally, had a habit of eating disobedient human kids who desperately needed to get up to use the bathroom in the night even when it was against dormitory rules. The ogre kids weren't truly evil like their parents, but they were malicious. They had names like Door Slammer, Window Peeper, Meat Hooker and, rather horribly, Doorway Sniffer. Most terrifying of all of them were the Lamp Shadow, the Smoke Gulper and the Crevice Imp, because they could be anywhere and everywhere. What house was there that didn't have lamps or a fireplace or the odd crack or two where something wicked could hide? It made every nighttime trip to the bathroom at the end of the long, icy hall an exercise in terror.

But that just goes to show you how even the worst things can have a silver lining, I told myself. It was excellent training for someone who might have to play hide-and-seek with zombies.

Nevertheless, I had worked myself into a good state of pre-hysteria and heart palpitations when Ambrose reappeared from the agitated surf. I was so grateful to see him—sans zombies—that I forgot to be bothered by his nudity.

"Did you see anything?" I called, a hand at my chest in a protective gesture that was probably a bit theatrical but still comforting. The wind tossed my words back at me, but he seemed to hear them anyway. I kept my eyes on his face. I wasn't ready for any other distractions.

"Not yet. But the sharks are definitely behaving

oddly." He picked up his damp shorts and shirt but didn't put them on at once. "Hand me the rifle," he said, and I bent to retrieve the shotgun.

"Okay, let's get dried off and have a bite to eat and then I'm going over to see the mangroves."

"*W-we're* going to see the mangroves," I corrected. My teeth had begun to chatter either from fright or the cold. I didn't mention the volcano. The smell was gone and the idea seemed stupid once I was no longer alone. Also, though it is anthropomorphizing, I felt that the island was grateful the wind had stopped its eerie moaning. A few birds appeared in nearby bushes and a long green lizard crawled up onto the rock where I was standing. He moved warily, as though expecting further assault. I sympathized.

"Okay, *we're* going to see the mangroves. But not until you've warmed up. I don't mind pale women, but you look like plasterboard. Gray just isn't your best color." He could probably also hear my heart galloping along like a wild horse with a lame leg.

The cold didn't seem to bother him, but I was beginning to shake and didn't protest when he lifted me down from my perch. His hands were still wonderfully warm as was his naked but wet body. "E-everyone's a c-critic," I muttered and then laughed. I had recalled Ambrose's entry on this subject in his *Devil's Dictionary:* **Critic,** *n. A person who boasts himself hard to please because nobody tries to please him.*

"Come on," he said, taking my hand and pulling

me close for a comforting hug. He held me close for a minute and I felt something like scar tissue rise up on his chest. It was his lightning scar, the ceraunograph imprinted on his body when he was electrocuted by the Dark Man. "Excuse the liberties, but you'll freeze if we don't get you warm."

I excused the liberties. I even welcomed them. Being in his arms was like being wrapped in an electric blanket turned up to an unsafe but toasty setting. I needed that badly.

Brandy, *n.* A cordial composed of one part thunder-and-lightning, one part remorse, two parts bloody murder, one part death-hell-and-the-grave and four parts clarified Satan. Dose, a headful all the time. Brandy is said by Dr. Johnson to be the drink of heroes. Only a hero will venture to drink it.

Rum, *n.* Generically, fiery liquors that produce madness in total abstainers.
> —Ambrose Bierce, *The Devil's Dictionary*

Chapter Four

Ambrose was dressed and had made or procured a pot of hot chocolate by the time I was out of his shower. Feeling infinitely better, I joined him at the small table near the French doors that overlooked the beach, and accepted a vibrant blue mug from his long-fingered hands. A quick sniff told me the hot chocolate was laced with brandy. Fortunately, a quick sip assured me that the chocolate was strong enough to defend itself against the liquor, and the drink was smooth and luscious and completely unlike the stuff I got at the greasy *ptomainery* where I had often grabbed breakfast and sometimes a late afternoon hot chocolate laced with peppermint schnapps.

"Have you noticed that there's a support group for every problem? Except this one," he added.

"I don't know," I hedged, trying for a bit of lightness as I sipped again at the chocolate. It was delicious. Usually I am surly when fatigued, but this time I was too shocked by what had happened and too fascinated with Ambrose to feel any of the low-grade peevishness that might be cruising through my body. "They might have a Zombies Anonymous chapter in Haiti."

"No. I've checked," he said.

"Well, that's just disappointing." Maybe it was my mind protecting itself, or perhaps the hot chocolate, but I seemed unable to return to my previous horrified state. In fact, I felt exhilarated.

He turned to me with a small smile. "Oh, I don't know. It's probably a good thing that zombies aren't all that common. The world has trouble enough with cockroaches and termites."

I nodded at this bit of prosaic wisdom and took refuge in my cup. We watched in companionable silence as a small bird flitted by the window and alit on a flowering bush just outside. It was a strange silvery white shade that I associate with the ghostly winter weather in Munich, and its eyes were red. I found its gaze a bit unnerving and wondered fleetingly if it suffered from albinism.

"Ambrose, is that all that zombies do? Track people, I mean."

"Pretty much. They do whatever they are bidden—as long as it involves hunting and killing and eventually eating whatever they find. They're not smart enough for anything more sophisticated . . . at least not the ones I've seen. You wouldn't send one to rob a bank or break into a computer." We weren't looking at each other. Instead, we watched the bird as it hopped closer, its red gaze intent on us though our images could not have been clear through the glare on the glass.

"That's a very strange bird," I said at last, forced to voice some of the discomfort I was feeling.

"Very. I've never seen one like it," Ambrose said slowly, beginning to rise. At the first sign of movement the bird hopped back from the window. Its posture was wary.

"Is it an albino? Can a bird be born without pigmentation?"

"Yes, but that isn't the only way they turn white. Look at my skin. It's a side effect of Dippel's treatment."

"But . . . you think this bird got electrocuted somehow?"

"Maybe. Saint Elmo's fire isn't selective with its targets. If an animal just happened to be nearby. . . ." His gaze was fixed on the bird. "I think that it might be best if I had a closer look at our avian friend. It's native to these islands, so it hasn't flown in from anyplace far away."

"Good luck with that," I said just as the bird again took flight. This time it landed in the highest branches of a spidery, broad-leafed tree. It stared at us for another moment and then flew away.

"Why did you come here for Christmas?" Ambrose asked me abruptly, resuming his seat. His gaze was bright like a searchlight on an escaping prisoner and about as welcome. Sensing my discomfort, he looked away. But I knew that out of sight wasn't out of mind.

"I didn't. I came the day after," I corrected, not wanting to get upset again. My body was already filled with tension; I didn't want my emotions adding to that.

"You booked two days before." His voice was mild but I suspected he'd be insistent. It occurred to me that my arrival had rather coincided with the zombie's, and that maybe he was wondering about possible connections.

"You had a cancellation."

"Yes. A fortuitous one."

"Well, that's debatable."

Ambrose raised a brow.

I thought for a moment before saying anything else, deciding just how much I was willing to share to put his mind at ease—at least, put it to ease regarding whether the zombie had or had not been after me. Usually life's small hurts and indignities roll off my shoulders, but this last one had been crushing, and I still felt a bit bruised and disinclined to share anything about Max or my lost baby.

"I am an only child. My parents are dead. They died on Christmas in a plane crash a decade ago," I said baldly, because there was no way to soften this story without having it sound like a plea for sympathy. "I expect that somewhere inside I must feel badly about this, but I think it is probably more that I feel sad I never had real parents to begin with." I cleared my throat. "They should never have had a child. Society doesn't like to hear this, but some people just shouldn't. As it was, I was given to nannies and then to schools to raise. I saw my parents only twice a year."

Why hadn't my mother just smothered me in the crib and put me out of their misery? I wondered this for the millionth time. With my bad heart, no one would have ever asked questions about a crib death. If I had to take a guess—and was feeling unusually cheerful—I would say it was my father who stayed my mother's hand, and sent me away as soon as he could so that she couldn't harm me. He seemed okay with imperfection as long as he didn't have to confront it daily, and it hadn't been his genetic flaw that had been passed on to me. My mother could barely stand to look in my direction.

I have sometimes wondered if maybe she didn't try smothering me once. All through childhood I had a terrible time sleeping, and feared the dark. When I had nightmares, I never cried out, fearing my parents would hear me and be angered. Nor did this fear go away when I went to school. Even now I hate to recall all those long nights in bed in the dorm room surrounded by the bodies of sleeping classmates but still feeling all alone and cold in my soul because the certainty existed that if the monster came and got me, no one would really care. I often imagined that I died, and thought about how my belongings would be divided up amongst the other girls.

In my fantasies, my parents never came to get my body. Some coroner would cut it up—a classmate's father was a forensic pathologist, and Miranda often regaled us with tales of strange and highly implausible autopsies. The butcher would discover that while most girls were made of sugar and spice, I was actually stuffed full of slugs and snails and puppy-dog tails. And Miranda would tell all the other girls what her father had found and they would laugh at me.

"Don't look so . . . whatever you're looking." My voice was too fierce and I moderated it immediately. I was looking at Ambrose but seeing my mother with a pillow in her hands, and at her side was a masked coroner holding a scalpel. "I never lacked physically—for anything, but . . . they had all the parental affection and instincts of a cash register. I was flawed bodily and they didn't love me," I ended flatly. "And because a large part of me believed them when they made the judgment that I would never amount to much in my short life, I never expected to live to adulthood. Not too surprisingly, I didn't develop a lot of the normal social skills other people have. I don't make friends easily. Especially male ones." I swallowed. "When the dazzling Max Ober swooped into my life I jumped at the chance to be *normal*. When this got taken away I . . . let's just say that the erosion of the illusion that I could ever be entirely normal was swift and horrifying. It made me rather bitter. And sometimes cruel." There was probably more I should have said, but I could go no further.

"Were your parents related to my late unlamented wife, do you think?" he asked after a moment. "Or is it just wealth that makes some people compassionless assholes who have no patience for anyone with flaws?"

This obscenity startled a brief laugh from me.

"They may have belonged to the same heartless social clubs," I conceded. It took some effort but I forced lightness into my tone. "You know, we're not unique. Not for this, at least. History is full of disasters, and disastrous lives and disastrous people."

"Sure. Like Pompeii," my companion said agreeably, and took a gulp of his own hot chocolate.

"The *Hindenburg*," I suggested. He apparently liked natural disasters, but I preferred man-made ones. Most people had screwed-up lives because of something they had done or had done to them by the people they loved; it wasn't accidental or random.

"Hurricane Katrina."

"The *Titanic*." I was beginning to smile.

"And my wife and her blasted mother—and apparently your mother and father." Ambrose sipped. "A bad relationship shouldn't inform one's every moment, but . . ."

"But it does." I sighed.

"For a while," he agreed.

"I'm fine now, though. I'm over it." There was absolutely no proof of this, but it seemed obligatory that I say it.

"So, it wasn't the sudden lack of parents that sent you to this island." Ambrose didn't comment on my assertion that all was well in my brain.

"No," I said.

He waited. I waited too, but he was better at it and eventually I loosened the vise grip on my tongue and told him what he wanted to know. "Have you ever spent winter in Munich? At Christmas?" I asked.

"Yes. It was charming if rather cold." I had the feeling he was going to be unyielding about this particular point, so I decided to go ahead and get it out in the open. Then I'd post a no-trespassing sign on this topic.

"A few months ago I . . . had a miscarriage." That sounded better than losing a baby. Babies were people and their loss had to be mourned. Miscarriages were medical mishaps that didn't require expressions of sympathy from him or admissions of grief from me. "My relationship with her father was already on life support when I found out I was pregnant. He stayed because although he is a philandering, self-involved jerk, he isn't heartless or entirely irresponsible. He knew I had no family to help me. But once I miscarried there was no reason not to pull the plug on things, so we did." I looked Ambrose full in the eye, daring him to ask even one more question. I didn't tell him that my hateful recriminations had started before the first tear could dry on my cheek. That would make me sound like his wife. She had also been a hysteric. Let it remain all Max's fault.

"I lost two children, one to suicide," he said softly. "And I ran away from home too. Hell, I even bought an island so I wouldn't have to go back and deal with my old life. If you were looking for a lecture on the sanctity of relationships, you won't get it from me." This reminder about his losses took some of the hot wind out of my sails. It was rumored that he had told H. L. Mencken that he kept his dead son's ashes in a cigar box on his desk. The boy had been only sixteen when he killed himself.

"Don't feel bad about getting away," he said. "It would have been worse had you married him. Men who are morally maneuverable are the least likely to change with wedlock."

"Was your wife really that bad?" I asked, glad to change the subject. Normally, I wouldn't have been this bald with my questions, but he had rather invited such a tack. Perhaps it had all happened so long ago that it just didn't matter anymore.

"Yes. She was the daughter of a hard-rock miner, and that pretty well describes her heart and soul. In my day, you didn't live with a woman before you married. In fact, you rarely had a chance to visit with them without some chaperone nearby. I took her measure only weeks after our marriage and did my best to steer clear of her after that. Unfortunately, the children always brought me back. Her beauty did the rest. It's why we had three children and not just the one. I used to call her Miss Mollie," he said reminiscently. "She hated that, said it was vulgar—which was reason enough to do it."

"History has been kind to her. She's usually painted as the wronged party," I said gently. Was I really still thinking of doing his biography? A part of me probably was. Observing others and telling their story was part of my nature.

"I know, and I've let that fiction stand for my daughter's sake. My ex-wife died soon after the divorce, and though she may have been devious and cold-blooded where I was concerned, she did love her children in her own selfish way. I couldn't take away my daughter's illusions. And, to be just, I was an utter bastard at times. Most times. And it got worse after I took that bullet to the head. I pity everyone who had to live or work with me before I was resurrected. Frankly, it's a miracle the marriage ended in divorce and not homicide."

Resurrected. The word made me shiver. Seeing this, Ambrose frowned and poured me more hot chocolate out of his small porcelain pot.

"Your . . . treatment helped with the head wound too?" I found myself rubbing my chest in sympathy, and stopped immediately.

"Yes, a great deal of the rage went away. I can't view it as an entirely bad thing, though it rather took away the urge to write. My career was fueled by vitriol, you know." His smile was wry, his voice self-mocking.

"So it's not an entirely good thing."

"No, especially not when you throw in the lycanthropy." He paused. "Also, I don't think the human brain is designed to suffer from the kinds of loss that come with extended life. It isn't just the deaths of friends and family that amass. It's the extinction of your era, your culture, even your preferred style of dress and speech. The world keeps evolving and so must I. It's wearying, though." He shrugged. "Who would have guessed that I'd end up being one of the things that goes bump in the night? It's probably what I deserve, but not at all what I expected. At times I have even wondered if I am entirely sane anymore."

I stared at him and took his measure, appreciating his toned if pale body but also remembering his mind. I'd always loved his mind.

After a moment I said, "I'm not that surprised you've ended up this way, I guess. You used to write vividly about some pretty creepy things. It was tempting Fate. Look at your last letter to your niece, when you predicted you'd end up facing a firing squad in Mexico."

His strangely twisted writings had delighted in being enigmatic and often deceptive. But ultimately the messages of the stories were straightforward, and he herded the reader toward a definite goal—usually the discomfiture of someone he disliked. But sometimes he drove people to confronting the weird and unexplainable that went on all around them. I wondered if he hadn't had a premonition of what was to come when he wrote "The Eyes of the Panther," a story about a man afflicted with lycanthropy. He had been prescient about other things that happened in his life, certainly. The foremost example of his prognostication was predicting the assassination of President McKinley.

"And as ye seek so shall ye find?" he asked, again seeming to read my thoughts.

"Sometimes." I yawned loudly, unable to fight off a sudden exhaustion rolling over my body. "Ambrose, is the full moon the only time you . . . change?"

He stared off over the water. "Yes. And no. I avoid changing as much as possible now, though I experimented in the beginning. It hurts, you see. And it gives me hell's own hangover sometimes for days after." He took a breath and then went on, I thought with some reluctance. "I can change at will, but don't."

"Because of the pain?" I asked, to clarify. This was morbid curiosity that I wouldn't normally indulge, but he had set the ground rules by prying into my personal affairs, and I figured I would ask my questions for as long as he would answer them.

"Yes, and the danger of being seen. And . . . well, the urges."

"Urges?" I had to ask.

"Of both a violent and sexual nature. They shouldn't be indulged. Sex makes the wolf want to kill. Killing makes the wolf want sex. And food. It's always hungry. It's a vicious cycle." Ambrose wrenched the top off a jar of olives and upended it over his mouth. Half the jar's contents disappeared. The rest he handed to me. Apparently he wasn't worried about me catching any of his werewolf cooties.

"Can you describe it?" I set the jar aside for later. The current subject matter was not stimulating my appetite.

Ambrose swallowed. "Yes. Imagine having every

tooth in your head extracted without anesthetic, while getting an all-over body wax. The hair doesn't so much push free as get ripped out. I grow a tail from the end of my spine—it's prehensile, by the way. My knees reverse themselves and joint backwards. And then I have to undo it when it's done— shove all the hair and teeth and claws back in again. I have to collapse the bones in my tail and pull them into my body. . . ."

This last part sounded especially horrible, and I started to say so but was overcome by another huge yawn. He continued talking, saving me from having to comment.

"Then I wake up with the most god-awful tastes in my mouth and I start remembering that I've been eating ghastly things. Sometimes I find blood under my nails and I have to recall what I've killed. And sometimes I know I've done other things, but can't always recall with whom."

Though I tried to suppress it, another yawn threatened to split my jaws as it forced its way out of my body. I apologized. "Sorry. It's not you. I'm just very tired. My head is getting so heavy."

I need my sleep. So does everyone, of course, but when I get very tired, things start going awry in my body. Among other problems, my blood pressure drops and I have blackouts. Adrenaline can carry me for a while, but even terror has its limitations. My hunch—and it was a real elephant-sized intuition—said I'd better nap as soon as I could because there was every chance I wouldn't be sleeping much once the other zombies reached the island. The other zombies . . .

I tried very hard to put the matter back out of my mind, which was a mostly useless exercise, but I succeeded in shoving it aside enough to relax my knotted muscles. I was so relaxed that I slumped in my chair.

"Come on, you need to rest," Ambrose said. "I'm amazed that you've made it this long." He stood up and took my arm, guided me to a small sofa made of bamboo and covered in batik cushions.

Part of me really didn't want to nap because I feared that I would dream, but I needed rest and my body was making me sleep. The swimming and snorkeling, the fear—it all added up to exhaustion. Not even the possibility of zombies invading the island could change that. My enervated remains collapsed down on the sofa, and I went bye-bye for a couple of hours. The last thing I felt was Ambrose pulling some kind of cover over me and smoothing back my damp hair. A small weight landed near my feet and I heard a loud purring.

"Don't worry," he said. "Ashanti and I will keep watch while you sleep."

That was the first time in my life that anyone had said this to me, and it brought a comfort that no words can describe.

Lunarian, *n*. An inhabitant of the moon, as distinguished from Lunatic, one whom the moon inhabits.

Werewolf, *n*. A wolf that was once, or is sometimes, a man.
> —Ambrose Bierce, *The Devil's Dictionary*

The hour of departure has arrived and we go our separate ways, I to die and you to live. Which of these two is better only the gods know.
> —Socrates

Chapter Five

I woke up to a sinking sun and an empty stomach that wasted no time in telling me its tale of woe. True to his word, Ambrose and Ashanti were nearby, though only the cat was laying on my body in a possessive manner and blowing hot breath into my ear.

"What time?" I croaked, squinting against the orange light. It had the same peculiar color of a southern California sky when the Santa Anas are blowing and terrible fires roar. My last had been a short but memorable trip because of the evacuations. I sniffed now but smelled no smoke.

"Dinnertime," Ambrose answered with a smile, setting aside a paperback. He was reading a novel by Lynsay Sands, which rather surprised me. I wouldn't have thought her to his taste. "I selected lobster for you. May as well enjoy a last sumptuous dinner before the cook leaves."

I nodded, but didn't mention that this sounded a bit too much like a condemned man's last meal: *Eat, drink and be merry, for tomorrow we die.* I promised myself that I would make an effort to appear enthusiastic about consuming it.

"I have to change," I said.

"Only if you want to. Many of the female guests dine in little more than a bikini."

"I am not most guests," I heard my half-awake voice reply primly, and then I carefully moved the cat off my chest, threw back the covers and stalked toward the bedroom. I could feel my hair curling around me like Medusa's angry snakes.

Ambrose laughed softly. He was amazingly lighthearted given what we had just recently been through, and I began to wonder if he had ADD.

Before dinner, we stopped back by my cottage so I could change. I skipped the stockings and garter belt but did put on a new linen sundress and heels. It's stupid, but I wanted a chance to wear it before everyone left and I no longer had an excuse for dressing up. The thought also crossed my mind that I should drop someone a postcard and let them know where I was—just in case—but other than my publisher, I couldn't think of a soul who would care. The thought was lowering.

Brooding doesn't usually solve problems but I sometimes do it anyway. I looked at my reflection as I slathered on some lip gloss, and didn't like what I saw peering back. Fear eventually leaves traces on the face, as certainly as pain does, and the marks are every bit as unattractive. Pain comes in a whole variety of flavors, as I have discovered through the years. I hadn't understood until that day that fear did, too. Having sampled several varieties lately, ranging from chronic angst all the way to mortal terror, I decided that I didn't need second helpings to confirm my lack of enthusiasm for such fare.

I was probably going to get them if I stayed on the island. The thought made my reflection scowl.

Dinner was lovely. Knowing it was the last night and that anything not eaten would go bad before people returned, the chef laid out an amazing spread. The delectables were appealing to the eye, but I found my appetite limited. Subconsciously, my body was sending out the message that it didn't want to be slowed down if I had to run for my life. Of course, by that logic, I shouldn't have wanted to wear a dress and heels.

About halfway through dinner, just as the sun was sinking into the sea, a strange fog rolled in over the island. It stopped at the ring of torches where we dined and didn't venture onto the lighted paths that led to the cottages, but it cocooned the rest of the islet in gray. It was too easy to think of it as a winding shroud and imagine that the whole island was about to be buried at sea.

I watched Ambrose as he studied the mist, baffled by his expression. I couldn't be certain, but I was willing to bet that every rock, every tree, every clump of grass and cute green turtle was covered with fog, smothered in the sinister earthbound cloud that smelled of sulfur and reawakened my fear of volcanoes. For the time being the sun was all but extinct. Twilight ruled, and would until true night fell. If the fog remained dense, we wouldn't see the moon. And Ambrose seemed happy about it! Except that it was too utterly ridiculous to even consider, I might have assumed he had somehow arranged for the fog.

Every now and then something large splashed out in the water. That I couldn't see it was only to be expected. After all, I was living in a horror movie, and those are the rules. The boogeyman is twice as scary if you can't see him coming.

I smiled at my silliness. Still, even with Ambrose beside me and a scotch in my stomach, the unknown was troubling. And it remained so, no matter how often I told myself it was just the fish or some seabird hunting in the shallow waves. I vowed to my sniveling inner child that I would stay far back from the shoreline and move as silently as I could when I went back to my cottage so that no one would chase us through the fog.

If I went back to my cottage, that was. I was thinking earnestly about spending the night behind Ambrose' thicker walls and metal shutters.

"I don't smell anything." He *was* pleased. I could hear it in his voice. He liked the damned fog.

And "anything"? That was code for *zombies*.

"Me either," I answered. Unless you counted the

nasty volcano smell. The candles' flames seemed to dance drunkenly in their cut-crystal bowls, but it may have been a shortage of oxygen and not the wind that made them gutter. I realized that my chest hurt and I had to force myself to breathe. I did not need to have a cardiac event in front of everyone.

"Do you hear anything?" I asked quietly.

"Yes. I think we have a crocodile out there."

"What?" I almost forgot to whisper.

"We get saltwater crocs sometimes. They swim over from the Solomons."

"Are they big?" I asked fearfully. *Crocodile,* like *cancer,* is one of those words that invokes atavistic fear in most people. In this, I am wholly normal.

"Well . . . not especially. But this one is an eighteen-footer."

"What?" Again I came close to shrieking, and this made him grin. I guess giant crocodiles aren't scary if you're immortal.

"Don't worry. She's staying offshore. She'll probably head for the mangroves soon. Crocs don't like people in large numbers. In a way she's good news."

"Yeah?" I sounded doubtful. Sorry, but to my way of thinking, an eighteen-foot crocodile roaming at large in thick fog just couldn't be a good thing when you had tourists roaming too.

"She's a sort of watchdog. Nothing is going to get past without her raising a huge ruckus." *Raising a ruckus.* That was code for having Hell's own fight. "And given this cold fog, I doubt anyone will be trysting on the beach, so we needn't worry about any close encounters between reptiles and humans.

Everyone will go from here to bed and then from bed to the plane."

Trysting. That's on old-fashioned code word for . . . well, you know, right?

He sounded so sure of these facts that I almost demanded to know if the chef had put something other than Bordeaux in the wine sauce. I glanced at my lobster, wondering if it was glazed with sleeping pills.

"You're a scary man, Ambrose."

"I know." And he stopped smiling.

"What did you tell the staff?" I asked. He lifted an enquiring brow. "About why they have to leave so suddenly."

"I told them there was a giant crocodile nesting in the mangroves and that we had to leave so that nature could safely take its course. They aren't complaining. It's happened before and they get paid for their time off."

"She's been here before?"

"Yes. These are her nesting grounds. There are very few giant crocs left. Humans have killed them all." He shrugged. "The island is large enough to share, so I don't mind granting refuge to another creature who needs it from time to time to raise her babies."

And just like that, the crocodile became an animal instead of a monster. Albeit, a really large, caution-inducing animal.

"I like you. You're gallant," he said unexpectedly. His dark eyes were suddenly fastened on mine, and I swear that they looked right past my body and into my soul. Radiant heat welled up inside of me, urging me to get comfortable, to take a place at his fire and never leave. "I didn't think I would take to you. Not this way. But that's life, isn't it? Unexpected."

I couldn't think of any reason why he had taken to me—or I to him. But I didn't think about it too much just then. These things happen, right?

I nodded reluctantly and looked away, beginning to be fearful of something other than zombies and crocodiles. I wasn't sure if I welcomed the distraction of more mundane concerns like the possibility of falling in love—or at least lust—with an inappropriate person.

Hard lessons had taught me that personality, identity, it's all about keeping clear edges, definite borders that outline who we are. *Here, here, here and here*—this is me; daughter, Democrat, dog-lover, whatever. But heedless and hopeless and often completely blind love smudges those boundaries. Sometimes it rubs them out altogether and you begin to blur into the other person, to blend your tastes, schedules and even beliefs. Next thing you know, you've moved to a foreign country and agreed to write a biography about a person you don't like just to please someone else.

It was probably good that I did this once with Max, since love is an important and almost universal part of the human condition, but I felt resistant to the idea of risking such entanglement again. It isn't a pleasant fact to admit even now, but at that point Ambrose's personality was stronger than mine—hell, he was practically a superhero who had saved me from a flesh-eating zombie—and only a fool would have ignored it. I could be an idiot—this was already proven—but I have always tried not be stupid in the same way twice. There would be no more blind, unquestioning love for me, I assured myself with a confidence I almost believed.

I did like him, though. Something about him fascinated me as no person ever had, and physically I reacted to his presence in ways that I never had before. That was probably partly because of who he was—Ambrose Bierce, the great American writer.

As though guessing both my wary thoughts and my unease with the sudden intense attraction, he added: "That wasn't a proposal of marriage or anything. You needn't look so concerned."

He blinked, and his eyes were again just eyes, although very dark ones. I smiled ruefully and nodded while I finished my scotch. What was I thinking? Of course it wasn't a proposal of marriage. Bitter Bierce would never marry again. He liked me. He probably even wanted me. Which was okay. I could do *like* and *want*.

"Why is Saint Germain doing this—coming after you?" I asked, changing the subject. "I know he must be crazy, but even crazy people do things for a reason."

"I've given this a great deal of thought while you were sleeping, and I believe that he wants a new viral ally."

Viral ally. That was code for . . . I couldn't even guess.

"What?" I was saying this a lot. *What?* That was code for *whatthefuckareyoutalkingabout?!?*

"I think that he has been looking for a way to raise and control the dead that doesn't involve magic. There were some suspicious goings-on in Mexico a couple years ago in a region known for having vampires. Rumor on the supernatural grapevine at the time was that he ended up killing the local death god and taking over his vampire priestesses. But someone—several someones—took the vampires out shortly after he made his power play. They also sabotaged some of his clinics where he was doing genetic research down in South America."

Is this chilling you as you read it? It chilled me as I heard Ambrose say it. I think it was that combination of words: *death god, vampires* and *genetic research.*

"Why?" I asked again. Maybe if I kept asking I'd eventually hear something useful or even understandable. "Why does he need another way to raise the dead? How is it that you can help?"

Ambrose shrugged. It wasn't a gesture of indifference but rather to show that he didn't know where to begin.

"As I understand it, magic limits the number of zombies he can raise and control at any one time. Even Saint Germain, powerful as he is, has limits on his psychic strength and how many balls he can juggle at once. If he had been able to establish vampiric mind-control—a sort of telepathic command system—he could have manipulated many more entities and even changed their instructions by mental remote control. As it is, once he creates a zombie or ghoul and gives it instructions, the thing is on autopilot and Saint Germain has no way of altering its objectives should the situation change. They are also stupid. He could try to create people like me, I suppose, but he never has. I think he fears what the reaction of any thinking person might be. Or perhaps he doesn't have the Dark Man's secrets of resurrection."

I didn't know what to say to this latest impossibility, so I opted for silence.

"His clinics do a lot of work with cloning and DNA manipulation. Vampirism should have worked, but has apparently failed him for some reason. I think he wants the lycanthropy virus now. He wants to be the alpha werewolf of a new kind of pack and breed instinctive obedience into his ghouls who could serve as his generals. As it is, he has only marginal control over them when they are out of sight, and he may worry about them turning against him eventually. Ghouls are not inherently loyal, and they are just smart enough to plan a coup—as the Dark Man eventually learned. Of course, Saint Germain may just want the virus for himself, so he can become stronger and faster than he already is."

"And if he succeeds?" I asked reluctantly. On the bright side, I had stopped worrying about the crocodile. Ambrose's suggestion was so much more terrifying by comparison that I couldn't work up much fear of a giant reptile that could eat me.

Ambrose shook his head. "Nothing he wants can

be good." He exhaled loudly. "Damn it. We need somewhere private to go while I decide what to do. I hate the idea, but it may be time to try to contact others who know about this kind of thing and ask for help."

"The supernatural grapevine?" I asked, using his term.

"Yes, there is such a thing, you know. I think all of us subscribe to *The Weekly Weird News*. You see some very strange ads there sometimes. I can put my own online ad in it from here, of course, but it would take time for people to see it and then react. Unfortunately, if Saint Germain has found this island then he has probably found my other retreats. I need a place where he would never think to look while I wait for some answers."

"I have a house in Maine." The words were out without any pause for thought. A house, not *my* house. I owned it now, but it was really the place where my parents had lived for six weeks every summer. I'd sold the other properties in Sedona and Charleston a few years back since they had no memories for me, but I had kept the Bar Harbor house because on a few occasions I had been allowed to visit there and had liked being near my father.

"In your name?" Those dark eyes were intent, distracting, and it took me a moment to follow his thoughts. Fear kept me from being too laggard, though, and I got what he was driving at.

"No. The house is still in my parents' names— even the utilities. I never got around to changing it. It's all paid for out of the trust fund."

"That's handy," he said slowly. "I suppose we could meet there later."

Later. That was code for stuffing me on a plane in the morning along with everyone else and facing down a zombie invasion alone. I let it pass for the moment. The trick with winning a fight was not only to choose where you drew the line in the sand, but when you drew it.

"It's an old stone barn with thick walls and small windows. It's very . . . defensible." And call me paranoid, but this seemed an excellent thing just now. Ambrose was right. It wouldn't take a lot of digging to discover which guests had been on the island at the time of the attack. From there, it was a short step to discover that Audrey Athenaeum was a *nom de plume* and that my real name is . . . something else. Something common. There are, in fact, thousands and perhaps millions of us that share the same last name. But even if Saint Germain started looking for me tomorrow, the chances were good he wouldn't think of me in connection with Fergus and Desdemona Somethingverycommon.

"What is your real name?" he asked, almost as though he heard my thoughts.

I resisted for a moment and then answered him truthfully. I half expected him to laugh, but all he did was shake his head. His voice was sympathetic.

"Parents. Did you know that my middle name is Gwinnett?"

"Yes, and that's pretty mean too." I recalled another fact about Ambrose Bierce. He was the tenth of thirteen children and his parents had christened them all with names beginning with the letter A; Abigail, Amelia, Ann, Addison, Aurelius, Augustus, Almeda, Andrew, Albert, Ambrose, Arthur, Adelia and Aurelia. His father had gone alliteration mad. Maybe other kinds of mad as well.

Okay, I've changed my mind. I'll tell you this part because this won't be my name for much longer. It is—was—Joyous Jones. That was my name. Really. Sounds like a porn star, doesn't it? It was a mistake too. I was supposed to be Joyce, after my paternal grandmother, but the Jamaican nurse at the hospital misunderstood my mother, and thinking my parents glad that their flawed child hadn't died after all, I had ended up as Joyous.

A less appropriate name would be hard to find.

"It was an accident. That's what they always said." I told him about the Jamaican nurse.

"But they didn't correct it," he pointed out—not cruelly, but he didn't seem inclined to sentimental-ize my childhood and pretend that it had been happy. I was grateful in many ways. I'm not into revisionist history. Sooner or later a lie, however well intended, will come around and bite you in the ass. Sticks and stones will break the bones, but words . . . Well, frankly, my mental beatings were always worse.

"They didn't care that much," I agreed. "The doc-tors told them there was every chance I wouldn't survive my infancy, so why bother the lawyers?" I wondered sometimes—not often but once or twice during the terrible teen years when I had several painful cardiac events—if they didn't want me, why they hadn't just put a pillow over my face while I was still in the cradle, and made sure of things.

"Your heart?" he asked. There was tension between his brows and his head tilted slightly as if he were listening. Probably no one else would have noticed, but I was beginning to know his expressions.

Unable to stop myself, I touched my chest and willed my heart to remain steady and calm.

"Yes. Though it turns out the defect wasn't as bad as they thought. I won the lottery and got only the mildest form of birth defect. My baby wasn't so lucky." I bit my lip. Why the hell had I said that?

"Nature can be pitiless." There was no overt sympathy in his voice, but I knew that he was empathizing with my pain. He had lost children, too.

"Yes, utterly pitiless," I agreed. But not as cruel as people are to one another. And not as cruel as this insane Saint Germain. His shambling monster had taught me that. Imagine not being able to find peace even in death. Zombies sounded stupid, but surely there was enough awareness to know that their bodies were rotting around them. Can you imagine being trapped inside a corpse and unable to escape, compelled to eat people and do God only knows what else? It was too horrible to think about. I said the first prayer I had uttered in a long while that the zombies were too stupid to remember who they were and what they had lost.

"Ambrose, are you afraid of anything?" I asked abruptly.

"Hell yes. Just not large crocodiles or beautiful women with sad eyes," he said, confirming one of my assumptions. "But I have a very lively fear of Saint Germain. He could do far worse than just kill me, if he got the chance. I can't let him get hold of the lycanthropy virus. The world has enough trouble with AIDS and global warming. It does not need a feral zombie army."

No, we couldn't let that happen. Not ever. I had never thought there was any cause I'd be willing to die for, but now I knew differently. Ambrose's matter-of-fact statement of Saint Germain's goals appalled me at a gut level. Everything human in me was repelled by what this creature was doing.

"We'll just have to make sure that he never has the opportunity."

Ambrose glanced at me. His super hearing probably picked up that this wasn't a mere statement of intention but an actual vow.

"Eat your dinner," was all he said. "You're going to need your strength."

I nodded and stuffed some lobster in my mouth. I'm sure it was good, but that night everything tasted of ash and sulfur.

Homicide, *n.* The slaying of one human being by another. There are four kinds of homicide: felonious, excusable, justifiable and praiseworthy, but it makes no great difference to the person slain whether he fell by one kind or another—the classification is for advantage of the lawyers.

Sorcery, *n.* The ancient prototype and forerunner of political influence.
> —Ambrose Bierce, *The Devil's Dictionary*

Chapter Six

Though I had thought to spend the night with Ambrose, somehow I had ended up back in my own cottage and unkissed. It wasn't that the thought of sleeping together hadn't crossed his mind. Or mine. There had been leaning and tension and speeding pulses, but in the end Ambrose had pulled back. I would have been insulted, except that I knew he was frustrated with playing the gentleman. Or whatever it was that he was doing.

Last night I had been tired and accepted his decision. Today I wasn't feeling as complacent.

I still had a strong suspicion when I awoke in my own bed that Ambrose was going to try to stuff me on a plane with the rest of the tourists, so I made sure I was nowhere around when the plane landed.

I left a note that said: *Forget it. I'm not going. See you for lunch.*

This wasn't a day for bathing suits. The fog had rolled back about fifty feet from shore, leaving a clear patch for the amphibious airplane to land, but the air remained cold and the usually playful island zephyrs were unnaturally still as if waiting for the guests to depart. Grimacing, I donned a pair of jeans and my only long-sleeved shirt. I also stuffed my digital camera in my pocket. I'd decided that while I was hiding out, I would finally visit the mangroves and perhaps get a look at the mother crocodile. If I survived this vacation, I was going to have some amazing photos to share with . . . someone. Someday.

It shouldn't surprise you that I also took a gun. I figured Ambrose had left it with me for a reason.

Ashanti seemed inclined to follow, so I shut her into my cottage before I left and added a line to my note warning Ambrose where she was. I didn't want her turning into alligator appetizer or to be left on the island by mistake when everyone else evacuated.

Thinking of appetizers made me realize that I was hungry again, but I decided not to risk getting caught by Ambrose over the breakfast dishes at what was undoubtedly a hurried buffet. I went out the door and turned left. It was the shortest route to the mangroves and had the benefit of staying away from the pier where people would be loading up to leave, but it did mean passing by the place where Ambrose had roasted the zombie.

Unable to help myself, I detoured by the pit and took a quick peek inside. There was nothing to see. The crater had been emptied of bones and ash and refilled with dried grass and driftwood. The sight of fresh timber had me shaking my head. With everyone gone, there was only one reason to have this fire pit prepared.

"Damn it." I looked back toward the cottage and the pier where the white and blue plane was waiting. I could still leave. Physically, it was possible. All I had to do was turn around and pack my suitcase. That would take all of five minutes.

However, I found that mentally this course of action was as impossible as ever. No matter how horrible things would get, I had to see this through. Ambrose was one hundred percent correct that we couldn't let Saint Germain get hold of any lycanthropy virus. And if he did—well, there had to be someone to tell the tale. Also . . . well, I just needed to do this. I turned my back on the plane, rejecting my familiar place on the sidelines.

The Spanish word for mangrove is *mangle*. I rather like this term because the mangrove forests on the island were dense, tangled into woody webs and filled with brackish water, black mud that was rich in rotting organics, and secretive animals like miniature red crabs living in the pendulous roots that are heaving the small warped trees out of the salty water.

There was also a bit of sandy beach, about four feet below the raised wooden walkway that was little more than a narrow bar, and I had no trouble seeing where the mother croc had been excavating a nest. I kept a wary eye out as I took a picture of the hidden beach; four feet was nothing to an eighteen-foot crocodile if she thought her eggs were threatened. I left her bit of seashore strictly alone, except for the mild molestation of my camera flash.

Though I thought I was being cautious that morning, in reality I was nowhere near cautious enough. I've done some research since then and have learned that saltwater crocs can swim about eighteen miles per hour underwater and will eat sharks if those are dumb enough to get in their way. That they can be damned fast and silent on land was something I had already learned from my in-flight reading, and they are responsible for about three hundred human deaths a year. The recitation of these facts doesn't begin to touch on the reality. They have one other trick. They can jump three quarters of their body length out of the water when they are going after prey.

I was dangling over a rough railing about fifty yards from the beach, photographing an obligingly frozen bird that looked a lot like a white ibis, though it was much smaller, when I suddenly had a strong sense of being observed. Half expecting to find an annoyed Ambrose waiting to escort me to the plane, I finished my shot and then turned nonchalantly, preparing to brazen it out.

It wasn't Ambrose sitting in the mudflat to my right. It was the huge, giant, massive, enormous mother crocodile that had managed to sneak up on me without making a sound. The walkway was only about eighteen inches above the water at this point and I had no trouble seeing every one of the horny plates crowning her mammoth, tooth-filled head.

The part of me not immediately terrified into babbling idiocy made note of the fact that this crocodile looked a great deal like an American alligator. It was broad in the chest—immense, colossal, bigger than any gator I had seen or ever wanted to see—and had a fatter snout than other crocodiles, which, my gibbering brain shrieked, was broad enough to accommodate my shoulders or hips, whichever it chose to swallow first.

My hands, which seemed to have independent thought, decided that they would perform a last act and take a picture of the creature that would be having me for breakfast. It would make for an exciting obit column and might even put my books on some best-sellers lists—posthumously, of course. This task involved glancing down at the viewer to make sure she was in frame. I needn't have worried. No matter where I pointed the camera, there was only smiling crocodile filling up the lens. She obligingly turned her head into profile and opened her jaws so I could see all of her enormous teeth. My handgun, tucked into my pants, felt totally inadequate for the situation, and I didn't even reach for it.

I expected death, but she didn't attack. Not even when the damned flash went off. Twice.

After I slipped the camera into my pocket and gulped a few breaths of air, I whispered a tentative hello. The beast swung her head back around but made no move toward me, and it goes without saying that I made no move toward her. Instead I began a slow retreat up the wooden walk, placing my feet quietly and praying that the railings were sturdy enough to catch me if I backed into them on accident. Once around the bend and out of her line of sight, I did some undignified fleeing until I reached the edge of the mangle and was again under an open sky.

There I dropped to my knees and did some heavy breathing and muttering prayers of relief and gratitude that I hadn't ended the morning in the creature's belly. There is a saying that there are no atheists in foxholes. There are none in crocodile-infested mangroves, either.

I heard the plane take off a few minutes later, and figured it was safe to return to my cottage and have some breakfast, or at least something hot to drink since my appetite had vanished again. This was a good plan, and would have been easy enough to execute except for two things. My line of retreat was blocked by a monster crocodile, and the damned fog came rolling back in the moment the plane was gone, making it impossible to see her or much of anything else.

I had two choices: circle the island in the other direction—not recommended in the tourist's guide-book, since parts of the three-mile shoreline were rough and had tricky tides—or scrambling over the mountain thrusting up in the center of the island. I looked at the hill behind me, visibility down to about ten feet and getting worse all the time, and wondered, if I climbed high enough, whether I could break out of the suffocating mist.

"Damn." I looked at the path back into the mangroves. It was filling up with fog too. The eerie gray presence had waited only for the plane to leave and then moved swiftly to retake the island.

Belatedly I recalled the fact that there could be zombies roaming around on the beach as well as crocodiles.

I needed to get to the far side of the island, where there were big guns, hot chocolate and Ambrose, and with the one shoreline path definitely in reptilian hands and the other possibly now zombie territory, there was only one way to get there.

The island's "mountain range" would cause sniggers from anyone who lived in the Rockies or Alps, but the incline on the side of the ancient volcano was steep and slippery enough to be dangerous on a day when the fog was sufficiently thick to cause an early twilight. Fortunately, I wasn't headed for any particular landmark. I needed to go up and then down, and there was a path somewhere, I assured myself. Even in the fog I would be able to find it eventually. I would go slowly, not strain my heart, and in no time I would be eating pancakes with Ambrose and a shotgun.

The ascent wasn't too bad, though I managed to tear my clothes while doing a panic dance induced by some giant insect dropping onto my shirt and squirting me with a noxious, stinging fluid. I shrieked in an unwisely loud voice and fell on my butt. Not content with a pratfall, I rolled a few feet in the mud, but was spared severe damage when the flaps of my jeans caught on some painful outcrop of volcanic rock. The pockets tore, but I was saved from injuries more serious than a bruised butt.

The poor beetle scrambled away as soon as I quit thrashing. Hurting a bit but more determined than ever to get the hell off that mountain, I rolled to my feet and moved on. I chanted a soft mantra: *nomorebugs-nomorebugs-nomorebugs.*

The summit was eventually reached but without any diminishment of the fog, and I celebrated my mastery of the mountain—and my not falling into the volcano's basin, which had appeared quite suddenly—by having a lie-down on mossy stone and gasping for air while my heart calmed itself. If I had been doing this at a higher elevation I probably would have died. As it was, the strain was greater than I'd anticipated and I needed to rest for several minutes.

Eventually I stopped wheezing and rolled back onto my feet. I didn't stay upright for long. There were too many birds—I think they were birds—flying about in the fog in what could only be described as blind panic. The noises they made were awful, a sort of hissing-choking sound that made me think of tear gas or some other kind of poison. After getting slapped a few times and having my hair pulled by passing talons, I dropped back to my knees and made up some German curses that were completely ineffective in quelling the avian chaos.

Cussing is fun and relieves stress, but my lungs began telling me that they really needed to get out of the sulfurous damp and away from the falling dung being dropped by the panicked birds. Also, my sniveling psyche, who seemed to be always with me on the island, kept whining that maybe the crocodile had followed me up the mountain and was even now sneaking up on me with its giant jaws agape. That was a highly improbably scenario, but there was no reasoning with my inner terror-stricken child.

I managed to make most of the descent of the steep side of the volcano on the seat of my now pocketless jeans, though a lot of unwanted sliding and rolling in gritty mud was involved. I think I also managed to hit every tree and rocky outcrop on my way down, but broke nothing, not even any skin. I didn't fall in the ocean when a cliff appeared—after I had slid off of it—but that was only because there was a stretch of sand and barrier of swamp grass warning me that it was time to stop my panicked rolling progress.

Slowly, the sound of blood pounding in my ears began to fade. My vision improved somewhat upon exiting the thickest ropes of shrubbery and entering the feathery sea grass near the shore, but not so much that I immediately recognized where I was. I thought about shouting for Ambrose but decided to save my breath. His hearing might be acute but was surely of no use with the wind shrieking along the beach like the voices of the damned. The earlier calm was gone, and the sea itself was in torment and thrashing loudly as it hurled itself at this side of the tiny island with blows that I could feel beneath my unsteady feet. The waves were fanning the fog away, beating it back little by little. Which was odd, because the mountain behind me was as foggy and breathless as ever. The wind seemed unable to find it.

The slowly revealed sight of the wreck-strewn shore and the white hellbroth beyond, dim as it was, would have daunted the bravest heart—which mine is not—so I was feeling pretty desperate indeed. Especially when I noticed that I was not on the beach near my cottage. Somehow I had gotten turned about on the mountain and ended up coming down elsewhere on the island.

I rested on hands and knees, trying to catch my breath and also decide which direction to travel. Without the sun, I had no way of judging my location. Thick shadows that shouldn't have existed at all fell heavy across the fungus-smeared rocks and dilapidated shrubbery that appeared silver in the thinning mist. Nothing looked familiar. Strings of something like cobweb but slimier dripped in strange crisscrosses on the sagging limbs, underneath which scuttled what I thought were rats but proved to be crabs fleeing the beach with a haste I had never guessed possible.

Gradually I became aware that my hands were stinging from the slime. They demanded that I put them in cold water at once, but something else kept my frozen arms in place while my eyes made a frantic search of the beach. Some part of my brain knew danger was near even if my eyes had yet to perceive it. Tears pooled in my eyes but I waited.

Suddenly, walking into view on the crab-strewn shore, I saw the most beautiful creature I have ever laid eyes on. He walked out of the surf, uncaring of what the salt water would do to his linen slacks and shirt. He stopped just beyond the tide line and stood very still, head cocked as though listening to distant music. He was blond, radiant, a fallen angel who commanded the wind to still so that he might listen. For me. I was morbidly and irrationally certain that he was trying to hear my heart.

Beautiful he was, but terrifying too. I stopped up my breath and ordered my heart to still and my hands to stop burning. I slowly lowered myself into the sand and tried to pretend I was a rock. He turned slowly. The blank, black pits where eyes should be passed over where I crouched. They rested on me for only a second, but I swear the touch of his gaze burned worse than whatever was on my hands.

It seemed inevitable that I would be discovered. He didn't see me, though. Apparently I was wearing enough mud, dung and other detritus to pass for a smelly sand dune. Or else he saw me and I wasn't his object.

My ears popped as the barometric pressure fell and the creature spun back in my direction. The dying wind shifted again, and the faint scent of brimstone, a ghostly whiff of breath laced with cognac and blood and other rot reached out to tickle my nose. I wanted to sneeze, to scream, to run as fast as I could and not stop until I reached Hawaii. Instead I remained still and nearly breathless until the gaze passed on.

Pleaseohplease, I prayed. *Don't let him call to me.* As horrified as I was, I had the awful feeling that I might actually answer if he bade me to come.

An eternity later, he turned away and strolled toward the bushes at the far side of the clearing. I allowed myself one gulping breath and then listened again with all my might. The air in my tortured lungs tasted of the bitter-sugar nectar of carnivorous blossoms that were dying, poisoned by the stringy slime that was still eating away at them and at my reddened hands.

It was dangerous, but I ran for the water, tiptoeing through the mass of crabs that seemed to be having some kind of seizures. I had to get the poison off of my hands, which now felt like I had laid them on a griddle.

Kneeling in the surf and tending to my burning fingers, it was several moments before I looked up again. Observation wasn't coming to me easily that morning, but this wasn't something I could fail to see despite the tattered remains of mist. Clumping toward me through the surf were . . . monsters. Fantastical, horrible monstrosities pieced together out of the odds and ends of humans and animals. I saw every variation of obscenity imaginable. These weren't zombies; these were something else even more awful.

Ghouls, my brain whispered. Just like Ambrose talked about in *The Devil's Dictionary.*

Only, he hadn't been joking.

Thank God for adrenal glands, because without the flood of chemical energy, I might have crouched there, riveted by horror, until something bit me. Choking back a scream, I fled back into the fog that still clung to the mountain, this time grateful for the sulfurous cloud that clogged up my lungs. It never occurred to me to draw my gun and shoot them. I was too afraid of drawing Saint Germain's attention. For some reason, I knew he would be worse.

Where the hell is Ambrose? I wondered as I ran.

A new fear dawned in my heart. Surely he would be on the beach repelling the invasion—if he was able.

Longanimity, *n.* The disposition to endure injury with meek forbearance while maturing a plan for revenge.

Longevity, *n.* Uncommon extension of the fear of death.

Misericorde, *n.* A dagger which in medieval warfare was used by the foot soldier to remind an unhorsed knight that he was mortal.
                    —Ambrose Bierce, *The Devil's Dictionary*

Chapter Seven

Maybe I got lost in the damned fog again, or maybe it was just sheer bad luck dogging me. Whichever, I soon found both the monstrous crocodile and Saint Germain.

As I crouched on the ground, my knees having failed me, I thought again that he was, without any competition, the most beautiful man—no, most beautiful *being*—that I had ever seen. Lucifer, the reputedly bright yet fallen angel would have nothing on him.

At the same time, he was also the most hideous thing that ever walked in Heaven or on Earth.

Fortune favored me in as much as the two monsters were very busy with one another and neither seemed to know I was there in the dripping shrub-

bery, trying to stay more or less upright by grabbing vines that I hoped weren't snakes or covered
with man-eating ants. Coward that I am, I was just
beginning to back away from the showdown that
had popped out in front of me in a most unpleasant
way, when I stumbled into one of the odd and infre-
quent clearings in the mist. Then I noticed something odd. *More* odd. Saint Germain was moving
but the crocodile was not. The giant reptile might
have been stuffed for all the life it showed.

Muttering, he approached the crocodile with
some sort of sword heavily carved with runes. He
handled the blade with easy familiarity, suggesting
that either he used it regularly at historical reen-
actments or had been a warrior in another life.
Ozone was thick in the air, and every hair on my
body stood on end as it rolled over me in a prickly
wave. I knew in my gut that I had stumbled into
magic—and not just any old magic, but true diablerie. Don't ask me how I knew this, but I realized
that Saint Germain had somehow bespelled the giant reptile and was planning upon slaying her. Or
worse. I had noticed that things didn't stay dead
around him. Ask me what's worse than a giant
crocodile and I'll tell you: A giant zombie crocodile who could be ordered to eat me.

I didn't think. If I had, my brain would have defeated me because it was also half enchanted by
Saint Germain's beauty and wholly fascinated by
whatever he was uttering in that bewitching voice.
And I was terrified as well, filled with the kind of
fear that makes you fall on the ground, screw your

eyes shut and mewl. But—thank all the gods and goddesses—my hands once again seemed to have a will of their own and they had the gun. They shook with dread as they took aim at the lovely stranger, but they kept on task even as my brain was panicking.

Understand that, just like you, I never wanted to shoot anyone. And if someone had told me that I would end up shooting someone—more than once—I would have laughed at them and then moved away from the wacko who suggested such a thing. I am not a killer.

Until I have no choice but to kill or die.

A head shot is best, I heard my father say, and I raised the gun up and squeezed the trigger before I could change my mind.

I missed his skull but managed to blow an ear off. The stuff that sprayed out of his head did not look like blood and it smelled awful.

Saint Germain snarled and whipped around to face me, sword still raised. In that moment, I knew I was dead. I could feel power, raw and evil, coming at me like a nuclear blast. He no longer looked beautiful. He said one word—I can't recall now what—and it backhanded my psyche with a force that stunned me into immobility.

OhmyGodohmyGodohmyGod, was all my brain could think or do. It forgot how to breathe or even make my heart beat as I saw that giant sword swinging down at me.

Then karma came to my rescue. I tell you, it pays

to be kind to animals, even giant reptiles. I had distracted Saint Germain long enough for the crocodile to shake off her paralysis. With a grunt that shook the ground, she leapt at the once-beautiful monster, grabbing him by both legs, and jerked with all the strength in her eighteen-foot body.

The whiplash snap should have broken his spine and crushed every rib in his carcass when it smacked into the stony ground. Saint Germain fell, but he didn't cry out, nor did he drop his sword, which clanged down entirely too near my body.

With any other creature, I would have put my money on the huge crocodile winning this fight. Really, you have no idea how huge she was! But this wasn't a human or even a zombie that she battled, and I couldn't count on her managing to kill him.

Sobbing with terror but again possessed of a beating heart and mobile limbs, I raised the gun between my splayed knees and shot again. And again. I pulled the trigger until the gun was empty, but Saint Germain continued to thrash and flail about with his sword in spite of the many large holes I had punched in him, including one that blew off his left hand just above the wrist. The damn thing dropped onto the trail and then scuttled into the bushes like a hungry crab after its lunch.

Not sure what else I could do that the crocodile could not, and having used my last drops of courage and every bullet, I turned and ran into the jungle. Panic lent me winged feet, and I managed to travel several hundred yards before I collapsed.

That was when Ambrose found me. At the time, I thought it a miracle.

"How badly are you hurt?" he asked urgently, rolling me over and lifting me into his arms. The now-familiar heat from his body washed over me, warming my insides and calming my heart enough that I could speak.

"I'm not hurt. I shot him. I shot him and shot him, but he didn't die. Maybe the crocodile ate him."

"Him?" His eyes widened. For the first time ever, he looked shocked. "Saint Germain is on the island?"

"Yes, and he has ghouls with him—a dozen or so. They were slimy and they poisoned all the crabs on the beach and burned my hands with their ooze." I wasn't explaining myself well, but a display of my blistered hands made my point for me.

"Damn. And he brought that many zombies as well. I got half a dozen already but there are as many still wandering around," Ambrose said, helping me to my feet.

"I need more bullets," I said back, trying to locate my knees and having only limited success. "And bigger guns. Much bigger guns. The Colt hardly did anything."

"Let's get back to the cottage and restock—for all the good it will do," he said, leaning down to pick up the largest rifle I'd ever seen. It had a very high-tech, futuristic look to it, and I was betting it wasn't available in your average gun shop. "I think I'll have to rip these bastards limb from bloody limb."

"Not bloody," I said, shuddering. "He had black ooze. Not blood."

"Point taken."

"Did you find Ashanti?" I asked, as I stumbled along with Ambrose. Without his arm around me, I would have fallen. As it was, my feet hardly touched the ground.

"Yes, and she left on the plane—which you should have done too. What possessed you to run off like that?"

I didn't answer, since he didn't really expect me to. Anyway, I was saving my breath for important things like screaming if we saw a ghoul, and running blindly through sulfurous fog if a zombie crocodile chased us. Thankfully Ambrose could find his way through the mist and kept moving at a brisk clip. The fog was thinning quickly now that we neared the water, and I began to think that I might actually be able to manage on my own. If I wanted to—which I didn't.

Admittedly I was somewhat distracted by heaving lungs, running on boneless legs, and residual terror at nearly being eaten, or killed and then eaten, by several different and horrible creatures, but I would have had to be acutely unobservant to have missed the way that Ambrose was scanning the nearby shrubbery watching for danger. It dawned on me that I had been found but not rescued. We were still in a lot of danger, and if he was being ultracautious, so should I be.

"What are you thinking?" Ambrose asked as I finally managed to regain command of my legs. This time he did want an answer.

"That I know what really chased Ichabod Crane through Sleepy Hollow."

He turned his head and actually grinned down at me. His usual calm had returned; nothing knocked him off balance for long.

"It might well have been," he admitted. "Why shouldn't a ghoul be a horseman too—especially if it's a zombie horse?"

I shook my head but was feeling better. No, we weren't safe yet, but Ambrose's cheerfulness was a bracing tonic. At some other time, I might have been annoyed by his refusal to feel a normal degree of human fear, but at that moment all outside courage was welcome since I was so short of it myself.

"I'm stopping off for some trench spikes. There's no need to waste the ammunition on the zombies. Let's save it for the ghouls. Spikes are also quieter. No need to ring the dinner bell for them." Ambrose seemed to be talking to himself as he said this, though I didn't actually see his lips move.

"I want some ammo anyway." My lips definitely moved as I answered. I didn't consider the ammunition wasted since I wasn't able to rip zombie heads off with my bare hands, but didn't say anything about his barbaric preference for hand-to-hand combat. If Ambrose wanted spikes, then spikes we would have. After all, as proved night after night on the evening news, some people favored bludgeoning and manual piercing to modern high-tech solutions. Guns were for wimps like me who weren't familiar with the older type of up-close-and-personal violence more common in other eras.

His head turned. Evidently he was surprised that I had heard him.

"You can have every bullet I possess," he agreed, speaking in a slightly louder voice, though it was still hushed with caution. "But I would prefer not to use them if we can avoid it. Sound attracts the ghouls and zombies, and I would rather not have the entire undead nation down on us all at once. Especially not if the crocodile has failed to digest their fearless leader."

"He had put a spell on her," I said, feeling stupid for uttering these words, but suspecting that this was something important I needed to impart, even if it meant using imprecise language. "He was going to kill her with some kind of sword. That's when I shot him. I blew his ear off. That made him angry."

"I imagine it did. What did he do then?" I had Ambrose's complete attention.

"He turned around and tried to knock my head off with another spell, until the crocodile grabbed him and they started fighting. I shot him until I was out of bullets but he wouldn't die. I think the thing that hurt him most was blowing off his left hand, but even then he never screamed. The hand crawled away." I reported this last bit especially reluctantly, almost looking for sympathy, but Ambrose didn't take me up on it. Crawling hands were apparently too common to merit comment.

"No screaming? Too bad. I should have enjoyed that. Good effort anyway. We'll have to work on your aim, though. It's hard to work magic if you don't have a head to talk with. Best to go for a head shot when you can." His practical calm, or something, was pushing my remaining fear back into normal proportions. My supernatural dread was gone. I felt that we would be able to cope with whatever came our way. Somehow.

"I didn't want to shoot the crocodile," I defended. "And they were thrashing around a lot. I couldn't get close without getting smashed by the croc's tail or Saint Germain's damned sword." I thought of something else. "I was serious before. He doesn't bleed blood. It's some clotted black stuff that stinks 'til hell won't have it."

"Black clots? Damn." He shook his head. "Well, that's sort of good news and sort of not."

"How so?"

"The real Saint Germain bleeds. What you saw was probably a golem."

"A Gollum?" I repeated, thinking of the *Lord of the Rings* movies.

"No, a g-o-l-e-m. It's a clay statue brought to life with magic—another kind of Frankenstein monster, only much nastier. They can be made of earth or twigs or even stone."

"This thing didn't look like clay."

"The good ones never do."

"Oh, look. We're here." I spoke happily, as I suddenly recognized where we were. A moment later the corner of Ambrose's well-fortified cottage peeped out of the thick tangle of swamp grass that still clung to a bit of the eerie fog. I felt myself relax a bit more once sanctuary was near.

Ambrose grunted something in agreement. My relief proved premature, though. We could see as soon as we rounded the corner that something had ripped the cottage's iron door off its hinges and thrown it twenty feet down the beach. We stopped cold outside the small building and Ambrose wrinkled his nose as he listened. After a moment I smelled it too. Rot.

"Ghouls," I whispered. I pointed to the trail of sludge, the burning slime I was now familiar with. "Don't touch it. It burns."

"Someone's in a bad mood. Why the temper tantrum when they could just walk in? It wasn't locked." I thought I head Ambrose say this, though again I didn't see his lips move. He could have taken the ventriloquist act on the road and made a fortune.

"Do you think they took the guns?" I asked, trying not to sound frightened, which is difficult when you're whispering in the first place because some nasty beastie might hear you.

"Not all of them. And they probably didn't get the ammunition. I keep it up in the rafters. It would be hard to find." Avoiding the worst of the slime, Ambrose slipped into the cottage and headed for the bedroom. As was getting to be my habit, I followed a safe pace or two behind him. I also did a lot of looking back over my shoulder, praying I wouldn't see whatever had ripped the door off.

One of the first things I noticed was that Ambrose had left an electric teakettle by the sink, but this served to make me realize that I no longer had any urge for food or drink. I laid my empty Colt down beside Ambrose's designer gun in the middle of the kitchen table. Unable to help myself, I looked about nervously, even though there was no place for a monster to hide in the bare room. Maybe it was paranoia, but I still felt observed.

There was a soft grunt and the sound of Ambrose hitting the floor.

"Catch," he said, and as I turned he tossed a box of shells in my direction. Wasting no time, I reloaded the Colt. "The shotgun?" I asked hopefully.

"Gone."

Ambrose walked out of the bedroom, donning a belt that was half filled with giant shells that looked about right for the gun he had chosen to carry, and half loaded with something that looked like bayonet spikes. He looked like an extra from *Blade*.

"Ready to kick some zombie butt?" he asked.

"Hell yes," I lied. We didn't have much choice. If they had gotten into Ambrose's reinforced cottage, nothing on the island was safe. My best hope of survival was to stick with the zombie-butt-kicker and hope he could kill Saint Germain's handpicked army before I got eaten or had a heart attack.

I knew that before the day was over, I would use the gun again. This didn't fill me with as much dismay as it should have.

Body-snatcher, *n.* A robber of grave-worms. One who supplies the young physicians with that with which the old physicians have supplied the undertaker. The hyena.

Grave, *n.* A place in which the dead are laid to await the coming of the medical student.
—Ambrose Bierce, *The Devil's Dictionary*

Some thought that being last thrown over the [gallows] and first cut down, and in full vigour, and not much earth placed upon him, and lying uppermost [in the grave], and not so ready to smother, the fermentation of the blood and heat of the bodies under him might cause him to rebound and throw off the earth.
—Lord Fountainhall, recounting the hanging and subsequent resurrection of a gypsy at Greyfriar's Kirkyard in Edinburgh

Chapter Eight

They say that sex sells, but I think fear is an even greater motivator. What do you think convinces healthy adults with functioning taste buds to eat plain oatmeal for breakfast when doughnuts are readily available? I'm not saying that light doses of fear don't have some good uses; it can keep us out of a lot trouble when temptation is whispering lo.

But too much fear is crippling. For me, that is in both the figurative and literal sense, but our enemy seemed to have none that bothered him. Saint Germain—or his golem—had faced down that monster crocodile and never even blinked. Nor did zombies or ghouls back off from guns or spikes or any weapon we had so far used against them. And that really sucked.

Some people grow incoherent when frightened. Others incontinent. I was neither—so far—but then I'd spent most of my time worrying that I would pass out and get eaten. I had a worthy distraction. Still, just in case, I used the bathroom before we left the cottage. There was nothing to do about possible incoherence, except to rely on statistics that said two writers would never run out of pertinent things to say, especially when every word might be our last.

We searched the guest cottages first. They had all been gone through, including mine. There were slimy trails on the floor and rot in the air. Most of the buildings had their doors ripped off. This was unnecessary, because none had been locked. I would also not be wearing my pareu again. I don't think ghoul slime ever washes out. Fortunately, my computer seemed unharmed.

I had a moment of epiphany as we were searching for bogeymen under the beds of the last cottage. I had willingly left the comfort of my known life to chase a bloodthirsty maniac who would let his ghouls eat me, and though terrified and hating every moment, I wasn't going back to my old life when this was over—assuming it ever was over. We might win this one battle, but what about the war? That was less certain. I was needed in this fight and I would answer the call, however ill-suited to the task I might be.

To this day, I still find it somewhat astounding that I mentally walked away and left it all behind without even a pang of regret. That's what rage and determination—and, I'll admit it, growing lust—will do for you. Like a migrating bird, I headed south for warmer climes and a better choice of mates. This was doubtless because Ambrose was near and his presence kept the worst of my terror at bay. Thanks to him, fear had me energized and wary, but not paralyzed. And, I'll be honest: Dread of confronting zombies wasn't as great as my secret fear that I was a damaged person and would never have a normal life with any normal person. The walking dead I could deal with as long as I had a gun. Relationships were trickier. A shadow of doubt would always precede me when it came to dealing with the opposite sex.

"What are you thinking?" Ambrose asked. That, and *Are you ready?* seemed to be his favorite questions. The latter is normal for a guy; the former is not.

"Things seem a bit . . ." I searched for a word. "Sticky. A bit tight. But you're very calm. Heroic even. It gives me hope."

"You poor deluded woman. A hero must do more than fight. He must be wise and capable of compassion."

"And your point is?"

"I'm neither of these things. My life has been nothing but rocks and hard places for the last century. Most of them of my own making," Ambrose answered. "I'm almost used to it by now. But you . . ." The dark eyes turned my way. I had gotten to a point where I could feel their weight whenever they were on me.

I pushed open a bathroom door, gun at the ready. It was a matter of form. Had there been anyone in there I am convinced that Ambrose would have heard them—or smelled them. There is a reason that no one markets zombie-scented aftershave or ghoul-flavored Jelly Bellies.

I said: "I understand. I've also had my share of choices between devils and deep blue seas. Only, my devils were emotional ones. This is the first one I've faced that has actual teeth. They're nasty, but at least I know what I'm grappling with. I can see it. All things considered, I think we're doing rather well." I sounded so brave, so calm and logical, when in reality I presently had all the will of a sock puppet and was keeping erect because Ambrose willed it. Newton's proverbial apple falling on my head had left me with a concussion. Personal detachment, the friend and constant shield of the nonfiction writer, was gone.

Perhaps running away from my old life would prove to be an epic misjudgment, but there was nothing I could—or would—do about it. Ambrose and I were in this together. Leaving aside my growing feelings for him, and that was an awfully large thing to ignore, the situation was beyond being dealt with by local authorities. Or *any* authorities. There was no legal reprisal—no human reprisal—that could set this situation to rights. Saint Germain was raising the dead and forcing them to do murder! What could the police do about this? Even if they believed us—which they wouldn't—no human laws were going to stop this madman before it was too late. The innocent had no protection I could see beyond Ambrose and me.

I have never felt myself to be called by a higher power to any particular life choice. But I felt a weight of responsibility that day and understood for the first time what it meant to be your brother's keeper—or at least his guardian at the gate.

I didn't kid myself that all could be put right by us in this most horrible of situations. There was no way to make up for the horror I now believed Saint Germain had caused untold blameless people. We'd probably never even know all those he had hurt. This man was the alpha asshole of all time . . . and almost no one knew about him! This was stunning to me. Evil was the foundation on which he had built his house, his corporations and charities for which he was lauded as a hero and benefactor, with not one word on CNN of his evil deeds. There was a deep abyss in Hell that already had his name on it, if we could ever kill him. Yet still he walked among the living, and had for over a century, doing evil at will.

No, we couldn't make up for the past. All that could be done now was to stop him so that he never had the chance to hurt anyone else with his sick diablerie. That meant Ambrose, because he was able, and little old me, because I was there and not going to pass the buck and refuse to help do what clearly needed doing. Not when Ambrose was in danger and needing backup. Not when I had a chance to finally do something that really mattered to another person. I was frightened and this would be hard and dangerous, but it was the right thing to do. I believed this with a conviction that bordered on religious faith.

"Unfortunately, the sea has some fangs too," Ambrose remarked, looking toward the shore through a broken window. He smiled, but his dark eyes didn't agree with his mouth's lighthearted perjury. Not too surprisingly he added: "I should have sent you away whether you wanted to go or not. I never suspected it could be this bad, but I should have guessed. After all, as the saying goes: if I didn't have bad luck, I'd have no luck at all." He paused and turned my way. "Of course, you're damned stubborn."

"And that's why I'm here?"

"It's certainly contributory."

"And that is the pot calling the kettle black." My verbal defense mechanism was kicking in, but the counteraccusation only amused him.

"Okay," I continued. "I admit that self-preservation says I should have gone. But I didn't. Couldn't. And neither could you. You know what's at stake. So here we are. The last of the great patriots, at least on this island." I looked out the window. Clouds were thickening. We were going to have a severe storm, and soon. I added seriously: "Even if we come to a bad end, I don't regret staying. My life was . . . just a lot of nothing. I haven't felt truly alive for a very long time."

There was a bit of silence. I hoped I hadn't sounded melodramatic. This urge to confide in anyone was new and confusing.

"And now?" he asked. I could tell that he wanted the truth, and I was certain he would know if I lied. There is a scientific name for this ability. It's called Hellstromism. It's the art of muscle reading, the study of small muscular giveaways that tell a body reader if you are lying or nervous. But was that how he did it?

I settled on saying: "And now I recall why I want to live. If we get out of this I am going to be making some changes."

I turned and looked back at Ambrose. I wanted to say something else but courage failed me. I was more afraid of his rejection of this mild declaration of newfound affection than I was of being killed by ghouls.

He nodded as he dropped to the floor. Again, checking under the bed was strictly for form's sake; we had yet to run into any monster that chose hiding over attacking. I think he just wanted a moment to think.

"Me too," he said at last. "You have made me recall why people seek out companionship. There is a powerful allure in being with someone who knows your history and all your flaws and accepts you anyway. I've been reluctant to get close to anyone for a long time. My changed nature was just too unpredictable. Too violent." He unfolded his limbs and rose in a fluid movement. He reached for me and I took his hand, knowing that I would feel the strange life current flowing through his body. In a very short time I had become addicted to that feeling.

"But now?" I wanted to ask about his past and what had happened to his last "companion".

"I hope—believe that my control is better. And we are a fair way from a full moon." He said abruptly: "It's probably pointless, but let's check the kitchens, dining room and lobby of the main building next. They're on the way, and I'd like to know we don't have something creeping up on us from the rear."

"Sounds good." It didn't, but what were the options?

We stepped outside and turned abruptly toward the shadowy mangroves where an unnatural wind blundered in and out of trees like a drunk with staggers, flinging handfuls of stinging sand at us from time to time. I set my jaw. We had a rendezvous with a rising storm and the evil creatures crawling underneath. Darkness could hide danger, but it also induced wariness. I wasn't worried about Ambrose being careless if dark fell; he would never underestimate this enemy. And my nerves were amped up enough to give off electrical charges, so exhaustion wasn't a problem. Not yet. We were ready.

"I'm not a patriot, you know," Ambrose said suddenly. "Not one of the new kind, anyway. Perhaps I used to be, but the definition has changed. I don't understand the recent breed of media darlings cast as heroes. Sometime in the last century the meaning of patriotism distorted."

I nodded. "I am often baffled by who is chosen for the cult of 'patriotic personality.' Their recent poster boys have seemed like self-interested jerks to me. These days it is politics that is the last refuge of scoundrels."

He nodded. "Most of our leaders seem to have decided that capitalism rather than invention should be America's defining trait, and they value it more than the personal freedoms that countless soldiers have fought and died for from the very beginning. Washington—and much of the rest of the world— is filled with narcissistic cowards who send the deluded to fight for them. Bah! To willingly do battle for these selfish men is idiocy, and as far as I am concerned, spreading their kind of social disease to the rest of the planet is just plain immoral. And what of the poor fools sent off to die for whatever economic plan the politicos have cooked up?" He snorted. "Maybe it is just that this is a young man's game and I got it all out of my system years ago. It took a while, but I finally figured out that, for me, there was more power in the pen than any weapon I used while soldiering. Words and not bullets will most often carry the days that matter." He paused. "This situation is an exception."

I wasn't certain what Ambrose was thinking of, but the war in Iraq was on my mind. In some ways, it was easier to handle than zombies and ghouls.

"I know the kind of person you mean," I said slowly. "Personally and morally cowardly, unwilling to go and fight their own battles, they still think they're patriots because they wave flags and have lots of pictures of dead presidents on the hundred-dollar bills in their pockets, and they have lots of political stickers on their SUVs."

"They don't want to expend any great effort comprehending any other point of view—"

"—but they hate and fear everything they don't understand and are just as happy when the government sends someone to bomb it." I stopped as I finished his sentence, shocked that this much vitriol was inside me. Was Bierce's bitterness contagious? Or had I always felt this and kept it hidden because there was no one to share these thoughts with?

He grinned. It wasn't a smile so much as a baring of teeth in a kind of snarl. "And they're busy high-fiving one another over the fact that there is fast food in the Forbidden City in China and on Princes Street in Edinburgh, and that Wal-Mart is a dominant global power where they can buy cheap socks and DVDs—and they are not at all distressed that a quarter of our nation's children live in poverty because our jobs have gone overseas, or that their cheap goods are being produced by slave labor imprisoned in other countries for having differing political views. They are consumers and not citizens, not neighbors, not caretakers of the only planet we have to live on. They feel entitled to everything and feel no requirement to ever pay anyone back for the privileges they enjoy." His voice had grown softer, sadder.

I nodded. "So, okay, we're not that kind of patriot. I don't think either of us is personally or morally cowardly." This was a bit of stretch. I *was* a dreadful coward, but I had chosen to stick around for this fight, so I was giving myself some bonus points. "Not that I'm looking to die for the cause of stopping Wal-Mart's conquest of the world or anything. I believe in free trade and so forth. We've just gotten unbalanced."

"Thank God—and I mean that sincerely. The world has enough martyrs. One needn't die to demonstrate that one has principles and feels answerable to a higher power than wealth. Sometimes living and speaking the truth is the bravest thing we can do. And the most powerful. It may be cliché but it is also true that, even in this day and age, the pen can be mightier than the sword."

I nodded, thinking of the small statue of Lazarus I'd seen in Ambrose's room "The pen *can* be mightier than the sword—if it writes for television." I was thinking sadly of the number of people who chose to watch television instead of reading.

"And it may be time to start doing that," he muttered. "I think it is time for a new career."

Ambrose stopped me as we neared the rear entrance of the resort kitchens. I had been so distracted by our conversation that I hadn't realized we were there already. Sand slithered down the leeward slope of the rocky outcrop where we waited—or rather where Ambrose waited and I cowered with splayed fingers that were trying to become one with the up-thrust stone.

The wind was blowing hard now and it hurt to face it. Suddenly my thoughtless, greedy body couldn't seem to get enough oxygen. No matter how my lungs bellowed air in and out, there wasn't sufficient oxygen. I wasn't near fainting, but I felt like it had been hours since I had been able to fully catch my breath.

I put my back to the wind and swiped at my tender face. I noticed that the world had a funny red glow about it. I would have said that there was a fire somewhere, but I smelled no smoke. Maybe my brain had just started wearing Hell-colored glasses all the time so I wouldn't keep being surprised when new devils appeared before us.

There's something inside. This time I was watching Ambrose's profile and was certain that his lips hadn't moved. Either he had one hell of a bent for ventriloquism or he was somehow managed to speak to me inside my mind.

The thought was disconcerting, but not entirely impossible given everything else. I decided that there were better moments to ask about this, though, and kept silent.

We sidled up to one of the shuttered windows and took a peek through the slats. The room seemed as empty as the rest of the buildings, but Ambrose remained alert, his posture tense, so though suddenly exhausted, I stayed focused too. We didn't discuss a strategy but that was fine. I never get hung up on the whole Plan B thing. If I thought things through, nothing would ever get done. Ambrose seemed to be of the same school of action. The situation was fluid; we would have to be extemporaneous and think on our feet.

The air that leaked out at us through the shutters smelled awful, far worse than it had in any of the cottages. Part of it might be that the spilled food on the floor had begun to rot—unnaturally, considering the short time it had taken. A quick peek suggested that it was mostly staple items, flour and sugar and so on, but it had been slimed with something yellow and puslike, and the resulting mixture had a pronounced odor of decay.

"Ewwww," I complained, but very quietly. Nothing rushed out at us, but still Ambrose waited another ten-count.

Finally he went to the door and eased inside. He hadn't told me to stay out so I followed close on his heels, my left hand clapped over my mouth and nose. We were careful not to track through the mess on the floor as we headed for the storage room. As we got closer, I began to hear a sound that was at first difficult to place because it was so oddly juxtaposed with the cacophony of blowing sand, thrashing flora and agonized waves that were pummeling the nearby beach.

It wasn't until I smelled something especially vile, a cross between rancid oil and rotting meat left in the sun, that I placed the noise. Someone had turned on the microwave (a shameful time-saving device, Ambrose explained later, that they kept in the pantry where food critics wouldn't see).

Ambrose stepped into that storeroom and made a place for me in the doorway. He didn't attempt to keep me from seeing what had happened in the pantry, though I could tell he didn't like being so equal-minded; if his cottage had been left as a sanctuary, he would have locked me up there. I didn't hold this whole protect-the-little-woman attitude against him, first of all because it came with the era he was born into, but also because I *wanted* to be protected. He was the superman, not I. Let him catch the speeding bullets. Or zombies.

"The evil bastards."

"Oh good God." My eyes latched on a red blot that had crusted against the glass door. I don't know what had been put in the microwave, but it had exploded, and clotted gore and bits of bone were glued to the small window. I prayed that, whatever it was, it hadn't been living when it went in there. The act was malicious and required thought—not what I had come to think of as standard zombie activity. The average zombie seemed about as bright as a Mr. Potato Head doll.

Eventually I pulled my eyes away from the glass window and noticed that every cupboard large enough to be used as a hiding place had been emptied with violence; canned goods were smashed and the shattered glass of jars spilled onto the floor. A part of me wondered who was going to have to clean this mess up and whether the damage would be covered by insurance. Could you get a policy that covered fire, flood and zombies?

A small beep announced that the microwave was

done cooking, but neither Ambrose nor I reached for the door. This was beyond weird, beyond explanation, beyond psychosis or any ring in Dante's Hell.

But it was not beyond Saint Germain or his ghouls. And besides, if something was still alive in there, we didn't have the tools to deal with it.

Shaking his head in disgust, Ambrose began picking out a path through the glass to the walk-in freezer at the back of the room. This time, I didn't follow. It was a dead end, and if there was anything living—or undead—in there, I was going to let Ambrose cope. I was busy trying not to toss up the hollow part of my stomach where my nonexistent breakfast should have been.

Reaching the brushed metal door, Ambrose laid his ear against it and stopped breathing. For a moment he was as still as a statue and appeared almost as lifeless. Looking back at me after a moment, he nodded his head once. It took me a split second to realize that he was signaling there was something moving inside the freezer.

Unprompted, my hands brought the Colt up and my body braced itself. Theoretically, cold should make a zombie slower, but I was taking no chances. I nodded back.

Try not to use the gun. The sound might attract others.

I nodded again, in response to Ambrose's mental words, but didn't lower the weapon.

Ambrose wisely shifted to one side, drew out a spike and then opened the door. Something huge and hissing and inhuman filled the opening and spilled out into the room.

At the same time, something just as large came up behind me and bit my shoulder.

For those who share my typical twenty-first-century academic resumé, which does not include a self-defense class, gang-banging or any practical experience with hand-to-hand combat, let me explain the physiological changes that happen in the body when it is assaulted or even just threatened with physical violence. Reaction time in a deadly encounter can be divided into a trifecta of critical responses. The first is when the mind recognizes that it is in danger. Many people die at step one because they don't even realize they are in peril and fail to react.

The second step is to formulate an appropriate response to the threat. Again, very difficult when one has no training or experience with violence.

The third is to carry one's plan through without hesitation. All of this happens faster than most crises in one's average daily life when you face different sorts of non-life-threatening emergencies, like a backed-up toilet or a flat tire, or even something large and dangerous like a blizzard or hurricane. Unlike normal life, there is rarely time for cogitation in a combat situation. Nor do you get to phone someone for assistance with your problem. We had no AAA or 911 to call.

Had we been outside and standing downwind, the smell or sound might have warned me sooner that evil was near. As it was, the only hint of danger I had was the fall of a hulking shadow over my left shoulder. My subconscious—which thinks faster than my conscious does when my life is at stake—said that giant shadows in an abandoned building on an abandoned island could only belong to something dangerous. Moving out of its way seemed the correct response to this threat, and I did so with all the speed my adrenaline-laced muscles could give me. I moved very quickly indeed—know this—but it still wasn't fast enough. The zombie was on me before I could twist around or shoot it. In less than a second, I was involved in a life-and-death struggle with a monster that was twice my weight and a foot taller, and who was doing his level best to bite through my clavicle. The pain was excruciating.

It shoved me against a counter. I shoved back and spun hard, managing to get my back to it again. My shoulders hunched down tight, trying to make me as small a target as possible for clawing fingers and teeth. I had the tiniest instant of hope that Ambrose would turn and rescue me, but then I heard a terrible screeching from the freezer and the sound of bodies hitting the floor, and then more of those dismembering-chickens sounds that had turned my stomach. Someone or something was getting ripped limb from limb. Ambrose was busy and I was on my own.

Most of you won't know this—and pray to whatever god you worship that you never do—but this kind of fighting is very personal. You look into your enemy's rotting eyes, smell his rancid breath . . . and in this case his decomposing body. This is horrible beyond description, but it does do one thing for you; it makes you focus. It also makes you angry. No, more than angry. Enraged. My very soul was offended by this thing. I was so filled with revulsion and wrath that I had no trouble forgetting about babying my damaged heart, and giving my full attention to dealing with the creature trying to chew on my shoulder.

Fortunately for me, its lower jaw was mostly torn off, so it was having trouble getting a grip with just its upper teeth through my thick shirt. Evidently realizing that this tactic wouldn't work, it next tried to gets its bloated hands around my neck. Again, fortune favored me. Several of its digits had fallen off and, as it squeezed, more of the skin sloughed away and its finger bones poked through. Not that this ended the assault. Zombies have no off button. They just keep doing what they're told to do until they fall into little pieces, and then the little pieces still keep trying to kill you.

I felt the wiry hair on his swollen forearms as he wrapped those about my face when his hands failed to get a grip. He'd seemed to be going for a snap of the neck, or perhaps to bend me back far enough that he could tear my throat out with his few remaining fingers, but I'd dropped my head in time and he only got my face. Three long, filthy fingers wrapped around my chin, and strips of dead skin slipped on my cheek as he tried to turn my head in a way it was never designed to move. In spite of the shedding skin, inch by inch, he was succeeding in forcing my neck around.

Knowing it was dangerous, that I might actually kill myself if the gun slipped even an inch, I brought the Colt up and aimed it as best I could over my shoulder. I felt the barrel enter rotting flesh—was it the creature's face?—and pushed a bit harder until I met with bone. A human would have backed off at this point, but not the zombie. It wrenched its head from side to side but didn't let go. It was much more difficult to pull the trigger in this position, but fear and anger lent me strength. I didn't even flinch when I felt the flash of heat on my cheek and the explosion deafened my left ear. Only later did I find that I had dislocated my index finger when the gun bucked.

The first bullet removed about a third of the creature's skull. This didn't kill the thing, but stunned it enough to loosen its grip. I shoved backward hard with my elbow, using the creature's toppling body to launch myself toward the freezer where Ambrose and some other monstrosity were wrestling. Not that I wanted to get close to that fight, but it was the only open spot I had in the pantry. My abused shirt tore at the sleeve when the zombie refused to let go. I didn't like leaving my skin exposed, but at least I was free to move.

Turning, I took aim at the thing that had assaulted me. It was standing there, almost naked, holding my shirt sleeve in its right hand. My vision began to darken at that point but I ordered my body to do what it must. Feeling like I was being guided by unseen hands, I switched my middle finger to the trigger and followed Ambrose's instructions. I put the first bullet in the thing's heart and then a second in what was left of its head. Thank God it did what was expected and fell to the floor. It kept twitching but didn't get up.

I glanced up at the door to be sure that no other creatures had followed us into the kitchen—I did not want to be surprised twice—and then spun around to help Ambrose with whatever was hissing like a giant snake.

The spirit was willing to keep fighting, but my body was ailing. It was an off-balance spin and I fell to the slimy floor, banging my left knee. My clumsiness was partly because the floor was covered in slop, but it was also my damned heart, once again failing to pump enough blood to my lungs. I could feel it shuddering, jittering in my chest. At least I didn't drop the gun when I hit the tile, though the Colt was now useless because I couldn't see clearly enough to risk a shot.

I lay there and wheezed while the nasty sounds went on.

Gradually my vision cleared and I got an up close and way too personal view of the mortal—or maybe I mean immortal—struggle between Ambrose and another of the monsters that had invaded the island. It was hard to tell at first what was happening because there was blood everywhere and my more or less horizontal angle presented me with a limited view of the freezer's mostly dark interior. I could see by the one remaining light that the stuff leaking out of Ambrose was a normal blood color. The ichor running out of the creature was a nasty dark brown.

It took a moment for me to realize that not everything on the floor was blood. A great deal of the mess was the creature's intestines. That didn't stop the creature's giant claws from ripping into the metal of the door, though. No wonder Ambrose was bleeding. Human flesh would shred like silk under those claws.

Ambrose was on top of the beast, and as I watched he reached for his belt and pulled out another of the spikes he carried. Drawing back his arm, he drove it into the thing's chest. It went through the body and punctured the floor of the freezer, causing some kind of gas to swirl up around them.

Swearing, Ambrose reached for a second spike and this time drove it upward from the beast's lower jaw, pinning the lower teeth to the skull. The thing kept thrashing, but Ambrose refused to be unseated. He pulled out the first spike and threw it aside. With a deliberation that was chilling, he drew his arm back and, making a fist, drove it into the thing's chest, shattering the bones of the ribs and sternum. More gore spattered him as the ribs exploded, rendering him all but unrecognizable. He finally jerked out the thing's heart and the thrashing eased.

Ambrose rolled off of the body and looked at me. He had a hole in one cheek, about an inch-long tear through which I could see his teeth, but as I watched, the wound began to mend.

"Joyous?" His voice was rough.

As though responding to a tug by invisible hands, I sat up straighter, managed to stay upright with the help of the wall. I was covered in canned cherries, which at first glance looked alarmingly like blood, but I seemed to have avoided the glass of the broken jars they had been stored in. My face and shoulder hurt, but a quick glance showed me that the zombie hadn't broken my skin with its teeth.

"Joyous—damn it! Are you all right?" he demanded.

I laughed once. The left side of my face protested, and I couldn't hear out of that ear, but all things considered the news was pretty good.

"Oh yeah. Never better." My voice was weak. I found that annoying but couldn't think what to do about it.

"You look gray." He crawled toward me, ignoring the shards of glass. It crunched under him but he never flinched.

"You should see the other guy." I tried to smile but failed. My left cheek wasn't cooperating.

Not taking this for a joke, Ambrose looked past me and spied the zombie. I glanced back briefly. It was a mess. I had done a fairly thorough job of ruining its head and chest.

"Good clean hits. You're getting better. Did it bite you?"

"No, it tried. But I killed it first. Ambrose . . . would it be okay if I took a nap for a minute?" I asked as the world again went black and fuzzy. "I need to rest. Just for a minute."

"Go ahead," he said, and got there in time to ease me down to the floor. I felt it as he pushed my dislocated finger bones back into place but was too weak to cry out. I was also aware of being bathed in heat and feeling my heart synching up to a new rhythm that was not its own. My grateful lungs finally filled with oxygen that finally began to circulate to the rest of my body.

When I came round again a few moments later, Ambrose was dragging the freezer corpses outside. He didn't retrieve the spike he had driven through the second thing's jaw and out the top of its head. Maybe he had plenty of spikes left in his belt, left over from . . . an old tent? Actually, I couldn't think where these spikes were from. Again I thought that they looked rather a lot like bayonets, only with handles. I think they must have been designed for killing, not camping.

"Are they like vampires?" I asked, looking away as he dragged the body past. I didn't like to think about the strength necessary to drive that thing through so much bone—and floor. Ambrose was one of the good guys, and I had to be glad for whatever had changed him into this inhumanly strong person, even if it was very, very weird.

Ambrose turned to stare at me. He had rinsed his face. I got a distracted smile. His head was cocked and he was listening. I remembered then that I had fired my gun and that might have attracted other monsters.

"In what sense?" he asked. He didn't say anything about how I shouldn't be silly, that vampires weren't real, and I made a note to ask about this later, along with how it was he could sometimes talk to me without using actual words.

"Do you have to leave the spike in . . . like a stake in a vampire?"

"I don't know. I haven't a lot of experience with ghouls. I know they're harder to kill than zombies. The main thing is that this one kept trying to bite me even after I destroyed the heart. I'm afraid it rather pissed me off and I got a bit violent." He winked. "I don't want that stake back. It's covered in blood and brains now."

One thing processed. "That's a ghoul, then? I thought it was." I noticed the creature's teeth and malformed jaws. It was like someone had taken a set of large teeth and stuck them into a smaller skull. I could have pulled back the lips to check on this, but even with the spike in place that action seemed the dumbest risk since Icarus thought: *Why not fly to the sun?*

"Yes. Look at its legs." Ambrose dragged it farther down the passage so I could see its lower body. From the hip bones down they were warped, roped with muscle and covered in dark hair.

"They're . . . What are they?" I shuddered. It was a weak effort but I was still very tired. The skin of my chest was sore and I looked down, unsurprised to see a handprint. Had Ambrose had to give me heart massage?

"Not human. Maybe gorilla."

Gorilla. I pulled my eyes up from my chest and

looked at the face again. That's what this was. The lower half of the head was ape, the top half human. Those weren't tattoos on its cheeks; those were staples holding the two halves together. A wave of nausea rolled through me, but I was getting better at accepting horror. My chest hardly hurt at all now.

"Why the hell would anyone do this?" I meant Saint Germain, of course. There was no need to use his name. There couldn't be that many corpse raisers in the region.

"Because he can. Because he's insane." Ambrose shrugged and confessed: "I don't know. Dippel was evil but his son is . . . I don't have a word for him. 'Demon' maybe. Except, demons are controlled by overlords. I don't think anything controls the Dark Man's son. There seem to be some people out there attempting to keep him in check, but the best they can manage is stalemate after stalemate."

Not the best news he could have shared at that moment.

"Can we do any better?" I asked.

"I don't know." This wasn't the comforting response I had hoped for either.

He went on to relate: "By the way, I checked the lobby and dining room. The radio has been smashed. The satellite phone, too. Not that I could have used them, but maybe you could have. I don't suppose you can fly a plane if anything happens to me?"

I shook my head. Fly a plane? That wasn't on my resumé. I had few skills that were of use in this situation. If he had any need for an expert in Microsoft Word or using a Cuisinart to make cookie dough, though, I was his girl.

"Why? I mean, why wouldn't we be able to use them?" I asked. "If they weren't smashed."

"Because one of the other side effects of the Dark Man's treatment is that I short out all electrical equipment I come in direct contact with—microwaves, cell phones, computers, CD players, all of it." He paused. "And I've been . . . helping you. Keeping your heart steady. I think that I have probably messed up your electrical field a bit. Still, there was a chance." He stood up and looked around.

So, he had been keeping a very close watch on this heart of mine? I had almost suspected as much. I had never felt as strong as I did when near Ambrose.

"Oh well." I didn't know what else to say. I believed him. When my heart went wonky it took drugs and a defibrillator to get it back online. Something had pulled me back from the brink of disaster several times that day, and it wasn't my faulty mitral valve finally grabbing its own bootstraps and heaving itself back on course.

Ambrose dragged the bodies into the courtyard. He pulled his fancy rifle out of one—it was covered in brown gore—doused the corpses with kerosene and then, by some means, lit them. There were three in the pile. I had somehow managed to miss his killing the third.

At the time I told myself that he used some kind

of flare to start the fire, but I know now that he was able to call at will the heat and lightning right out of the stormy air. He could also direct the storm's currents into my heart. I don't think any flares were needed with so much electricity in the air. He was simply willing the corpses alight with some kind of pyrokinesis.

"I wish we could send the bodies back to wherever they came from," I said. "To their graveyards or families." I was on my feet again and trying vainly to scrape the drying cherry muck off of my shirt and jeans. I left my face alone; it was regaining mobility but still hurt. This was also when I noticed my sore knee and finger.

"Me, too. But then we'd have to explain what we were doing with them. Frankly, though I've written fiction for more than a century, I think it is a tale that is beyond me to tell." Ambrose pulled off another shirt, wadded it up and tossed it into the blaze. Zombie-fighting was hell on the wardrobe.

I nodded, punch-drunk. Returning them would also cause their families pain when they were reinterred. And would they feel compelled to change their headstones? I could just imagine:

JOHN DOE, BELOVED FATHER
BORN 1952 - DIED 2006 (AND 2009)

Ambrose interrupted my thoughts. "That should do it. They burn well once the bones catch fire."

"So, mangroves next?" I looked out at the horizon as I asked this. The sun had disappeared again and a wind, audible because of the peppering sand it carried, assaulted the front of the building where the resort lobby was located. I was glad we were on the lee side and protected from the worst of it. I noticed something odd about the trees, then. The upper limbs were alive with frogs, lizards and small crabs hanging on for dear life as the violent wind whipped them about.

"But no birds," I murmured.

Ambrose glanced upward. "They've fled. If these poor creatures had wings, they'd leave too." Reminded of our danger, the look he gave me was frustrated and a long way from the admiring one I desired. I understood, though. He wanted to keep me safe, and there was nowhere safer than at his side. He was my literal life-support system. I had no choice but stay next to the lightning rod and risk becoming collateral damage.

"Look, I won't freak out on you," I said. "It isn't fear that makes me faint. It's my damned heart overexerting itself—and you can deal with that."

"I realize this fact and am not at ease. A little fear from you would be reassuring. You keep rushing in where angels fear to tread."

"Hey, I didn't rush in back there. I got jumped. And I killed it! Anyway, I have a little fear. I have a *lot* of fear. I just don't allow myself to get hysterical, because it makes me pass out. I have had no choice but to learn self-control. I'd have died in childhood if I hadn't."

He actually glared at me. "You are the damndest woman." But then he sighed, and this took any heat out of the comment. "All right. Stay behind me. Keep checking our back trail and shoot anything that moves. Saint Germain can take over animals and birds, and we can't assume that anything or anyone is a friend."

I thought about the giant croc and swallowed. I wasn't sure that shooting it would do any good if it decided to come after us. I was barely able to kill a human zombie, and they were slow and weak compared to the crocodile.

"I heard a story once that the peasants of Scotland believed a corpse would bleed in the presence of its killer," I said randomly, wanting to think about something else but not having much success with a mental change of subject. "I wonder what these bodies would do around Saint Germain,"

"They'd probably get up and walk again. That's why we're burning them," replied Job's comforter. "Let's go. We're burning daylight."

Witch, *n*. (1) An ugly and repulsive old woman, in a wicked league with the devil. (2) A beautiful and attractive young woman, in wickedness a league beyond the devil.

—Ambrose Bierce, *The Devil's Dictionary*

The ineffable dunce has nothing to say and says it—says it with a liberal embellishment of bad delivery, embroidering it with reasonless vulgarities of attitude, gesture and attire.

—Ambrose Bierce on Oscar Wilde

I choose my friends for their good looks, my acquaintances for their good characters, and my enemies for their good intellects. A man cannot be too careful in the choice of his enemies.

—Oscar Wilde

Chapter Nine

We found the crocodile right off. She was lying on her favorite sandy beach by the wooden walkway, and something approximately man-size was thrashing around in her belly. Saint Germain's sword was stuck in the sand about five feet away. I was unable to stop my hands, which dug out my camera and took a couple of photos, though at the time I rather doubted they would actually capture the sheer horror of what we were seeing. One of the photos caught Ambrose in profile. His face was calm but grim. It wasn't the kind of thing you sent to your friends with a caption like WISH YOU WERE HERE!

I want to make a pitch for Nikon cameras here. My little digital camera had been tumbled down a muddy mountain, sodden with rain and had canned cherries crushed on it, albeit through the filter of my clothing, had had sand thrown at it, and the darned thing was still working. I was terribly impressed. Later. Of course, at the moment we ran into the crocodile digesting her golem dinner I wasn't feeling much of anything except a sort of disassociated horror that would require proof before I or anyone else would believe it.

"I knew a Wolfeschlegelsteinhausenbergerdorff back in college. He played football and they had to wrap his name around the shoulders of his jersey."

I don't know why I said this. Perhaps it was just that my brain had finally had enough of morbid things and was refusing to contemplate any more awfulness. My body was also sore and tired by the unaccustomed physical activity and multiple falls. I am not fond of exercise and, when I do indulge, I don't do it ferociously. I was completely unprepared muscularly for what we had been forced to do.

Ambrose pulled his gaze away from the crocodile by turning his head in my direction. I could see it took effort. And it was right about then that I noticed the lingering smell of rot in the air.

The crocodile belched.

"I wonder if she'll throw him back up. I would," Ambrose muttered. He didn't comment about my athletic friend with the world's longest name.

"Do you ever lie?" I asked absently, staring into his dark and mostly unreadable eyes until they blinked and focused on me.

"Constantly, and it's damned exhausting. I think it's why I spend so much time alone. You?" He sounded like himself again. I was relieved. I didn't like the idea that anything could shock Ambrose. I was counting on him remaining a superhero until we escaped from the island.

"Rarely. I expect I would lie more often if I cared more. Or if I had any really good secrets," I added. "You know, I'm getting hungry. I don't know why—today has been a total gross-out. It couldn't have been worse if I'd started the morning with a bowl of turd soup."

Ambrose gave a quiet laugh.

"What?" I asked. "I'm serious. This is the worst thing I've ever seen. The crocodile has eaten him and he's not dead."

"I know. Never mind," he replied. "I doubt you'd understand why this is funny to me."

"My sense of humor does seem to have been impaired."

"Understandably." He sighed. "You and I have a real problem here."

I was encouraged by the *you and I,* even if I didn't want to hear about any more difficulties.

"We can bury our dead, bury our mistakes and even our memories. But there is no guarantee that they'll remain discreetly hidden until the final trumpet if we do." He looked about the mangrove and then back at the crocodile who belched louder this time. A clear handprint—the right one, I assumed, since I had shot the left one off—appeared briefly in the croc's side, causing the scales to bulge. I thought he was going to say more on the subject, but instead he shook his head and added matter-of-factly: "We've got to find the rest of the ghouls and zombies and put them down. Then we'll decide what to do about Saint Germain or his golem—if he's still kicking. Burning is the only solution, but I'm damned if I know how to get him out of her."

I stared at the crocodile, unable to come up with any solution that didn't involve killing the beast. She was big and scary, but I hadn't forgotten that she saved my life.

Ambrose nodded, as if understanding. He finished, "Afterward we'd better get out of Dodge— and all before nightfall. We'll deal with the nightmares and your heart later."

I was sure he wasn't speaking metaphorically, about my growing affection for him, but decided not to ask what he thought needed to be done about my coronary challenge. It was my second least favorite subject.

"Okay—ready when you are." I was getting to be such a liar, myself.

The ghouls and zombies were not difficult to find. After all, their mission was to discover and eat us. Or eat me. Ambrose thought they were trying to capture him alive for genetic experiments, I remembered. Either way, they weren't trying to be quiet and sneaky.

"Are you really ready?" Ambrose asked, his skin changing tone as once again we felt the temperature drop and ozone build in the air. I could detect no breeze, but his hair shifted uneasily as if stirred by an invisible wind.

"Yes," I lied.

I looked at the zombies staggering through the sand and felt like I'd dislocated my brain. I wasn't panicked because Ambrose was near and keeping me calm, but my mind insisted that I had to be looking at something that was a trick, a distortion of reality. It couldn't be real. The things came shambling down the beach, a lumbering funeral procession until they smelled us; then they lifted their heads and began an eerie sort of hissing and redoubled their pace.

None of the zombies were exactly skeletons, but there wasn't a whole lot of flesh and bone left after their prolonged stay in the water. Gender was difficult to determine, since much of the identifying sexual characteristics had been eaten away.

I pulled up my Colt. It would do a lot of damage, especially at close range—as I had seen. The things shuffled on, getting closer, uncaring of our weapons or perhaps not comprehending what they were.

I chose a man, a white stick figure with a mustache like Tom Selleck's. He had on swimming trunks and what used to be a Hawaiian shirt. As I watched, an eel wriggled out what was left of his stomach and dropped onto the ground where it thrashed helplessly. Which made it hit home then that these things really were rotting corpses of once-living human beings, and I had to swallow hard against my rising gorge. These were zombies, the walking dead. And they were looking at us like we were the first stop at the free, all-you-can-eat buffet.

I had some range with the handgun, but I waited, not wanting to waste any ammunition. When the first was close enough, I looked into the creature's blank, watery eyes and felt relief. The soul had already departed from this bloated being. I was shooting flesh, but it wouldn't be murder. I told myself this fiercely and repeatedly: *You can't murder what's already dead.* I've since wondered if someone will one day look into my eyes and think the same thing. Some people's definitions of "us and them" can be pretty exclusive. Would I someday be seen as a monster?

Ambrose pulled the trigger of his rifle. It was surprisingly quiet, and I realized that it was silenced. The zombie in a filthy white dress standing next to my rotting Magnum P.I. snapped back, a small bloodless hole appearing in her gray head. She managed another step, but Ambrose fired again, putting a second round into her heart. He was quick, clean and efficient. The creature crumpled to the sand without a sound. I thought about complimenting Ambrose on his marksmanship, but decided what he really wanted to hear was my Colt dealing with our approaching enemies.

I swallowed again and then let fly. As I had hoped, my gutless Magnum zombie and the sexless creature behind him both fell over, blown back by what looked like a violent wind but was in fact lead bullets traveling at murderous speed. There was no blood on either in spite of the wounds, though an amazingly awful smell filled the air as the monsters were blown open.

Aim, fire, retreat and reload. Repeat as necessary. It was actually over quickly—five minutes at most—and yet I felt like I spent an eternity there. I'd had some bad nightmares before that day, but I knew that new ones were coming. I'd never think of the beach in the same way again.

There's always a price, isn't there?

Two ghouls, drawn by the zombies' baying and the sound of gunfire, rushed us from the overgrowth to the left, but Ambrose was swift in dealing with them. The gun couldn't kill them, but even ghouls have trouble attacking when their heads are blown off.

The wind, never entirely still, kicked back into action and blew the smell of gunfire away in one last angry gust. I was sorry to see it go, since what replaced it was nauseating.

Silence fell. It was not complete, of course, since the ocean was always moving, but an unnatural quiet fell over the island that had previously been filled with birdsong and the croaks of happy amphibians and the drone of insects.

I'd never been completely surrounded by death before. Few people in the modern, industrial world have. Historically there have been slaughters and plagues, but outside of that really bad tsunami in 2006, most of us modern-day urbanites face our corpses and mourn our deaths one at a time. But now I was surrounded by casualties, more fatalities than I had ever imagined could happen at one time and in one place. I was completely encircled by the dead. And they were indeed just corpses now. Whatever had been animating them was gone. Maybe this was because the croc had finally succeeded in digesting Saint Germain's golem, or maybe because the real wizard had decided to retreat and take a moment to rest before beginning round two of his assault.

On the bright side, Ambrose and I were alive and mostly unhurt, and we were about to handle these corpses so that they would never trouble anyone again. It would have been easier to shove them into the ocean and let the sea creatures do our work, but what might happen to animals that ate zombie or ghoul? Contaminating the water seemed a bad idea of *Titanic*—as in the doomed ship—proportions. Nor could we leave them rotting on the beach. Leaving aside the matter of land scavengers dining on them—again, the worst idea since Pandora said "Let's open this little box"—eventually the staff would return to the island and, though loyal and well-trained and used to doing without police, this many bodies would require an explanation, probably of an official nature since many of them had bullets in them.

"They might also get up again if Saint Germain

calls them," Ambrose remarked, clearly following my train of thought. We seemed to be communicating on an inaudible wavelength, though he was smiling and in control while I was not. For a moment I wondered if he was high on something.

He said quietly: "These aren't like the zombies I saw in Mexico. These are far stronger. We just can't take the chance they'll follow us back to the main island when we go. We have to burn them all."

I nodded wearily and began dragging driftwood into the nearest fire pit.

"The situation could be worse," I remarked.

"But only with an act of God."

"Or the other guy." I paused before adding, "It hasn't been your garden-variety vacation, that's for sure. But it has certainly been memorable. Even without the pictures, and those are going to make it extra special."

"If being near me hasn't ruined your digital camera," Ambrose warned, hefting the first body into a fire that had sprung up from nowhere.

The crabs began falling from the trees as soon as the zombies all were set afire. They landed awkwardly, crustaceans not being built for skydiving, then crawled for the shoreline as quickly as their damaged bodies would carry them. I took this as a good sign. If they thought it safe to get back in the water then maybe the invasion was done.

Not wanting to stress myself unnecessarily and therefore be unable to haul bodies, I went back to my cottage to see what could be salvaged. As I'd noted before, my laptop had survived the onslaught, along with my passport, which I had for some reason put in my computer bag. Chalk another one up for modern technology and microfiber bags. My clothes were another matter. Feeling repulsed at the slimy and torn fabric, I gathered everything up by clean corners and took them outside to be burned with the rest. I wasn't surprised to find Ambrose doing the same thing with his clothing. He was leaving no scent for bloodhounds to trace.

"The weather is weird," I commented, wanting to think about anything except what we were doing. The sun was going down, and where it poked through the cloud cover it was bright enough to induce a migraine after the twilight that had plagued us all day.

"Yes. The wizard and I have both been manipulating it." Ambrose looked up and frowned.

"Oh." The sky looked bruised, not surprising with a supernatural bad guy molesting it at will. "I didn't know you could do that."

"To a limited degree. I can draw an electrical charge out of the air. My body has become a sort of lightning rod. Usually I enjoy it, but I have to be careful when I'm not alone because someone else could get hurt."

"You mean, hit by lightning?"

"No. I mean that it can make me go furry. It's why I use the gun to kill these things when I can. I'm afraid that physical contact might draw the beast. Killing and storms are a bad combination this close to the full moon. I have to be careful for the first few days before and after the lunar event."

"I'll remember that," I said, and meant it.

An inky finger of gray smoke stretched toward us from the east. I couldn't identify what kind of smoke it was, though I preferred it to the stench of barbecuing zombies.

"Is that your cabin?" I asked.

"Yes, I set it afire." His voice was matter-of-fact, but his eyes still glittered and I could see raised tissue on his chest beneath his wet shirt. He jerked his head toward a large duffel. "That's what's left of my guns and ammunition. I'll bury what we can't take with us. Then we'd better get a move on."

"So, we're definitely leaving tonight?"

"Yes. I checked my plane and everything's fine. We'll spend the night on the big island and then leave for Maine in the morning. There is a flight out at eleven every weekday. It's never completely full this time of year."

"We can go? Just like that?" For some reason this surprised me. Maybe because it was so anti-climactic.

"Just like that. I'll call the manager from the hotel and warn him that there will need to be a lot of cleanup and that we'll have to cancel all bookings until at least February. You have your passport?"

I nodded. "Do I have time to shower?" I asked, looking down at my clothes that were covered in sand, slime, dried cherries, soot and sweat.

"If you're quick. I'd like to get out of here before we lose the light. My plane is old and doesn't have any computer guidance systems since I'm death on them. I can see all right even in the dark, but the officials on the ground don't like it when I land at night."

"I'll be quicker than quick," I promised, feeling like I had had quite enough death-defying adventure for one day without adding flying in the dark.

"Here. A souvenir for you." Ambrose reached down and tossed a clean T-shirt my way. It was large, a man's shirt and somewhat worn. On it was a quote from Stephen Crane's *"In The Desert"*:

BUT I LIKE IT
BECAUSE IT IS BITTER,
AND BECAUSE IT IS MY HEART.

And that finally made me laugh. Of course Bitter Bierce would have such a shirt.

"Thanks. I'll be right back."

Lord, *n.* In American society, an English tourist above the state of a costermonger. . . . The word "Lord" is sometimes used, also, as a title of the Supreme Being; but this is thought to be rather flattery than true reverence.

Abscond, *v.i.* To "move in a mysterious way," commonly with the property of another.
        —Ambrose Bierce, *The Devil's Dictionary*

Chapter Ten

Our journey was long, but I slept through most of it. Ambrose handled the seaplane well, in spite of it being a relic from the earliest days of aviation. For you airplane buffs, it was a Curtiss N-9. Ambrose had learned to fly it during the First World War and had kept the hydroplane as a souvenir.

Perhaps Ambrose was doing something to keep me calm, or maybe it was just that I'd had a surfeit of terror and could feel no more, but the short flight to the big island was neither scary nor exhilarating, though a strange sort of lightning danced over the plane for the entire trip and also made Ambrose seem to glow.

Ambrose was well-known and he had no trouble getting us a suite at the hotel on Nadi. I don't recall the name of the hotel, but it was on the beach in Smugglers Cove. The rooms were airy but that is all I remember. My exhausted body dropped into a light coma the moment it hit the four-hundred-thread-count sheets.

We had time the next morning to do some perusing of the gift shop for clothes, and have breakfast, and then it was time to leave. This time we were flying first class. I might have protested the expense, but Ambrose made all the arrangements. Maybe he thought he owed me a refund for the missed vacation on his island. I wondered briefly how his phone call to his manager had gone and how he planned to explain what happened to the bungalows on the island. I would have blamed it on the crocodile. That was the only thing that sounded even remotely believable.

During one of the flights I uploaded the photos from my camera onto the computer. They were amazing. If I were so inclined, I could have made a bundle selling them to the tabloids:

THE DEAD WALK IN FIJI!
CANNIBAL ISLAND CURSE STRIKES AGAIN!

No reputable paper or magazine would touch them of course. The subject matter was so bizarre that anyone sane would believe them to be a hoax. I had been there and I still couldn't entirely process what had happened.

The airplane was alright as airplanes go, but as a place to begin a romance—or at least the consideration of a romance—it was lacking in ambience. Still, I had a lot of slow, quiet time in which to consider Ambrose and the fact that I was taking him to what was the closest thing I had to a home.

Eventually we landed in Bangor and were able to stagger out onto real land with other real people, albeit a cold and dark place locked in winter. After renting a car, we took Route 1A to Ellsworth and then Route 3 to Bar Harbor. We could have chartered a private plane to take us to Hancock County Airport, but Bangor was much larger and only fifty miles away. Also, we knew for certain that it wouldn't be closed because of the weather. The snowplows were not always Johnny-on-the-spot in smaller towns that were largely boarded up for the winter. Once we were this close, we didn't want to be delayed because of bad weather at a small airport.

In spite of my residual bad childhood feeling about the place, Bar Harbor is lovely. It is under-sized as many cities and towns go, and consequently has escaped the retail monotony that has overshadowed much of the United States. It has retained an identity. Bar Harbor has shops and boutiques but no mega-malls. Unfortunately for us, most of these quaint tourist shops closed up at Christmas and wouldn't reopen until spring.

Having been unable to outfit ourselves with appropriate winter gear at airport gift shops, we made a stop at an outlet store near the airport to buy winter clothing. I had been living in a borrowed T-shirt and tie-dyed shorts for the last twenty hours and was feeling chafed and cranky. Ambrose didn't actually need a coat and boots since he didn't feel the cold, but it was good camouflage. I, on the other hand, did need a coat and jeans and woolen shirt and socks and snow boots. I threw in some sunscreen and tinted lip balm, too. I would have liked to shop a bit more for cosmetics and toiletries, but my nerves kept insisting that we were exposed and needed to get under cover. I decided I would make do with whatever clothing and shampoo I had at the house.

We stopped once more at a small market just outside town. The moment we stepped from the car, the cold rushed into my joints and made me realize how tired I was. My body ached all over and I was feeling that the old raised walkway in front of the store might actually defeat me.

Then Ambrose touched my arm and, as was always the case, I found that I had a hidden store of energy. Or, more likely, that he was sending me some of his own seemingly endless supply.

We picked up milk and eggs, bread and butter, frozen orange juice and coffee. And olives. They had three kinds displayed tastefully among a collection of antique lobster cages that were also for sale. The man behind the counter rang us up without idle chitchat, and for once I was grateful for the local inclination to be standoffish.

"Ready?" Ambrose asked me as I paused at the market door, surveying the disturbed snow in the tiny parking lot, looking for heaven only knew what.

"As ready as I'll ever be," I muttered, and pushed open the door to head back out into the cold.

Do you recall the opening credits to that old

soap opera, *Dark Shadows*? There are high-drama shots of murderous waves throwing themselves onto rocky cliffs—that's Bar Harbor. It's about forty-five square miles in all, and has about four thousand five hundred residents. In summer. There are only about half that many in winter, especially over the holidays. There's plenty of room for privacy. Perhaps too much privacy if we ran into trouble.

There is one sandy beach among the rocky cliffs and we passed it on the way into town. A conspiracy of ravens was gathered on the icy shore and eyed us openly as we passed. Usually I adore the giant black birds, but their boldness made me feel uneasy then, in spite of being exhausted. After what we had seen on the island, I would never be entirely trusting of birds again. Of any animals, really, since it seemed they could be signed up for the other team.

Downtown has only four main streets that block it in. My house was located on a small lane just off Main Street at the corner where Svenborg's—The Finest In Viking Cuisine—had set up shop two decades ago, and the food wasn't half bad if you stayed away from the lutefisk.

The house had been used as a barn when built in 1895 and was known locally by the unimaginative name of Graystone. I made note as we passed that most of the quaint houses and businesses along Main Street were shuttered, their inhabitants wisely headed for warmer climes. Even Svenborg's was empty, though there were Christmas lights in the window. We might have been traveling through the world after everyone had been removed by the Rapture.

The thought gave me the shivers.

"Cold?" Ambrose asked. He seemed to be enjoying driving the car, though we were unable to get any radio reception and the headlights refused to work.

"Only in my soul," I muttered.

We drove slowly through the deserted neighborhood. I noticed that some of the trees along the street were not bare of leaves and were bowed down under the heavy weight of the clotted snow. From time to time winter will come on so fast that it will rudely freeze the trees and shrubs before the leaves have fully turned and shed. This is when unnaturally heavy limbs snap and trees are toppled in high winds.

Some careless child had left a bicycle out in the snow in front of a charming red Victorian. The frostbitten handlebars looked forlorn as they pushed out of the snowdrift, an avalanche victim making a last cry for help. It looked sad. Perhaps it had been displaced by something newer.

A few brave narcissi, forced in a greenhouse for holiday decoration, huddled in pots on covered porches. But their heads were tucked low against the cold and they seemed uncertain about showing themselves to the cruel white world. The hawthorn hedge that surrounded the house on the corner was drooping under the white load, with only the smallest hints of green showing through the winter blanket. Some people might have called the scene peaceful.

As I had feared, the snowplows hadn't been through for a couple of days and, though the snow wasn't deep, we were obliged to slow to a crawl as we turned off of Main Street and onto the tiny side road where the house was. I directed Ambrose to park around back where the thick trees gave some shelter and the snowfall was still fairly shallow.

The silence when Ambrose turned off the car was strange and I felt a bit odd not to have the mechanical vibrations shaking my body after the last twenty-four hours of nonstop travel.

"Well, this is it. Home sweet home." My voice wasn't convincing.

Having no real luggage, we gathered up our few parcels and grocery bags and began tromping toward the back door through the crackling ice crust of undisturbed snow. I noticed that Ambrose was looking about carefully, and knew that he was evaluating the house in terms of its defensibility. He seemed satisfied, which pleased me in a vague way. Really I was just too tired to care much about anything except some food and then bed.

Our passage through the icy air was marked with a trail of vapor caused by Ambrose's extraordinary heat. I saw that it trailed along behind us for some twenty feet, a long foggy shadow that ended at the back stoop.

I'd lost my keys somewhere on the island, but I kept a spare in one of those fake rocks in the planter by the back door. The lock was stiff and reluctant to yield, but it finally saw reason when I swore at it, and reluctantly let us inside.

A caretaker who managed the property for the trust was supposed to keep the electricity on and propane in the tank, though he winterized the rest of the place just in case of power failure. I said a prayer that he had not been derelict these last couple of years and then crossed the threshold into the musty darkness of the kitchen.

For a moment I was ten years old again, feeling uncertain of my welcome but ready to be stubborn if my parents tried to send me away before the week was up. The paralysis of memory was broken when I felt Ambrose reach past me. The lights snapped on at once and dispelled the worst of the gloom though not the cold. Shivering, in spite of my new coat, I hurried to the thermostat and turned on the heater. Warmth as much as light would chase any lingering ghosts away.

Ambrose had closed the door behind us but stayed on the far side of the kitchen, slowly taking it all in. He drew in a deep breath and then cocked his head, listening intently for heaven only knew what.

I listened, too, but heard nothing suspicious. It was so quiet that we could hear the fall of ash in the cold hearth as ice forced the frozen soot from its hold on the old stone on the chimney. No one was home except my ghosts, and those wouldn't hurt Ambrose.

"This is unexpected." Ambrose smiled slightly and I knew he liked what he saw.

Physically, the place was charming. The pantry had been incorporated into the kitchen in one of the many remodels the house had undergone, and now served as a breakfast room. Warm wood cabinets with paned glass fronts stretched all the way to the low-beamed ceiling that was still tall enough not to threaten the averaged-sized modern man. I'm not tall, so the uppermost shelves are just out of reach, but I wouldn't change a thing. Efficiency be damned. The room was appealing.

The first thing we did was turn on the water. Everything seemed okay because the pipes had been covered in heat tape and if the temp dropped below forty degrees, a small circuit opened up and an electrical current warmed them. Fortunately, Ambrose knew what he was doing with the water pump. My experience with such things was only theoretical. I had never visited in winter.

Together we unpacked the groceries. Ambrose pulled out the small refrigerator while I reached around and plugged it in.

"Let me show you around," I said, my breath visible in the air even though the furnace had engaged and was puffing like the little engine who knew he could.

The furniture in the rest of the house was appropriately tasteful and simple, except for the porcelain centerpiece on the dining room table. The tribute to Bacchus stood about eighteen inches high and was composed of three small-breasted nymphs lolling about in a bunch of giant purple grapes and touching themselves in inappropriate ways. It was definitely an antique and probably valuable, or else my mother would never have kept it. I liked it, probably because she hadn't, and I left it on the trestle table in spite of its tackiness.

There was only one phone in the house. It was a black Bakelite rotary model located on a telephone-chair just inside the dining room, and it pleased Ambrose mightily since he could use it without shorting it out. I picked it up and was satisfied to hear a dial tone. Probably it was dumb to spend money to keep the house in readiness, but I'd felt safer going off with Max as long as I had this bolt-hole available if I ever had to retreat. Gee, I must have been psychic.

"And a gossip bench! I haven't seen one of these in years," Ambrose murmured, touching the aged oak of the telephone table. There was a current phone book on the tiny shelf and an ill-fitting drawer where I kept assorted keys and other odds and ends.

The bathroom had not fared so well as the kitchen and dining room. The giant bathtub was still impressive, but the wallpaper had been exposed to some kind of water damage since I'd left for Germany, and looked like it had psoriasis. It was still attached to the walls, but it had blistered and needed replacing.

The bathroom had another remnant from the days of antiquity that amused Ambrose, a hair dryer consisting of a bubble helmet fed by a hose with bellows that you pumped yourself while seated on a wooden stool. I rarely used it because it smelled vaguely of rotting rubber, though it had a place where you could insert a cotton ball drenched in perfume that was supposed to suffuse the hair with scent. It had been the height of high tech in 1920. My mother used it.

"Good Lord! I saw one like this in Constantinople the year I took the Orient Express to see the East. You could tip the boy who brought the coffee to pump it for you if you were feeling lazy."

"The bellows are kind of leaky, but it still works." My voice was neutral and Ambrose shot me a quick glance. "There's not much else on this floor," I said. "It's a small place. Humble."

"There is a second floor?"

"Yes, a loft where the maid slept. It used to be where they kept the hay, but it was finished off when the barn was converted."

I excused myself from Ambrose, saying I needed to use the bathroom, but really just to gain some time before we went on with the tour. I used the toilet though I knew the porcelain would be a punishment on my bare skin. What I hadn't expected was to see steam rising from the toilet bowl when I stood. I had wintered in cold places, but never in a building where the heat had been turned off.

My feet walked a little slower than usual as I rejoined Ambrose, and we went down the dark hall side by side. There were two "family" bedrooms in the house, one with a double bed, thick down comforters and a red velvet canopy with working bed curtains. The other was smaller and had a twin mattress with spooled headboard and badly faded patchwork quilt. I couldn't quite picture Ambrose sleeping in it, but knew I couldn't stand to be in the room myself. It was one of the places I still have nightmares about. I hadn't stepped in there since my parents died.

I showed him the master bedroom first, opening up the wooden shutters to let in the late afternoon light. The windows were frosted and the sunlight was cold when it touched me. I noticed that in spite of the shutters being closed, the Axminster carpet was beginning to show its age. I would need to do some work if I was going to keep the place.

"Very nice. I've always liked bedrooms with fireplaces." He touched with a gentle hand the handpainted tiles that surrounded the firebox.

I nodded, finding it increasingly more difficult to speak.

It took some mental exertion to force myself across the hall and to open the narrow white door to the other bedroom. Nothing leaped out at me and said boo as I reached in and flipped on the light. There was one twenty-five-watt bulb in the fixture in the ceiling and it did little beyond make the room look dingy. The narrow bed remained plain. There were no teddy bears or dolls on the coverlet. The whole room was impersonal, not a single memento or photo to suggest a child had ever been in the house. Of course, I rarely was there, and when I came my mother made it obvious that she couldn't wait for me to be gone. There had been no presents from her, no posing for family photos, no gifts of bedtime stories unless the maid had had time for me.

Every other room in the house was lovingly decorated, but not this one. The message of my mother's discomfort with the occasional visit of her unwanted child seemed clear to me even after all these years, and I feared to Ambrose also. It wasn't the room's fault, of course, that I felt unwelcome even now. Houses don't remember. But I did. I had thought that I'd made all the needed mental adjustments to come back to this parental domicile, but obviously I hadn't. It would be okay, though, if I just stayed out of that bleak cell of a room.

I sounded surprisingly nonchalant as I said: "You can stay here or sleep with me in the other bedroom. I never go in here myself. Eventually I'm going to make it into an office. If I keep the place. I've been thinking of letting it go."

Those dark eyes studied me for a moment, and I knew that he was picking up on all the things I'd left unsaid. His mouth looked a bit grim as he took a final look around the room.

"Let me start a fire in the living room and we'll talk about arrangements over dinner," he said at last. Again Ambrose reached past me, and this time turned out the light. He closed the door quietly. I knew he was thinking that sometimes it was better to let sleeping ghosts lie. How right he was. I thought I heard him add: "No wonder zombies didn't really scare you. This must have been like living in Hell."

"Only colder," I muttered.

"Let's get that fire started."

Feeling happier with the door shut on my worst

187

memories, I opened my mouth to protest that the woodpile was probably damp and would take forever to light, but then recalled that Ambrose wouldn't be troubled by a little thing like wet kindling.

"Will toast and eggs be okay?" I asked, pushing past him and heading back for the comparative warmth of the kitchen.

"As long as there's coffee and orange juice too."

"Well, naturally. I would never serve naked toast and eggs."

Mad, *adj.* Affected with a high degree of intellectual independence.

Ghost, *n.* The outward and visible sign of an inward fear.
                    —Ambrose Bierce, *The Devil's Dictionary*

. . . The other day they seized an odd man, who goes by the name of Count St. Germain. He has been here these two years, and will not tell who he is, or whence, but professes that he does not go by his right name. He sings, plays on the violin wonderfully, composes, is mad, and not very sensible. He is called an Italian, a Spaniard, a Pole; a somebody that married a great fortune in Mexico, and ran away with her jewels to Constantinople; a priest, a fiddler, a vast nobleman. The Prince of Wales has had unsatiated curiosity about him, but in vain. However, nothing has been made out against him; he is released; and, what convinces me that he is not a gentleman, stays here, and talks of his being taken up for a spy.
                    —Letter from Horace Walpole, 1745

Chapter Eleven

As tired as I was, I couldn't bring myself to sleep after our cozy breakfast. I urged a yawning Ambrose to go ahead and nap while I did the dishes. I think he would have volunteered to help, but he could see I truly wanted to be alone. Probably he thought I was needing some time to lay to rest some familial ghosts that our sudden visit had riled up, and that I would prefer not to have any witnesses, but it wasn't that at all. The only thing haunting me at the moment was the lingering smell of coffee. I just needed some time to think. About Ambrose. Without Ambrose possibly listening in and hearing what I was thinking about.

I'm all for a little healthy self-rationalization, but I'm not out-and-out delusional. I hadn't wanted another relationship after the last debacle, and had thought that after Max I'd posted a pretty clear collection of stop, danger, radioactive signs around me to warn off any stubborn males. But our unusual circumstances on the island had run our unusual liaison right through that romantic red light and into some rough off-road conditions. As much as I would like to ignore the inconvenient truth, the fact was that Ambrose and I were in a relationship whether I wanted one or not. Just what kind it would be remained to be seen, but I was fairly certain that it was going to be more significant than the one Max and I had shared. And this would have been semiokay if my feelings toward him were strictly platonic and dutiful. But they weren't.

Maybe it was because we'd just spent the last twenty-four hours semicuddling on various planes. Or maybe it was that he had saved my life repeatedly by fighting off monsters and also reaching inside me to mend my heart whenever it faltered. Whatever it was, half of my mind and all of my body thought it belonged with Ambrose, and would like to get a whole lot closer to his warmth and . . . whatever else it was that Ambrose had.

Logically, this seemed like a really bad idea. He wasn't called Bitter Bierce for nothing. They also say you shouldn't have an affair at the office because when something goes wrong on the personal side, working together could be difficult or even impossible. We were in a similar situation, minus the coffeepots or copy machines that come with the usual nine-to-five jobs.

There was also the matter of whether Ambrose was still a bit suicidal. Or entirely sane. Or even human. Sitting where I was, it was impossible to make a judgment call on any of these things. Until I was a little clearer in my head, sharing a bed with Ambrose seemed unwise, no matter how keen the body was to do just that—and then go in and jump his bones.

So, instead of walking down the hall and climbing into bed with the man who appealed to me above all others I had ever met, I got out my portable computer and forced myself to write the last three chapters of the book I had due. The chapters were short and not my best work, since my online notes were sketchy. What can I say? Pencils' limited fascination had already palled, and the woman who had wanted to write about them had gotten lost somewhere between Munich and Fiji.

I had to use the phone lines to connect to the Internet and it took forever to send the bloated file to my editor. This had me tugging on my hair in frustration, but I reminded myself that I wasn't going to go crawl into bed with Ambrose regardless of how long it took to e-mail the book, so it was fine to spend my time doing an online submission.

I knew that Harold would be about as thrilled with my electronic submission as he would be to find his name on a bathroom wall preceded by *For a good time call,* but I hoped he would forgive me when he read my e-mail explaining—okay, lying— that I was on a wildlife preserve in Fiji photographing endangered species for some future unspecified project, and that this was safest way to get the book to him on time. To bolster this story, I wrote a separate e-mail and sent him a cute photo of the green turtles playing at the Sylph's Hole and one of the giant crocodile—without Saint Germain in its stomach.

Fifteen minutes later, I shut the computer down and wandered into the bathroom. The house was warm enough by then that a wallow in the old tub sounded appealing. I rummaged through the brittle wicker cupboard where the towels were stored and found a small cut-glass jar half full of withered bath beads. Though visually unattractive, they still smelled appealing. I sniffed happily at the glass container with my eyes shut, sorting out the various faded hints of musk, black orchid and rose. The oils hadn't gone bad but they were only shadows of their former selves. Reaching into the billows of steam gushing from the taps, I upended the cut-glass jar and shook it until all the withered green beads had fallen into the frothing water and began to break apart in swirls of emerald color.

Further rummaging through the cabinet produced a razor—a little rusted in spots, but I was current with my tetanus booster so decided to chance it rather than go a moment longer with stubbly armpits and legs—and a large towel which was in fact my father's old terry-cloth robe. It had yellowed a bit, but the dried lavender bundles tucked inside the cupboard had left it with a nice old-lady scent.

I undressed quickly, hanging my clothes on the brass hooks on the back of the bathroom door. Humming "Can't Help Lovin' That Man of Mine," I turned off the gushing taps and slowly lowered myself into the strange-colored water. It was hot—too hot for safety, since my blood pressure tended to drop out from under me without warning—but I nevertheless folded myself into the giant tub and then stretched out to my full length, bracing my toes on the far end.

Sighing, I closed my eyes and pretended that I was in a natural hot springs. With Ambrose. At night. And we were all alone. It took a minute to lower my inhibitions enough to script a decent monologue of sweet nothings for him to whisper in my ear. I think maybe I fell asleep.

"Joyous?" At first I wasn't sure if the voice was real or in my fantasy. Either way it made my skin prickle in spite of the water's heat. "Joyous, are you okay?"

"I'm in the bath!" I called at last, realizing this

wasn't my fantasy Ambrose calling to me from my dream. I glanced down and found my body still obscured by milky green water. "You can come in," I added bravely. And probably unwisely, if I was really thinking I wanted to stay uninvolved.

At my invitation he opened the door and walked into the bathroom, but he stopped suddenly just inside the door, feet planted firmly on the black and white marble tile. I watched him close his midnight eyes and inhale deeply of the swirling steam.

"I had forgotten the pleasure—the pure blessing—of having the scent of a woman hovering about the house like a guardian angel," he murmured, opening his eyes and taking a step toward the tub. His face was smiling, his expression almost dreamy. I guess he had found some ghosts in the house as well, and he was pleased at the reacquaintance.

In my mind, I reached for him. He might have protested since my hands were wet, but since it was my fantasy he let me touch him, let me undo the buttons of his fly so he spilled out of crisp new jeans and into my eager hands. His flesh was glowing gold against my pale skin and hotter even than the bathwater. I rolled onto my knees and leaned forward. I set lips against him and began to—

"Joyous?" His voice was a question but also a bit shocked, and my eyes flashed open again. It was a relief to find that I was still on my back and modestly covered in green water. Unless you really squinted, my telltale nipples didn't show.

Disconcerted both by my thoughts and Ambrose's sudden stillness, I slid a little deeper in the bath and concentrated hard on the faucet whose fluted mouth was scaled with mineral deposits.

"Were you able to sleep?" I asked, hoping that the sudden rush of embarrassed heat to my face didn't mean I was about to faint. That would be adding insult to embarrassment.

"Yes." He retreated a step and then sank down gracefully against the wall, keeping his distance from the tub. He had one knee bent so that I couldn't see his lower body. Not that I turned my head, but I had this feeling amounting to certainty that somehow Ambrose had read my mind, and his body had reacted to my mentally copping a feel— and he was somewhat disconcerted by it.

"I finished my book and sent it to my editor," I said cheerfully. "He won't like the electronic submission, but I don't think he'll complain since I am so near the deadline."

"And if he does?" I think this question was asked randomly.

"I don't really plan on reading my e-mail for a while, so it doesn't much matter."

"We may have to," he answered, finally straightening his right leg. "Read e-mail, that is."

"Yes?" I allowed my head to turn in his direction. Only my eyes peeped over the rim of the tub, and I felt fairly safe behind my cast-iron barricade since I could only see him from the chest up. His eyes were again calm, his expression carefully blank. I hoped that mine were as unreadable.

"I placed a couple of . . . personal ads before we left Fiji."

"Personal ads?" I said blankly, at first unable to place these in a context that made sense. I was certain that Ambrose wasn't planning a garage sale or asking for blind dates with single white females.

"Yes. I asked that I be contacted at a public message board where I have previously found . . . interesting conversations."

"Would these be ads about our little zombie problem?" I asked, the last of my arousal fading away as I was brought back to reality.

"They would. I feel it is time to test my theory that there are others like me out there and that they are using *The Weekly World News* and other tabloids to communicate with one another."

Others like me. Translation: *other zombie-killing superheroes.*

"Oh!" This information made me feel a bit cheerful, and countered some of my letdown. I really liked the idea of us not being alone in this mess.

"Do you want to use my computer now?" I asked. "Feel free. It's on the kitchen table."

"Yes, but I can't touch it right now. I'm somewhat . . . agitated. Even if I wear rubber gloves I'll short it out, so I'm afraid the job is yours."

"I forgot about that." I also hadn't been thinking about what could happen to me in an iron tub filled with water if I actually reached for Ambrose while he was agitated. "Well, just hand me that robe and—"

"There is no hurry," Ambrose said, getting to his

feet. I watched him move, thinking that ballet dancers should be so graceful. He kept his eyes turned away from me. Perhaps it was simply good manners, but I suspected that he was as unnerved by the appearance of my suddenly libidinous thoughts as I. It was likely that he had been thinking of me as something fragile that had to be protected, not as a potential lover. I wasn't sure how I felt about that. A foolish part of me was inclined to be insulted at his failure to perceive me as more sexually attractive than vulnerable. "Finish your bath and then we'll take a look at the message board."

"Okay," I said, but reached for the robe as soon as he was gone. Proof that we weren't alone would relax me even more than lingering in hot, scented water. It might even keep me from having further dangerous thoughts about what I'd like to do to Ambrose.

No: you were fully and clearly warned. For your bad deeds, vicarious atonement, mercy without justice. For your good deeds, justice without mercy.
—*Don Juan in Hell* by George Barnard Shaw

Kill, *v.t.* To create a vacancy without nominating a successor.

Non-Combatant, *n.* A dead Quaker.
—Ambrose Bierce, *The Devil's Dictionary*

I will knock down the Gates of the Netherworld, I will smash the doorposts, and leave the doors flat down, and will let the dead go up to eat the living! And the dead will outnumber the living!
—*Epic of Gilgamesh*

Chapter Twelve

It took a while to get logged in to the lutinempire message board, mostly because Ambrose couldn't remember his screen name at first. It was *M7864*—an impossible to remember cyber-name, at least for my nonalphanumeric brain, so we changed it right away to *Bitter1*. His password was *devil*. Not the most original or secure, I admit, but it was something we could both remember.

Ambrose leaned over my shoulder as I typed. I

could smell his skin and felt the heat that always radiated from his body. It should have been relaxing, but wasn't. My continued arousal was annoying, and I was certain that it had something to do with his scent. He had to be packing some major pheromones.

Once we were on the board I had to scroll through the various strange messages and topics until I found the thread Ambrose wanted. Many of the discussions I bypassed were intriguing in an anthropological kind of way—especially *I HAD BIG FOOT'S BABY!*—but the one Ambrose pointed to made me smile grimly: CHILDREN OF THE DARK MAN RECOVERY GROUP

I clicked. The message was short, but it didn't need to say more to attract the attention of those in the know.

Bitter1 says: Looking for lost kin to start recovery group in New England area. Member of Paris chapter would like to help. Must be fan of 19th-century adventure novels. Shall we meet for New Year's?

"You've had a bite. Several bites," I said, at first surprised and pleased. My delight didn't last long. I scrolled past some obviously disturbed posters who clearly knew nothing about the real Dark Man—and entirely too much about Satan—until Ambrose stopped me. I thought at first he was pointing at a post about wanting to have relations with the Devil, but quickly reconsidered when it got pornographic. I realized that he was pointing out the post below it.

M7872: So bring my scarlet slippers, then,
And fetch the powder-puff to me.
Meet where and when?

I read the reply twice and then looked up at him. I knew this quote. It was part of a verse from a poem I'd read in college, but I couldn't immediately place it.

"Will you post back?" I asked, feeling suddenly a bit cautious.

"Yes." He hesitated, though. I understood his reluctance. The Internet is wonderfully anonymous. We had no way to know for certain if we were talking to a friend or foe. If I were better at computers, it might be that I could track this person down through an IP address or something. But I'm not better at computers, so we were stuck with average skills and probably worse than average luck.

"What is something peculiar to Maine—something that would give a clue about where we are without coming out and saying anything directly?" Ambrose asked. "Is there a state flower?"

"Um." I thought hard, trying to recall anything I had read at the Visitors Bureau. "The state berry is the wild blueberry. Let's see . . . The state animal is the moose—I think. That makes me think of that TV show, though, the one in Alaska. What was it called? *Northern Exposure*?"

"Maybe that's what unfriendly eyes will think, too." He told me what to type. I thought it kind of obscure but did what he asked.

Bitter1 says: I'm a huge Dumas fan. Can't wait to discuss a story with you over pancakes and wild blueberry syrup. I'll bring my pet moose if the harbor isn't barred.

"Are you sure we shouldn't add something about . . ." I began, but stopped when we got an immediate response. Gooseflesh rose on my arms as I realized that someone had been waiting for us to log in and answer.

M7872: Good enough. I'll find you. We heard about Cannibal Island. Deepest sympathies. You and your friend sit tight and do not post again. Cyber walls have ears too. The game is afoot! Aid is nigh.

Our responder obviously had no problem remembering obscure screen names and passwords, since he was sticking with his anonymous, randomly assigned alphanumeric name. He was also apparently conversant with the novels of Arthur Conan Doyle. Did that up our chances of being in contact with one of the good guys since he was a fan of nineteenth-century popular fiction?

There was a pause and then one more message for us. This one was very direct and I thought perhaps in someone new's more elegant language. Perhaps it was the person who had quoted the earlier poem.

M7872: There has always been enmity between the Dark Man's son and his father's patients. Possibly because we have free will and sufficient presence of mind to refuse an alliance with this zombie master. Also, as a wizard who steals power from others by absorbing their life force, we make very tempting targets. Be very careful. At least one of us will be there soon. I repeat, do not post again. It is not only the dead who travel fast.

"Well, that is blunt enough."

"Indeed. Perhaps unwisely so. The mention of zombies seems like tempting the gods. Can we erase this conversation?"

As though the computer was hearing Ambrose's words, our entire exchange disappeared from the screen, including the original thread start. I scrolled through the topics twice, but it was gone. I wondered fleetingly if the woman who wanted to know how to get a date with the Devil would be annoyed that it was missing.

"Someone knows his computers," I said at last. "Or her computer. I shouldn't be sexist about this."

"Is what happened hard to do?" Ambrose asked. This reminded me that he was anathema to all things electronic.

"*I* wouldn't know how to do it. Maybe he—

she—was the moderator for this board. Or owns the Web site. That could explain things." I closed my laptop and rolled my head from side to side, trying to ease some of the tension in my neck. I would have liked to ease some tension in other places, but with Ambrose's acute hearing I really couldn't picture doing so while he was in the house.

"Joyous?" Ambrose's voice was almost diffident. He continued to stand behind my chair where I couldn't see his face. I could feel him, though. Heat poured off of him and lapped at my skin. I felt my nipples tighten and was grateful for the thick fabric between me and whoever might see.

"Yes?"

"I'm sorry about earlier. In the bathtub. I didn't mean to eavesdrop on you."

Eavesdrop. Translation: *accidentally tap into my bathtub fantasy.* I did some mental swearing as I realized that he actually *had* felt/seen what I was thinking.

"I've just gotten into the habit of listening to your heart and hearing how you are coping with things. Sometimes I hear other things as well. I shall be more careful in the future."

Blood burned in my cheeks. I had another brief flashback to my water fantasy, which I repressed immediately, even though thrusting it back was almost physically painful and made my lower body throb in protest. I considered sending him out for milk or a newspaper while I either collected myself or let myself loose entirely.

"I know you're concerned about me—and I'm

grateful. It saved me more than once and I can never thank you enough. You just . . . caught me off guard." I took a slow breath. I meant to tell him that I had no intention of letting anything happen between us, but what came out of my mouth was: "Ambrose, you must know that I am more than just a weak heart that you have to babysit. I'm an actual adult with . . . with adult feelings."

He backed up a step. I didn't think he was listening to my thoughts, but he could probably hear the frustration in my voice.

"I know. And I find you attractive too. Damnably so." His blunt words caused a small, pleasurable contraction in my pelvis. My stupid body still thought it might get lucky. "But I am also more than just a man. I'm human in my head and in my heart, more or less, but in all other respects . . . I'm not really a human anymore."

"Oh, come on. Don't forget the opposable thumbs. Scientists think that's a really important human trait," I pointed out after a long moment of silence. I didn't turn to look but I had the feeling that this made him smile.

"Okay, I have human thumbs. But that doesn't alter the fact that the form of lycanthropy I am infected with can be spread more easily than you would think. Since I don't always have the best of control when I'm . . . when in an intimate situation, I tend to be cautious. We can't risk calling the beast. The tiniest scratch or nick could be enough to cause infection. Believe me, you don't want this to happen."

This was less arousing. My body didn't want to hear about infections.

"Ah. It's good to be on guard then." And that was all I could manage on the subject.

I did not turn around to look at him. Instead, I stared out the window over the sink and urged my lower body not to squirm on the chair. My voice was calm when I spoke again. "Look. It's started snowing. More snow."

"Snow," he repeated. "I wish I felt better about this." He moved to my side again.

"Does this feel unnatural?" I asked.

He shrugged and then shook his head. "Not really. But snow will make travel more difficult for our new allies."

"And our enemies," I reminded him.

"Maybe."

I fought an urge to glance behind me. "I could be wrong, but I'm thinking that if our new friends are anything like you, snow won't be much of a problem."

"If my enemies are like me, they won't have any trouble either."

I scowled. "You know, Ambrose, we're going to have to work on your outlook on life. Let's try to be a bit more positive."

He sighed in frustration. "As soon as we are on the far side of this mess, I promise I'll do just that."

Mythology, *n.* The body of a primitive people's beliefs concerning its origin, early history, heroes, deities and so forth, as distinguished from the true accounts which it invents later.

Reliquary, *n.* A receptacle for such sacred objects as pieces of the true cross, short-ribs of saints, the ears of Balaam's ass, the lung of the cock that called Peter to repentance and so forth. Reliquaries are commonly of metal, and provided with a lock to prevent the contents from coming out and performing miracles at unseasonable times.
> —Ambrose Bierce, *The Devil's Dictionary*

My price is one hundred thirty million dollars. If, when you are ready to pay, I happen to be out of town, you may hand it over to my friend, the Treasurer of the United States.
> —Bierce's reply to Collis P. Huntington when confronted on the Capitol steps with a demand to know the price Bierce would accept to not go public with proof of the railroads' effort to get a bill through Congress without public hearings.

Chapter Thirteen

Ambrose and I slept in my parents' bed, each of us being ridiculously careful to stick to our own sides and avoid any unintentional touching. I don't know how Ambrose fared, but I was exhausted and, the moment my head hit the old feather pillows, I pretty much went out like the power during a blizzard.

I dreamed that night. I dreamed terrible things as I so often had as a child in times of stress, but this time the nightmarish visions were playing out on a sewn-together backdrop of strange new emotions, incorrect memories and wildest imaginings, where I saw frightening things both real and unreal. And I did so over and over again. I woke several times, but the nightmare pulled me back under every time.

The worst vision by far was my mother standing next to Saint Germain as the wizard pushed a pillow over my face. The only difference in each performance of the nightmare was that the mood grew progressively more ominous with every repetition, until it wasn't my mother standing over me anymore, it was my mother's corpse. Her zombie had come to kill me. Her breath was full of dry rot as she hissed my name, her tissues being too desiccated for her to speak as she used to.

I finally came awake with a scream on my lips and my heart slamming painfully as it tried to escape its terror.

Hush. This was a thought, not a voice, but I knew it came from Ambrose. His hand was resting on my chest right over my heart. Immediately my pulse began to calm and each throb of the damaged muscle became less painful.

"What's wrong?" I whispered, my voice raspy with strangled screams and my booted and spurred pulse still dancing a jagged tango at my temples.

"The power's gone out," Ambrose answered, his voice also hushed. In the dark, his skin began to glow. Heat poured off of him and I could feel static crawling over my skin. I know he was listening intently even as he pressed more firmly on my chest. I could almost imagine his fingers gripping my heart and forcing it to calm. At his command, my heart slowed to its regular beat.

I glanced at the clock on the bedside table but it was ominously dark. However, the room wasn't completely so. I looked quickly toward the door, startled by the flash of red light. Before I could gasp or do anything else hysterical, I recalled that there was a smoke detector tucked in a corner up near the ceiling. It blinked periodically to tell us that it was on battery power, the flashing too slow to signal immediate danger, in spite of the warning color.

Ambrose also turned toward the door to see what had caught my attention.

"That light?" he asked

"It's the smoke detector. It runs on batteries when the power is out," I said, guessing what Ambrose was about to ask. "I guess maybe the lines went down in the storm. It happens a lot."

Ambrose grunted and jerked his head at the window.

"How strange. Other houses across the street still seem to have . . ." I stopped speaking, inter-

208

rupted by a powerful boom, and then the entire west side of town went black. "That's really weird."

Weird. Translation: *That was damn spooky.*

"That's more than weird. Get dressed." He propelled me into a sitting position and then rolled from the bed.

"You think this isn't an accident? You think that someone deliberately . . ." My voice was barely louder than the sudden wind pawing at the window. Once I was sitting up I could hear that the storm had worsened while we slept. I slid out of bed and reached for my jeans. For half a moment I considered excusing myself and dressing in the bathroom, but decided that this wasn't the moment for modesty. Also, it would be colder in the bathroom. If Ambrose didn't want to see me naked, he could turn his back.

Ambrose went to the window and pried it open. He was a dark shadow against the gray of the frosted pane. The sash shrieked a protest and wind rushed inside, hurling snow with angry fists. The icy confetti latched onto the drapes and carpet and clung with frozen claws. However, none stuck to Ambrose. I actually heard the small flakes hiss as they hit his glowing skin.

I smelled ozone. The taste was thick on my tongue and I thought of the unnatural storms that had surrounded the island when Saint Germain had come. If Ambrose hadn't called this storm . . .

"But it can't be!" I said, buttoning my flannel shirt and reaching for my GET LEID IN HAWAII sweatshirt to put on top. It was impossible to put on too many layers with the sudden cold seeping into my trembling bones. "Damn it! How could he have found us so soon?"

"I don't know. Unless that message on the computer . . ."

"Even if that was Saint—was him—he can't have gotten here already. He was in Fiji. Inside a crocodile."

"His golem was in Fiji," Ambrose reminded me. "He could have been anywhere. This could even be another golem or a clone or something." Ambrose slammed the window shut and went to the armoire. My father had kept a shotgun on the top shelf along with a Colt revolver. I had never moved either, though it was probably unwise to leave firearms in a house left empty months at a time. That Ambrose knew they were there did not surprise me; he had spent a fair amount of time exploring the house while I did my best to avoid him with fussing in the kitchen.

I stuffed my feet into my boots and took the guns from Ambrose as he sat on the edge of the mattress and pulled on his snow boots. He had slept fully clothed so didn't need to do more than button his shirt.

"I'm going out to check the car," he said, taking the shotgun back. He checked that it was loaded. I couldn't see what he was doing but the sound was unmistakable. "I want you to stand in the doorway while I go outside, and shoot anything that moves. Anything except me," he added.

"The snow is too deep to move the car. It's a front-wheel-drive wuss car," I protested, but followed him out of the room. No way was I doing the stupid horror movie thing and getting separated from him, not if there was any chance that Saint Germain was around. I had no illusions about my chances of surviving a fight with some psychotic wizard.

"Maybe. But we need to know for sure. I'd like to know we can leave if we have to." He paused at the telephone table and picked up the handset. "It's dead," he said. Somehow I wasn't surprised. Naturally, neither of us had a cell phone for backup, and none of my neighbors had shown any signs of being at home earlier in the day, so popping over to use their phones was out too. We could break in, but only as a last resort. The summer homes had burglar alarms and the year-round residents had guns and an inclination to use them.

"I guess we have to assume that we're really in trouble here," I said as Ambrose moved on to the door. I was hoping that he would contradict me.

"Yes, I believe the expression is *up Shit Creek.*"

That was almost enough to make me laugh. The vulgar phrase sounded absurd on his lips.

"Yes—but how far up?" I asked. "I'm not sure I understand, or even have the right scales on which to measure our situation. I just don't understand how he could have found us so soon. Do you hear something?" I asked as he paused, head tilted to one side as he stood silhouetted in the window.

Ambrose glanced back. I was sure he could see me clearly even if I could only barely make out his outline.

"It's worse than Fiji. We have civilians here in town. And cold that can kill you if you go outside." He turned away.

We walked quickly, being careful to avoid the dining table where the laptop still sat, the useless portable computer that wouldn't contact the outside world without a working phone line.

So much for running away from our problems so we would have time to regroup. I promised myself that I would buy a cell phone the first chance I got.

"Maybe help will get here soon. That last message sounded pretty confident." I was talking about the message board.

"Yes. But not soon enough," Ambrose said. "I can smell him now. That stench in the air is unmistakable." These words made me shudder, and I felt the cold burrowing deeper into my organs. The furnace was on but the sudden drop in temperature inside the house was more than it could cope with. Maybe it was as frightened as I.

Ambrose turned toward the living room and I followed his gaze. There was still a faint glow of embers in the fireplace and, with a wave of his hand, Ambrose sparked the ashes to renewed life.

"Throw on a log," he said. "You may need the light, and we will probably want the fire."

We will probably want the fire. Translation: *We might need to burn some zombies.*

"F-f-fuck a duck," I stuttered, recalling what my roommate at school used to say whenever she got weekend detention—which was often. She never did learn how to lie convincingly and was always cutting classes.

It was Ambrose's turn to laugh.

Feeling almost frozen, both physically and mentally, I hurried to do as he asked, using my left hand to throw on a log and a handful of kindling. My right was gripped tight around the Colt. It felt almost natural there. And that was good because—"Oh double fuck a duck."

"What is it?" Ambrose asked. He wasn't laughing now.

"I just remembered. We are only a half block from an old cemetery." Where my parents were buried. My dream came back to me with complete clarity, and my shudders almost knocked me over. "Z-zombies c-couldn't get out of frozen g-ground, c-could they? They couldn't dig through s-six feet of ice?" I was feeling nauseous as well as cold.

"Probably not. Unless someone thawed the soil." Ambrose was suddenly beside me, laying a hand on my hunched shoulders. His warmth helped still my shaking body.

"Could that be done?" I asked.

"I don't know. Perhaps with repeated lightning strikes."

As if receiving its cue, eye-abrading light strobed against the windows and a whole series of thunder bursts rolled over the house, making the walls tremble. I could feel the power in my fillings, and my mouth flooded with a horrible metallic taste.

I began to shudder again. The Psalm 91 suddenly

popped into my head and I heard myself say:
" 'You shall not be afraid of the terror by night, nor
the arrow that flies by day, nor of the pestilence
that walks in darkness, nor the destructors that lay
waste at noonday. A thousand may fall at your
side, ten thousand at your right hand; but it shall
not come near you. . . . ' "

"Amen, amen, amen. Now come guard the door,"
Ambrose said. His voice was bracing but his hand
dropped away from me.

"Okay . . . Ambrose?" I came up behind him. Unable to stop myself, I snuggled into his back. I was
still trembling. That made me feel ashamed, but I
couldn't stop.

"What is it?" he asked. His voice was calm and
patient.

"I dreamed of my mom. That she was a zombie.
Saint Germain was with her and she killed me."
This last part I could barely whisper.

"Your parents are buried in that cemetery?" His
voice remained calm, but I knew he understood
my growing horror without me speaking it.

"Yes."

He turned and both arms came around me. We
were careful with the guns but he held me tight
and I felt him kiss my hair. Instantly I calmed, my
heart slowing to a normal pace. *It'll be okay,* I told
myself. *Ambrose will protect us. Somehow he'll
make this go away.*

"Your mother won't kill you," he promised. "I'm
here and I won't let anything hurt you ever again."
He didn't say that she wouldn't get out of her grave,

214

though. Ambrose didn't make promises he knew he couldn't keep. "Are you ready?"

Ready? To open the door and maybe see my mother as a killer zombie?

"Hell, no," I said. "But let's do it anyway."

"That's my girl," he said approvingly. Ambrose turned away. And then time seemed to almost stop.

I know now that there were two kinds of time. One is the stuff that makes up days and nights. You mark it with minutes and hours on a watch or a clock, or by weeks and months on a calendar. That's normal time where most of us live.

Then there is the other kind of time, the kind that goes at once too swiftly and also too slowly for the consulting of timepieces. It is the variety that rushes at you in moments of peril. Flight-or-fight moments. That's where we were that night. The body understands this, even if it has never encountered it before, and I was sure that, like me, Ambrose was recalibrating to this faster internal stopwatch, sending adrenaline to his muscles, speeding up his heart so he was prepared for the shift into battle time where normal hesitation could lead to death.

Another moment and he was ready. And since he dragged me along with him, I was too—at least as ready as I could be given my fragile body and lack of experience. It could have been worse, but a dark and dangerous part of my personality, dormant until I met Ambrose, awoke in the face of this new threat and prepared itself for whatever horror I would have to face. That included my mother, if she was out there.

I checked my revolver, making sure it was loaded. Ambrose cleared his throat and time started again, seconds snapping into battle rhythm.

He said, "I discovered long ago that I was willing to lose my life in combat, but not my nerve. Not my honor. That's why we will do this thing— and do it fully—no matter how terrified or sickened we may be."

Translation: *We would do this no matter how terrified and sickened I might be.* He was speaking to me, testing my soul. And he was right. This had to be done. Especially if my mother really was out there. Saint Germain could not be allowed to win. Everything I had told myself in Fiji remained true; he absolutely had to be stopped. At any price.

"Let's go." It cost me to say that, but I managed it and in a calm voice that almost matched Ambrose's.

Shotgun ready, he unlatched the door and stepped swiftly onto the covered porch. Not hesitating, except in my mind, I stepped right after him, the Colt pointing safely away from Ambrose but ready to be fired at anything that moved.

Gallows, *n.* A stage for the performance of miracle plays, in which the leading actor is translated to heaven. In this country the gallows is chiefly remarkable for the number of persons who escape it.

Nihilist, *n.* A Russian who denies the existence of anything but Tolstoy.
>   —Ambrose Bierce, *The Devil's Dictionary*

With what anguish of mind I remember my childhood, Recalled in the light of a knowledge since gained; The malarious farm, the wet, fungus grown wildwood, The chills then contracted that since have remained.
>   —Ambrose Bierce

Chapter Fourteen

I made myself step onto the icebox porch, and looked into the supernatural storm that frightened me almost as much as Saint Germain himself. It was like the gale on the island but so much fiercer and colder. The wind also carried a smell of rot and sulfur that had me gagging. Could it be that it was stronger because the real Saint Germain was near?

Go back! We'll die out here, whimpered the part of me that feared the storm.

217

We'll die if we stay inside and pretend nothing is wrong, answered the part of me that feared Saint Germain.

And anyway, I wasn't letting Ambrose face this on his own. Our chances of survival were better if we stayed together. I'd watched monster movies. I knew how these things worked.

Lightning hit the yard a few feet from our car. The porch shook as it rattled the ground, and an expanse of loosely woven icy crystals immediately peeled off the slate roof and slid down like the cold blade of an icy guillotine between Ambrose and me, just missing my outstretched hand that held the revolver. I flinched back from the crashing ice, stumbling on the doormat now sheeted with unnaturally large spikes of frozen water. I noticed that the stone steps were also covered in what looked like miniature stalagmites thrusting up from the ground. I told myself it was just hoarfrost, but I didn't believe it.

I stepped sideways so I could see Ambrose but refused to leave the comparative warmth of the doorway. The final rush of falling ice hit the granite steps and came apart with a soft shattering sound.

This was just snow falling off the roof, jarred loose by lightning. Nothing more. Ambrose, with his keen hearing, hadn't even flinched. Saint Germain wasn't up there waiting to pounce. I had nothing to fear.

And then the world got darker and I realized that what few lights had been on in the houses to the north of us were gone.

Hands trembling, I kept my gun raised and my eyes watching the trees and shrubbery while Ambrose circled the car. It seemed to be intact, but the snow had reached all the way to the doors. It would be even deeper out in the street.

Saying nothing, Ambrose turned from our rental and looked at me. He jerked his head toward the road and I understood that he was going to see if there were any tracks leading up to the house from the street.

I nodded, wanting badly to follow him, but knowing that the cold would probably do something bad to my heart—and what Ambrose didn't need was to be giving me first aid if we were about to be overrun with zombies.

Ambrose ghosted into the trees. I wouldn't have known where he had gone except for the vapor trail he left behind. In spite of the heat at my back, I shivered violently as I watched the ghostly tail slowly dissipate. Lightning was illuminating the horizon again and the wind cut like an ice dagger, tearing through my clothes and into my skin, trying to find my heart. It seemed Mother Nature was cooperating enthusiastically with Saint Germain and making a serious attempt to kill me.

The gun was so cold. I wondered if it was possible for the Colt to freeze to my hand. That would be bad, but I refused to let go or step back inside the house. I couldn't see much in the dark and snow but I could still hear.

A plane passed high overhead, its tiny line of windows cheerily alight and silhouetting a small

219

crowd of heads. I had the foolish impulse to rush out into the open, waving my arms and screaming at them for help. But we would never be seen or heard by anyone in the plane. We would be lucky if the pilot noticed that Bar Harbor was dark and said something to the control tower in Bangor. And even if they did report something, it would likely be dawn before any rescue or utilities people were dispatched to investigate.

Looking away from the plane, I strained to hear any sound, but it was hard with my blood swishing in my ears and my heart thundering ever louder and increasingly more irregularly. I had to squint my eyes because the brutal cold was making them tear.

Then the bad thing happened. Ambrose discharged the shotgun. Ambrose wasn't careless, and he had proven he could handle zombies in twos and threes without using a gun. There was only one reason that he would resort to gunfire: something more dangerous.

Though driven by panic, I moved slowly into the yard, following in Ambrose's tracks. I had no choice. The storm had suddenly become aware of me and shifted to blow directly into my face, and the stone stairs were slick and dangerous with their icy daggers. These tiny hoarfrost knives of the assault were driven hard and almost parallel to the ground. The bitter airstream and stinging snow left me nearly blind as I sank to my knees and then crawled into the garden, trying to make myself small. Hoarfrost stabbed my hands, and I pulled the sleeves of my sweatshirt over my palms in an effort to protect my skin. It helped but I bled anyway, leaving dark patches in the snow, a track that anyone could follow.

I headed for the trees, trying to follow Ambrose's path, praying that he had broken a wide trail through the snow and that the foliage would offer some shelter from the gale. Crawling into the minimal protection of dark wood, I relied mainly upon the diminishing feeling in my ungloved hands to tell me if I was straying from the trail Ambrose had left.

The shotgun continued to sound. *Bang! Bang!* And then a pause while he reloaded. It was an older model and carried only two shots. I wondered how much ammo he had managed to stuff in his pockets.

I crawled faster, breath grinding in and out of my lungs like broken glass as my heart failed to carry the needed oxygen to my brain and muscles. The world began to dim, but I managed to find my way to the road and the dark shape that was Ambrose. Head tucked down, I made the final push, clambered up the side of the ditch, and as though stepping through a waterfall, I finally found a safe place at the back of Ambrose's legs. I took a moment to gasp a few breaths of ice air.

It was easy then to see what we faced. The storm, perhaps at Ambrose's bidding, had parted and was blowing around them and us, leaving an unobstructed view of the road and what blocked it. None of the shambling horrors coming our way were recently dead, but most were still partly fleshy and able to cause harm. The lightning that had freed them from their graves and surrounded them with an eerie silver light had failed to completely thaw them, and they staggered with stiff limbs like Frankenstein monsters. Their gray faces were frozen and bristling with spikes of hoarfrost and clotted earth. Their frozen vocal chords crackled and popped as they moaned. At the rear of the horde I thought I saw a figure in black, a hard shadow barely discernable from the night around us.

Unable to help myself, I scanned their faces, looking for the one. *Her.* My mother. And I was not surprised when I found it. But what was infinitely worse than my dream—and for some damn reason completely unexpected—was to see my father there too.

The mewling sound I made was startling enough to draw Ambrose's attention. Using his body for support, I dragged myself to my feet and pointed the Colt at my mother. I heard my father's voice: *Two hands, girl! Aim carefully and squeeze the trigger slowly. Realign after every shot. Don't just keep pulling the trigger. You don't want to blow your own head off.*

She was wearing her wedding gown I had chosen for her at the undertaker's suggestion, and what was left of her hair was in that long braid she had always favored. The rest was . . . horrible. She had no lips, no nose or eyes. Her flesh about the gown was also burnt, and her neck was broken. The damage was probably from the plane crash and I understood why we hadn't been able to

222

have an open-casket funeral. To me, she looked more dead than the others. And more evil. Maybe that made it easy for me to pull the trigger. I put bullet after bullet into her. Only at the second did I remember that I also had to shoot the heart as well as the head and lowered the revolver a fraction to shoot again.

The recoil must have hurt, but I was too frozen to feel. I did notice my father's corpse turning toward my mother and then swinging back to look at me. I say look, but he was missing his eyes. Nevertheless, I believed then and now that he knew it was me who shot her.

Life can be—in fact, almost always is—hard. In some ways I had a leg up on most people who had parents who protected them from this knowledge until they were grown and forced to finally care for themselves. I'd had to face the difficult and even the impossible from a very young age. But this was beyond what even my mind could withstand, and I knew I couldn't pull the trigger again, even if it meant that my father killed me.

"Shoot him, Ambrose," I said, my voice cracking. "Shoot him right now!"

Ambrose must have seen what had happened and guessed who these people were, because though other zombies were closer, the next shotgun blasts took off most of my father's head and drilled through his heart. While he did that, I took aim at the next closest zombies and pulled the trigger of the Colt until it was spent. I felt no guilt at all. Actually, I felt nothing.

"I'm out of shells," he said. "You?"

"I'm empty." And I was empty in so many ways. The Colt and I were both done. I found myself taking a head count as Ambrose pulled me backward. Twenty-eight zombies left. Thirteen on the ground.

"Too many to fight unarmed. . . . Is there any more ammo at the house?" Ambrose's voice was calm.

"I don't know. Maybe in the garage."

"Go back and look. Take this knife." We were both so composed as he pressed the weapon into my free hand. Ambrose was calm because he is always self-possessed and me because my world was going black. This time I didn't fight it. If I died I wouldn't have to see what we had done, wouldn't have to drag my mother's corpse into some bonfire and burn it while it twitched and moaned. And I wouldn't know if Ambrose failed and we were eaten by zombies.

"Sorry." My legs folded and I sat down in the snow. I think it is to my credit that I didn't drop my gun or knife. "No can do."

Ambrose touched my head in a fleeting caress. "All right. Then we do it the hard way." He dropped the shotgun and took a step away from me. "Don't look. And for God's sake don't touch me."

But, of course, I did look. My vision was fading, so that might account for why I didn't understand what I was seeing at first. Outnumbered, out of bullets and—in my case—literally out of breath, Ambrose did what he had to do to save us. He *shifted.* I heard a noise as every joint in his body popped and I was sprayed with a hot mist of something that might have been blood.

In seconds he had bounded away, leaving behind some torn clothing and what looked like an animal-shaped shadow on the ground. I fell sideways into the crackling snow and watched as a wolf—a grizzly-bear-sized wolf—laid into the zombies. Claws slashed, heads and entrails flew. It was unparalleled savagery, and yet the zombies kept coming. Not all of them headed for Ambrose either.

While I might have been ready to freeze to death, I found that when push came to shove, I was utterly unwilling to be eaten by former friends and neighbors. Forcing air into my lungs, I tried crawling for the ditch at the side of the road, thinking that maybe I could hide.

Stupidly, I paused at the gully's edge to look back at Ambrose. A zombie had nearly reached me. I recognized him. He was our former sheriff, Douglas Fields. They'd buried him in his uniform and he still had a star pinned to his rotting shirt. I did a second stupid thing, I wasted time and breath emitting a small high scream as Douglas grabbed my leg, and then I toppled all the way onto my back in the ditch, pulling Douglas with me.

My clothes were thick but his teeth and jaws were still intact and I could feel the bite on my shoulder. I screamed again and tried to roll into a ball so he couldn't get my throat. My attempts to stab him were feeble.

This time, aid arrived. Ambrose was suddenly there, another zombie riding on his back, but his claws were slashing and Sheriff Fields was immediately missing his head. Unfortunately, though I was distracted by the former lawman's still-thrashing body spasming on top of mine, I could feel Ambrose's talons doing what the zombie's teeth had not. His claws laid open my arm and back, cutting through the cloth like butter. Blood poured over me in a warm blanket.

I saw the shadow again, the thing that moved like a ghost but that had some substance. It seemed to be stalking Ambrose. Not sure why, but relying on instinct, I reached out with the knife and jabbed it through what would be the thing's feet. It whipped about like a snake for a moment or two and then disappeared completely, leaving me to wonder if I had suffered a hallucination.

I saw no more of the fight after that and am not certain how long it went on. Thank God for the cold and the stilling of the wind, because the smell would have been disabling otherwise. As it was, I turned my face into the painful snow and tried to make a small safe place for my nose. I could feel blood trickling down my side but was too weak to try to staunch it.

A horrible snarl sounded nearby, and Douglas's twitching body was dragged off of me. There was more snarling and tearing.

"Ambrose?" I called weakly. "Are you okay?"

The snarling stopped.

A moment later, an animal growled in my ear, something that sounded like my name. I turned my head and looked at Ambrose. His muzzle was bloody and full of fangs, his jaws were covered in gore and his body trembled.

"Are they all dead?" I whispered, wondering if he would spring at me.

The giant gory head nodded and he shook more violently. I think the beast and the man were at war. Clots of black leaked off his fur and spattered the ground and me. I turned my face back into the snow. I was ready to die. If Ambrose killed me, so be it.

Then I felt those sharp teeth move onto the back of my neck. I tensed. A tongue licked once and then Ambrose took hold of my sweatshirt just below the collar. As ever, my heart seemed to calm in his presence.

Ambrose dragged me back to the house, moving far faster than I had while crawling toward the road. I wasn't going to die out in the snow after all. He mostly kept me off the ground, but the hummocks of snow-covered shrubbery now scraped my stomach in a few places and I got bruises going up the steps that were still covered in hoarfrost. I wasn't complaining, though. A bruise on the body was better than a bruise on the heart. Ambrose was alive and so was I, in spite of impossible odds. The bites and scratches didn't matter.

Fuck you, Saint Germain, I thought. *You've done your worst and you still didn't win.*

And in a way this was true. To some people, his other misdeeds might seem more awful, but for me, having my parents pulled from their graves and sent to kill me was the worst thing he could do. I knew down in my soul that nothing else he ever tried to use as a weapon would horrify me half so much. There was a kind of awful peace in that knowledge.

I shortly found myself resting in front of the fire. Ambrose rolled me onto my back and laid a clawed hand—it was more hand than paw now—onto my chest. There was a flash of heat and I felt the last of the lead weight on my heart ease off. My lungs filled gratefully, glad to have a working heart to pass the oxygen on to starved organs and muscles.

"Stay here," Ambrose's misshapen mouth said, and he turned me onto my side.

I wanted to tell him that his pointy ears were kind of cute, but I just nodded and then went to sleep.

About, about, in reel and rout
The death-fires danced at night
The water, like witch's oils
Burnt green, and blue, and white
> —*The Rime of the Ancient Mariner*
> by Samuel Taylor Coleridge

All the yardarms were tipped with a pallid fire; and touched at each tri-pointed lightning-rod-end with three tapering white flames, each of the three tall masts was silently burning in that sulphurous air, like three gigantic wax tapers before an altar.
> —*Moby Dick* by Herman Melville

Love, *n*. A temporary insanity curable by marriage or by removal of the patient from the influences under which he incurred the disorder.
> —Ambrose Bierce, *The Devil's Dictionary*

Chapter Fifteen

I woke up to the smell of hot chocolate and noticed a saucepan on the hearth. Beside it was a mug with fragrant steam rising from it.

"Ambrose?" I rolled over until I faced the sofa. My movement was somewhat impeded by an old afghan that had been wrapped around me, but I felt no pain. Perched about two feet away was Ambrose. He had showered and changed into clean jeans, but something about him was still not entirely normal. Perhaps it was the golden glow of his damp skin and the steam rising from his head as his hair dried. There were no marks on him, but I had this sense that he was in some kind of pain; if nothing else, that there was psychic bruising that hurt him terribly.

His eyes studied me for a long while, their expression grave and perhaps a little angry. When he spoke, it was in the voice and style of the Ambrose Bierce I had become fascinated with in college. The old-fashioned tone and choice of words lent gravity to what he said. "Under the scar tissue and yards of barbed wire I've wrapped myself in, a heart still beats. It wants and yearns as it ever did—and I believe now that it can love."

I stared, speechless. Of everything he might have said, this was the most unexpected.

"You will hate hearing this, but it is your frailty that in part attracts me to you. From the first, I wanted to care for you and keep you safe while I studied this enigma of new love. How could a body so softly made hold so strong a will? I guess I needed an answer because I have been so very lost for so very long. And that is why I didn't send you away from the island. Away from me. Even when I knew I should."

I still didn't know what to say—didn't know what he was saying and whether it might be better to stop him.

Ambrose went on, his tone almost meditative. "What gives you the strength to endure your losses and loneliness when my own much stronger body and personality could not find the resolve to carry on? That I feel an attraction for you at all is astonishing. I have lost so much that I have simply given up trying to care for anything or anyone who is physically vulnerable. And you are all too vulnerable." His slumberous, still slightly wolfish gaze sent heat through me. I wondered, if he stared long enough, would I be immolated, just burned to ash where I lay? "But all the while I was surviving on my own, playing at being a lone wolf, I was also slowly dying inside, hating and envious in my soul of what others so readily have. Even before my physical death, I could not speak to friends or family without some venom of envy in my words. And after . . ." He looked at the fire and then back at me. "That changed with your coming. Your arrival on my tiny island was almost enough to make me believe it was Divine guidance that brought you to me. Until today, my old rage was left sleeping between cycles. My beast came only at the call of the moon and went away again without argument when the sun rose on a new day. We had made a kind of peace, the monster and I, and I foolishly thought I could let you near the beast during a waning moon without endangering you."

"Ambrose . . ." I held out a hand to him but, though he smiled briefly at my gesture, he did not take it.

"I thought I was fully prepared for the fact that time would eventually bereave me of you, as it has everyone I have known. Death is the natural end to life. I accepted this and told myself I would be happy with whatever days or years we had. But I can see now that I lied to myself. This is too soon for an end, and it lays unbearably hard on the conscience that I have anything to do with your premature death. I hate myself for letting this happen. I don't think that I can forgive myself." He said this quietly, expressionlessly, but I knew that he meant it. I could hear both rage and loathing in his voice.

"Why? What happened? What are you talking about? I'm fine."

"You were injured. By me. While I was a wolf."

Translation: *I had been scratched by a werewolf, and had probably caught Ambrose's lycanthropy.*

Well, I had more or less understood this when I first felt blood running down my arm and back. I just didn't feel like thinking about it then. Nor did I now.

"Lighten up," I said, still too tired to actually consider the full implications of what had happened. "You had to intervene, and you were in wolf form. Anyway, I could have been infected with something serious like rabies if you hadn't interrupted the sheriff's dinner plans. I'd rather be a canine than a zombie dinner any day." Ambrose's expression didn't change, so I added: "It isn't like I would leave you because I'm angry about an accident, you know. In spite of my recent behavior with Max, I try very hard not to misdirect my anger."

"I never thought you would leave because of an accident. You are far too forgiving and compassionate." He paused a moment and I looked at him, not understanding why he still appeared so somber. "Still sure that you're an optimist?" he asked. "Well, you're correct in one way. There is something I can do to mitigate this mess. I have learned that supposedly irrevocable death can still be gotten around."

"What are you talking about? Does it involve silver bullets?" I asked warily.

"No." There was another long pause. "Just electrocution."

"What?" I was finally startled out of the semitrance his words and my exhaustion had put me in.

"It's your choice, of course," he said. "But if you don't let me do this for you, you will die at the next full moon."

"But why? I mean, why would I die?" I had that nasty Alice-down-a-bad-rabbit-hole feeling again. "Why wouldn't I be like you?"

"Your heart," he said simply. "Very few humans are strong enough to survive the change into a wolf, even without a damaged heart. Why do you think the world isn't crawling with *weres?* Most die during the first full moon. Their bodies simply can't withstand the trauma of the alteration. The cells rip themselves apart and do not knit back together fast enough. They bleed to death, their organs turned inside out. It isn't a fate I would wish on anyone."

A wet splash on my cheek distracted me from Ambrose's words, and I realized I was crying silently with a mix of frustration, rage and fear. I scrunched down in my blanket so he wouldn't see.

"Damn it! Ambrose, you are not allowed to say you love me and then tell me I'm going to die. It's fine drama in a novel but this sucks." I gulped down a sob and then added fiercely: "Take it back!"

"But that's my point. I'm not saying that you'll die. I mean, you will. But just for a while. And we don't have to decide now, but it would be best to act while there is a storm system nearby. I need a very particular kind of lightning for the ritual. Saint Elmo's fire, of course." His voice was calm, though I knew that he was seething inside. His eyes remained a dull yellow, though the normal blackness was slowly spreading out from the center.

"That's like ball lightning?" My brain tried to grab onto some aspect of this situation that wasn't horrible. "The candles of the Holy Ghost. Spirit ire. Will-o'-the-wisps."

Translation: *The creepy light that had been crawling over the zombies. I didn't much like the sound of that.* But it was marginally better than having my organs turn themselves inside out and dying from it.

"Yes, it's called all those things. This kind of electrical phenomenon produces a form of electrical plasma that glows a violet blue with threads of green and white. You can get it in certain storms or volcanic explosions. It carries about thirty thousand volts per centimeter. It sounds different than regular lightning. It . . . sings." He added cryptically: "Storms are safer than volcanoes. We have more control."

It was my turn for a long pause.

"Are you sure this won't kill me?"

He hesitated and then hedged: "It's *supposed* to kill you."

"I mean kill me permanently."

His eyes as they met mine were anguished. "No. I can't guarantee that it won't. I've never tried doing this to someone else, let alone someone with a damaged heart. I watched the Dark Man do it many times, though, and know exactly what he did. I have also successfully reanimated myself when I've felt my body slowing." He added softly: "It's less violent than turning wolfen. It can work."

"If my heart is strong enough."

"If your *will* is strong enough," he corrected. "This is as much about spirit and mind as it is about body. Unlike the lycanthropy, which leaves you no choice, you have to want to come back for this to work."

So it was all on my head. Great.

"Will I be a zombie?"

"No!" His denial was swift.

"That's good."

"You might say that I am the lesser of two evils in this situation." He smiled again, but there was no humor in it.

"You aren't evil," I objected. "Crazy maybe, when you're a wolf, but not evil."

"Maybe." He nodded in acceptance.

I looked at the claw mark on my arm. It was already healing, knitting together without a trace of fleshy tearing. The virus was apparently alive and well and doing its work. I couldn't pretend that perhaps I hadn't been infected. Ambrose was telling the truth. I was going to turn into an animal at the next full moon. The only question was whether or not to let the next moon kill me. At the moment, though I was far from emotionally grounded, that seemed like a bad idea. Life—even an extremely altered one—was the better choice.

"Okay," I said. "Let's do it."

He showed misgiving for the plan once I had agreed. "We can wait until you've rested and had a chance to think—"

"No. I might come to my senses. Better we do this now. We probably have other trouble coming our way. That wasn't the only cemetery in town, and I need to be able to defend myself. The cold would have gotten me if the zombie hadn't. I'm too weak to fight them as I am. Maybe . . . maybe this will be for the best." I was trying to convince myself.

Ambrose nodded and glanced out at the window where the storm clouds roiled with green light. I was certain this time that he was calling them.

"I'll need a few things. I have my medallion, but some heavy chain would be good. We need it for a conductor. . . ."

"There's some out in the shed." A new thought occurred to me. "Ambrose, if my heart is healed . . . in this form, will it be possible for me to have a child?" I don't know where the question came from.

"I don't know," he admitted. He looked thoughtful now instead of sad. The change was a relief. "The Dark Man's get was always sterile, but lycanthropy seems to heal anything. Changing at the full moon might do something odd to the fetus, though. I don't know if a baby would be strong enough to survive if the mother changed around it. I don't know if it would change too."

"But it might work if both parents are lycanthropes and not human," I persisted. "There is still a chance."

"It might work. We could certainly try." He took a deep breath and then gave a half smile, which was genuine and made him appear a lot more human. "What the hell. Life should be a daring adventure or nothing, right?"

"Right." It was stupid, but I found myself feeling more optimistic. This was giving me a strong reason to fight if the endgame got tricky and I lost my nerve. I struggled upright, pushing away the afghan and reaching for the hot chocolate.

"You have your heart medicine?" he asked.

"Yes." I patted my pocket. "Will I need it?"

"I don't know. I have an adrenaline cocktail that should do the trick. That's just for backup."

"Any sign of the police?" I asked, sipping at my cocoa straight from the pan. It should have burned my mouth but I didn't feel it. "I would have thought we made enough noise to rouse greater Maine."

"No. I don't think anyone heard anything. The storm must have drowned out the gunshots. Or maybe they were forced to sleep."

"Could he do that?"

"I don't know what he can do. There have even been wild stories about him overseeing his zombies by astral projection."

I thought about the shadow, now less sure that it had been a hallucination.

"He might have done that tonight," I said.

"Possibly. He was definitely controlling things."

"We'll have to burn the bodies?" It was half statement and half question. I was thinking that my parents were out there and their disposal was something else I didn't want to consider. It was easy to push that thought away because I used both hands and feet.

"Eventually." Ambrose still crouched just out of reach. His expression was almost guilty.

"Is something wrong?" I asked. "I mean, something else? Is it about the scratch? Am I scarred in some way?" He shook his head, now looking bemused. I knew I sounded exasperated, but there was only so much that I could take in at one time. "What then? Does the lycanthropy mean that I will somehow belong to you? I mean, you said that Saint Germain wanted the virus to make his ghouls obedient. What does that mean exactly? Will I be your slave?" I asked this last part hesitantly, because I didn't want any more bad news that might dissuade me from this course.

"I've never made a wolf before. Or taken anyone into the fire. But I know from my own experience that creation does not mean ownership. Adam begat Cain, but he didn't own or control him. The Dark Man never controlled me."

Translation: *I had free will*. It was a small mercy, but I took mercy any way I found it.

"But I am going to look out for you, Joyous. For

a while I will be your constant shadow. No one should have to face this alone. I wouldn't want you to . . . be like I was. So, you're stuck with me whether you want to be or not."

"I want," I said briefly, because I had decided that the less I heard about the transformation, the better it would be. Suffice it unto the day the evil therein and all that. We still had to deal with a bunch of zombie bodies—*don't think about your parents!*—and with Ambrose's declaration of reluctant love.

It probably hadn't escaped his notice that I had said nothing back about my own emotions. I wanted to, but I wasn't at all sure just what I was feeling, and Ambrose had sounded more angry than pleased that he had feelings for me. This wasn't a typical Hallmark moment.

"Okay. Let's just do it." I got to my feet. I felt remarkably sturdy considering what I had been through.

"Come to think of it, there is one really good thing about being a lycanthrope." Ambrose also rose. His movements were strong and fluid. If he had been hurt in the fight I could see no physical signs. His skin was as perfect as ever.

"Yes?" I wanted to hear something uplifting, like I would always have a flawless complexion, smooth thighs and gain fifty points of IQ.

"Wolves come into season only once a year."

I blinked.

"You mean that I'll only have one menstrual cycle a year?"

"Exactly. Think of it as Nature's apology for the other thing you'll have to do once a month."

Having my organs turn inside out and hair sprout all over my body seemed a lot worse than PMS, but I said: "Well, then. I guess every cloud really does have a silver lining."

"And if I hang around you long enough I might even learn to look for them," he muttered.

"Is there any other upside to being a werewolf? Shiny hair? Strong teeth? Flawless skin?"

"Well, I can finally catch a Frisbee with my teeth."

It was a small attempt at lightness when I knew there was no mood for it, but the pessimist deserved a reward for trying, so I gave him a small smile. "As the old saying goes, what can't be cured must be endured. Let's get that chain. We still have a monster to kill." And I wasn't talking about zombies. Even with all the personal trauma, I hadn't lost sight of the fact that Saint Germain was still free and able to go on causing trouble.

Me, *pro.* The objectionable case of I. The personal pronoun in English has three cases, the dominative, the objectionable and the oppressive. Each is all three.

—Ambrose Bierce, *The Devil's Dictionary*

I had thought there could be only two worse writers than Stephen Crane, namely, two Stephen Cranes.

—Ambrose Bierce on Stephen Crane's *Red Badge of Courage*

Chapter Sixteen

We were waiting up in the loft. The window that had once been a door for winching up bales of hay was wide open to the night. Ambrose had fed the lengths of chain we found in the garage through the old block and tackle above the door lintel. The air was cold but still, and with Ambrose beside me pouring out heat, I didn't feel much beyond a slight chill.

"I used to have trouble believing in the intangibles." His expressive voice had flatlined and that made me pay special attention to his words. He turned away from the scaffold that now looked entirely too much like a gallows. I hoped that whatever he had planned wouldn't involve me hanging from the damned thing.

"Like love?" I asked, trying to distract myself from what was coming. I had been thinking positively that I wasn't going to let a little thing like lycanthropy ruin this relationship—and end my life—but I was still feeling very nervous about the temporary suicide thing.

He shrugged. "Not so much anymore. I have learned that love, or at least infatuation, has observable side effects."

"Those can be faked," I pointed out, trying to sidetrack him from whatever subject was making him so grim. Feeling nervy, I began pacing. But not too far because I got cold if I got too distant from Ambrose.

"No. Not with me. I can hear a speeding pulse, feel the change in temperature of your skin when you think of me in a certain way. That would be hard to feign." I felt a pang of what I assured myself was simple hormonal lust and not anxiety about what we were about to do. I noticed he didn't mention reading my mind.

"Yogis do it," I said, still playing devil's advocate.

"Yogis slow their hearts and breathing. You . . ." The dark eyes began to gleam, and I don't mean that in some metaphorical way.

What? I stopped pacing and really looked at Ambrose. He seemed exceptionally purposeful. Lustful. And he'd been that way since his transformation into a wolf. He had walked away from me when I was in the bathtub, but I wasn't so sure he would this time. After all, the worst had already happened and I was infected. I wondered if perhaps he was annoyed that I hadn't said anything about my own feelings when he declared himself. Or maybe he was just looking for the warrior's reward.

"I what?" I demanded.

He wanted me. I had thought I wanted him, but was that just situational pique because at the time I thought I couldn't have him? Surely I was not that shallow. I tried to drag my mind away from what was about to happen and really consider this question. Did I want him? Why did I want him?

I'd been talking about trying for a baby, but were we ready for the whole relationship thing that went with that? We had only known each other for a few days. And pick a moment out of any novel or movie, and I promise you that the love scene wouldn't happen right before the goody-two-shoes heroine was electrocuted by the hero. I was a physical and emotional mess. He was still partly werewolf. Now that I was really looking I saw it. Slightly long ears and fingers, rough voice, weird eyes.

My own eyes dropped down to the front of his jeans, and I recalled his body from earlier. Not to be crude, but he seemed more proportional to his wolfish form, which was about seven feet tall— long—than he did as a man. Nature had been more than generous. Too generous?

What should I do? I was used to being Miss Modesty—a vanilla, bring-me-flowers-and-candy, no-kissing-on-the-first-date girl. Nothing had prepared me for this moment.

"Maybe you should do what you want and not

what's expected," he said softly as I turned to look outside; not that I was actually seeing the approaching storm. "As you already know, time can be very short."

Maybe I should just let go. I thought about it—probably because it was better than the other things I could be thinking about. Like shooting my mother's walking corpse, or dying by electrocution as soon as Ambrose called up enough lightning to kill me.

What would hold me back from this step? Parental values? Ha! Even if I had managed to attract my parents' attention long enough for them to try to teach me anything, my past was now as irretrievable as Ambrose's was. Time had placed it beyond mortal—or even immortal—reach. I wasn't the same person anymore. Miss Modesty's beliefs and mistakes had nothing to do with me as I was that day. I had to make a decision given my present circumstances, which were rather dire.

Perhaps it was all rationalization, but when the past is beyond fixing or even recalling, it makes looking forward a lot easier. Screw the right moment or being some kind of a good girl. It was time to toss over some of that heavy emotional baggage I'd been hauling around. So, what did I want?

The answer was obvious, now that I admitted it. Ambrose. I wanted Ambrose.

I turned back and smiled at him. The expression must have had a fair share of come-hither in it, because before I could do more than blink, he was there in front of me.

In spite of his earlier words, the look in his eyes had nothing to do with love—not the romantic kind we dream about as adolescents. I didn't mind that, though. That kind of love would only get in the way of what I needed and wanted. If I was going to die—perhaps permanently—I wanted to go out on a high note.

We kissed. Desire attacked me but I didn't fight it off the way I normally would. It was a violent meeting that left blood on the lips and my heart hammering. The effect was stunning, or more accurately, shocking. His hands, alight with gold fire, that touched my unprotected skin burned as he pulled my tattered clothes away. I wanted to cry out but my voice was throttled by the current that passed from his lips to my mouth. He stole my breath. I kissed him harder and stole it back. His slightly shocked expression told me he hadn't expected that to happen.

It surprised me too. Maybe I was already more of an animal than I thought. Or maybe I was turning into one whose instinct to mate was stronger than fear.

Surprise didn't keep him away long. His skin was smooth wherever I touched, eerily perfect, as though he had waxed it. Until I felt the first ridge of scars, the weird erectile tissue that laced his chest as he grew aroused and started pulling the storm's power out of the air and drew it into himself. He blazed with the power of storm and lust.

I laid a hand against his groin and felt the pulse

there. The bulge was thick and long beneath his jeans.

"Ambrose," I whispered as the smell of ozone grew thicker in the air. "But is there time before . . . ?"

"We'll make time." His hand fisted in my hair and he made a small sound that was not quite a word. Not quite human. In the distance, I thought I heard thunder tolling. There might have been lightning as well but I couldn't see it beyond the radiance that surrounded him, a golden white light that danced over his skin. I knew the name for this light, this spirit light: Saint Elmo's fire. It made him look like a fallen angel.

He kissed me again, my back to the wall beside the window, and this time I tasted storm on his lips. I would have fallen but he held me up with his body and I could feel my heart synching with his.

I pulled my mouth away and moaned into the curve of his neck, burying my face in the radiance, knowing I should be afraid or shocked or embarrassed about what we were doing, and yet incapable of reaching the logical state where I could pull away or even think to say no, whatever the potential dangers might be.

I felt his skin roughen and wondered for an instant if he would shift again and let his beast free. He pulled back from me and I saw his eyes. They were no longer black but pure feral gold. His jaw also looked heavier and shadowed and his teeth were longer and sharper. Had I actually been kissing that? And enjoying it?

"Ambrose?" I whispered again, not exactly afraid but feeling more cautious as I looked at his teeth. I was attracted to this part of him, but I wasn't stupid. The beast was dangerous.

He stilled, breathing hard as he struggled with himself. After a moment his lashes lowered over his eyes. He held me against the wall, a hand still fisted tight in my hair, but he did nothing more.

I didn't want him to do nothing. The dampness between my legs said that I wanted him to do something and do it right away.

"It's all right," I said softly. "Do what you want. I know it won't hurt me. Not now." Not now that I was also part wolf.

He took me at my word. My remaining clothes were torn free. I closed my eyes, not wanting to see if his hands were again fearsome claws. As though guessing what I feared to see, he spun me around and lowered me to the floor, not sparing me his weight as he came down on top of me and pushed my legs apart.

Then he was in me. Blood hot. No, far hotter than any blood that my cold, wounded heart had ever pushed through my body. I could feel small shocks inside my loins and reevaluated my stand on kinky sex. I decided to enjoy the electrical molestation and worry about being embarrassed later. Sex, and whatever else we shared on that rough wooden floor, was a sweet narcotic moving through my veins, burning away the person I had been and leaving someone new in her place.

Afterward as I lay there, too exhausted to move,

Ambrose reached over and looped the cold chain around my wrists. He rolled me onto my back but I didn't open my eyes. I felt something cold and heavy over my heart and then a sharp stab as some kind of prongs were driven into my chest. The wound was shallow but painful. I parted my eyelids once and saw some kind of a medallion pressed into my flesh. Small trickles of blood ran down the valley between my breasts, but it slowed and then stopped even as I watched.

He put his hands under my butt and pulled me forward. His expression was rapt. He glowed so brightly that I could have read by the sheen. He had become a beacon and I said a quick prayer that his light would be bright enough for me to find. Because I wanted to come back—for my own reasons, of course. But also because I didn't want Ambrose to be alone again. How cruel it would be to have him love me and then take it all away.

"It's coming," he said. If he had any fears or doubts they didn't show. "Just close your eyes and concentrate on coming back to me." With that, he pushed back into my body and began moving again. Stunned, I could do nothing but look into his yellow eyes. Then, seeing the lightning rolling toward us, I did as he asked and lowered my eyelids. I didn't think there was much chance of my losing track of Ambrose while he was actually in my body.

The light grew brighter, picking out the pattern of the veins in my closed eyelids. I felt Ambrose changing under my hands. I felt him changing inside of me too. He seemed to be growing hotter and had to fight for every inch he had inside of me as my body tried to adapt to the alteration. My own skin tightened and I could feel the small hairs all over me erect themselves. Electricity was crawling over my skin, in my skin. I climaxed and was so caught up in the radiance that pushed through my eyelids and the feeling of fire inside my body that I didn't feel the lightning strike.

Then I heard myself scream, and my back arched off the floor. It sounded partly like pleasure but mostly like pain. The noise was also closer to a wolf's howl than any sound a human would make.

Thunder and lightning were loosed on the inside of my body and mind. And it seemed that all the light in the world—even the cold moon hiding in the icy clouds above us—screamed aloud and then stabbed through my skin. It entered every fiber of my physical being and perhaps my soul too, spreading pitiless fire. It was the blaze of a laser. But it didn't burn; rather it melted my heart, drawing away everything that wasn't essential to survival. It filled the head with merciless white noise, a clamor not understood by the ears themselves, but rather a vibration that distorted tissues, distressed the molecules of the body and drove them into violent rearrangement. I could feel myself being remade, reordered into something stronger, something that perhaps wasn't entirely human. I think that the newborn werewolf inside of me wanted out.

Then a flock of blackbirds, a murder of crows, swooped in and buffeted my brain, tearing at my thoughts with talons, confusing and distracting me until I could no longer tell what was happening to my body. I fought to keep my soul in place. There was no proof but I believed that the reaper was closing in quickly. I snarled a warning and this sound was purely animal.

But then it was over; the tearing claws were gone. Lightning danced over my eyelids and died out slowly, a last climax of eerie, incandescent light that was as soft as a kiss. My body spasmed once more and then the world went black. I was blind and breathless. Dead, I realized, but not gone from my body. Something had tethered my soul.

I thought I felt Ambrose pull the medallion away from my chest and then something long and cold stabbed me in the heart.

Pain returned along with breath! Terrible pain as the adrenaline hit me! But my heart did what he demanded and began to beat again almost immediately. I started to shudder with cold. The propellers of normal thought started back up in my head, their sharp blades revolving through my brain as it pulled me back to wakefulness, slicing up the lingering veil that cloaked my feelings. Lucidity returned. I regained control of my body.

"It's over. You're alive." I knew the voice was Ambrose's but suspected it belonged more to his wolf-self than the human man. I didn't care. His wolf would never frighten me again. It had fought for me, had saved me.

Trembling, he picked up my shuddering body and staggered down the stairs. A moment later I felt him laying me on the floor in front of the fire-place. I was sandwiched between the twin heats of the fire and Ambrose's body.

"Open your eyes," he said. "Joyous, look at me. I need to see your eyes. I need to know if it worked."

Feeling reluctant, I nevertheless complied. As I suspected, Ambrose was still partially in wolf form. His ears were slightly pointed, his eyes burning gold. He was also naked.

This should have been unnerving, but I've never seen any sight I loved more.

Then I looked lower and was nonplused. Damn, if he still didn't have an erection. Instead of inter-rupting the mood, the vicious lightning had acted like some kind of electrical Viagra.

I shook my head, amused. "You have a one-track mind," I muttered.

"At the moment, that seems to be true." He shook his head and sounded chagrined. As I watched, his features again began to draw inward and become human.

"Then I guess I'm a very lucky girl," I murmured. My voice was rough. It sounded passionate, but I suspect it was half the effects of the lightning con-stricting the muscles of my throat when I screamed and howled.

And then—Heaven only knows why—I started to giggle and blush. Maybe Miss Modesty was back in the driver's seat and she just wasn't ready to deal with an aroused he-wolf. Again.

Academe, *n.* An ancient school where morality and philosophy were taught.

Academy, *n.* (from academe). A modern school where football is taught.

—Ambrose Bierce, *The Devil's Dictionary*

Dear Lora,
I go away tomorrow for a long time, so this is only to say good-bye. I think there is nothing else worth saying; therefore you will naturally expect a long letter. What an intolerable world this would be if we said nothing but what is worth saying! And did nothing foolish—like going into Mexico and South America.

I'm hoping you will go to the mine soon. You must hunger and thirst for the mountains—Carlt likewise. So do I. Civilization be dinged!—It is the mountains and desert for me.

Good-bye. If you hear of me being stood up against a Mexican stone wall and shot to rags please know that I think that a pretty good way to depart this life. It beats old age, disease or falling down the cellar stairs. To be Gringo in Mexico—ah, that is euthanasia!

With love to Carlt, affectionately yours,
Ambrose

—Letter from Ambrose Bierce to his niece

Chapter Seventeen

"Ambrose?" I asked after a while. "When you said that the Dark Man had a ritual for changing his . . . patients? Well . . ." I trailed off and kept my face buried in his chest. I wasn't sure how to frame my next question. There didn't seem to a polite way to ask if the ritual always involved sex.

"Yes?"

I could feel the painful heat of an embarrassed blush burning through my cheeks, but my verbal filters were definitely not working at full efficiency because I went ahead and asked.

"You didn't mean that he had sex with the bodies while he electrocuted them, did you?" Translation: *You didn't have sex with him, did you?* While I was okay about what had happened with us in the minutes before I died, the image of Ambrose and the Dark Man together was . . . well, *eww*.

Ambrose started laughing. His chest shook hard enough to dislodge me. I was relieved to hear it.

"No. I just thought it might be more pleasant to have the lightning pass through me first so you wouldn't suffer from the kinds of burns that I had. They heal quickly, but they're disconcerting and painful that first time. And though I know you're stronger now and could take more damage . . ." He stopped. "I just wanted it to be as pleasant as possible and thought maybe a distraction would help both of us."

"It worked." *Mostly.* Seeing his sudden concern, I wasn't going to mention the pain like no other that had rounded out my climactic moment and spoiled some of the fun.

"Besides, I wanted you. Lust has been attacking me pretty much since we met." His voice was still amused as he confessed. Probably because my face was still hot.

I swatted him without looking up. "So, you were being selfish and doing what you wanted. That's typical. Men!"

"Partially selfish. If the beast had really done what it really wanted . . ." He stopped, no doubt deciding that it was wiser to keep his own counsel on this.

"You . . . wanted to . . . what? Kill me?" I asked in a small voice. I didn't look up. "Really? I thought earlier, out on the road. . . ."

"No. Eat you, maybe . . . and we would have done a great deal more, a great deal more violently than we did."

"What do you mean?" I was under the impression that he had done just about everything that was legal.

A hand slid down over my behind and gave it a pat. I gasped as several ideas occurred to me. Lack of oxygen forced my face up to the air and I found him smiling at me. His expression had never been so relaxed. I wondered if he was teasing me but decided not to ask.

"You perv!" I joked.

"I fear so. You bring out my worst impulses."

This idea was oddly flattering. Miss Modesty wasn't used to being the object of perverted fantasies.

"You're staring awfully hard at me now. I'm going to get a complex," I said, raising a hand to my wayward hair and wondering if it was doing a Bride of Frankenstein thing.

"You look rather different," he answered. "I think I like the changes."

"I do? How do I look different? Is it my hair?" I rolled to my feet and scurried for the bathroom and the mirror there. Ambrose followed, pulling on his jeans. He was probably expecting me to freak out, though I had told him time and again that *I do not get hysterical.*

I didn't get hysterical, but it was a near thing.

"Well." The gods had apparently listened to my request for flawless skin. They had given it to me in spades, along with an extreme shade of pale. My eyes were also black and missing pupils. Just like Ambrose's. Excepting that Ambrose's eyes were mysterious, dark and dangerous, and I looked about as scary and enigmatic as a gerbil. My hair had also curled itself into a golden nimbus that wouldn't flatten no matter how many times I shoved it down.

"I look like a God-damned fuzzy hamster," I said, a shade of dismay in my voice. "Look at this hair! Will it always be like this?"

This cracked Ambrose up, making him actually double over with laughter. It was then that I realized that my lover was still more than a bit high from the storm. For that matter, I was too, though my buzz was quickly fading. I waited patiently for his hilarity to cease.

"You don't look like a hamster," he finally managed to say. "Nor any kind of a rodent." As compliments went, it left a bit to be desired. Ambrose realized this and added simply: "You're beautiful. Now more than ever."

That was slightly better. I reached for the door and pulled on a robe. I wasn't actually cold. It was just force of habit. Miss Modesty didn't go prancing about in the nude.

"What do we do now?" I asked, dreading what he might say. In his present mood, suggestions could be anything from an indecent and unnatural sexual proposition to a discussion about how to handle the many corpses littering the roadway. I wasn't sure I was ready to hear either.

"Eat. Everything. I'm ravenous. Shifting always makes me hungry," he said. And I suddenly realized that I was absolutely starving too. My little bit of hot chocolate had been consumed a long time ago.

"We don't need to do something with the bodies first? I mean, what if the snow plow comes around first thing this morning?" This was a token gesture to my conscience, in case it wasn't in a deep coma and would chide me later.

"I've been thinking about the bodies," he said, herding me toward the kitchen.

"Yes?" I didn't ask when. Or how much.

"There is no way to disguise that the cemetery has been disturbed." Ambrose opened a cupboard and got down all the jars of olives. He popped open a lid, ate a handful, spilling brine on the floor and on his bare chest. "Take these," he instructed and then went to the refrigerator and grabbed the eggs.

"I don't suppose there is any way to hide it," I agreed as I fished out an olive. Nothing had ever tasted so good.

Ambrose picked up a frying pan and then started for the living room. It took me a moment to figure out that he was going to cook in the fireplace. It was then that I realized my vision was better than before. Much better. I hadn't even noticed that we were wandering around in the dark.

"Whoa. This is great. I can see everything," I muttered.

"So why don't we haul the bodies back there?" Ambrose went on. "I'll still burn them, just to be safe, but at least they'll be where they belong and no one will ask about what they were doing in the road."

"They'll be looking for vandals and not zombies," I said, fishing out another olive. It tasted *sooooo* good. I almost moaned.

"And probably not until spring if I arrange another snowfall. We'll be long gone by then." Ambrose was being deliberately callous and I appreciated it. If he acted sensitively I might feel that I had to cry or something, and that would be dumb, because my parents turning into zombies and trying to eat me was a situation way beyond tears. "If we are very lucky, they might blame it all on the freak lightning storm. If I were the local sheriff, that's what I'd do. To say anything else would be to invite in the tabloids, and the locals would hate that."

Just then a knock fell on the back door. Ambrose and I froze and looked at one another.

"I didn't hear anyone coming," Ambrose said.

"Zombies don't knock," I replied. "Could it be . . . ?"

Putting down the olives and the frying pan on the hearth, we walked back toward the kitchen. Standing in plain view of the narrow side window that framed the door were a tall man and a petite woman. Actually, they were more than a man and woman. The man radiated some kind of otherworldly power that I could feel even from across the room, and the woman was the most beautiful creature I had ever seen, with hair the red-gold that autumn leaves blaze right before their death. Both had the familiar jet-black eyes that had looked back at me from the bathroom mirror only moments ago, though neither looked remotely like a gerbil.

"Well, I'll be damned. I recognize her," Ambrose said softly, and opened the door. His tone was one of shocked wonder. "Ninon de Lenclos. Welcome—welcome. This is more than a surprise."

It took a moment for Ambrose's words to sink in, but when they did, I felt my brows rise. Ninon de Lenclos? The seventeenth-century French feminist?

"Hello, Ambrose Bierce. I assure you that the pleasure is all mine," Ninon said. Her voice was vaguely accented, soft, the stuff of which wet dreams are made. At another time I might have been jealous of the way Ambrose stared at her; as it was, I was too stunned. "I'm sorry we're late. The storm was violent and we didn't dare interfere from the plane since these new machines are so full of sensitive avionics," she apologized. "It seems we missed the party thanks to this delay. You are both well? No injuries?"

"Not really," I heard myself say. "But we're having a zombie roast later if you'd like to stay. I wouldn't mind giving it a miss myself. Two of the soon-to-be-grilled are my parents. I'm still rather angry about that."

Both the man and the woman looked my way. They did not appear upset at my words, just curious. Ambrose's hand settled on my waist. I welcomed it, though of course I wasn't that upset. I don't get that upset. It was just the electrocution. It had affected me like a dose of Pentothal.

"It's shock," Ambrose said. "Literally. She's just risen, and we are both still a bit punch-drunk. The lingering storm isn't helping, either. My IQ took a nosedive when the storm came in and hasn't recovered yet."

"And I've been turned into a werewolf, but please don't worry. We're glad to see you. Hi, I'm Joyous Jones," I said, belatedly stepping forward and offering my hand. The woman took it first and then the man. I could feel a kind of power in them. They were like Ambrose and I, but somehow slightly different.

"And I'm Miguel Stewart. I'm . . . a vampire." His touch was gentle, as though he expected me to be frightened at this announcement. I wasn't, but that was because Ambrose was at my back and I had come to have utter faith that he would protect me. Also, I realized that I really was feeling a bit intoxicated and incapable of prolonged fear. Maybe Ambrose was right about the storm making us high. "I believe we spoke in the chat room last night."

"Ah," Ambrose said. His hand stroked me. I appreciated the warmth of his touch. For some reason I was starting to feel cold inside and the beginnings of a hangover headache were forming behind my eyes. "I thought that perhaps it was Alexandre who would come. I was sure he was . . . one of the Dark Man's get."

260

"He is, but we were closer," Ninon said. "Dumas is still in the Philippines, but we were visiting New Orleans and able to get a late flight out. Alex is also death on computers. Much worse than the rest of us. Miguel is only newly changed, and the best suited among us for using modern electronics, so he contacted you on Alexandre's behalf."

"I understand," Ambrose said. "I short out everything too. It gets worse every year. I fear that someday I won't be able to travel by plane."

They might have been discussing the inconvenience of seasonal allergies. I smiled politely and wondered distractedly what would happen the next time I tried to use the laptop. Or the phone. I thought that it was a good thing that I had sent in my book before I was changed. What if I had ended up erasing the damn thing?

Suddenly self-conscious about doing chitchat in my bare feet and bed-head, I tried smoothing down my hair. Just to further embarrass me, my stomach let out a loud rumble.

"Would you care to join us for breakfast?" I asked, tying my robe tighter. I felt more than disadvantaged standing about seminaked with wild hair while Ninon looked like she had stepped out of a safari shoot for *Vogue* magazine. "I'm afraid it's just olives and scrambled eggs. I haven't had time to grocery shop, what with the zombies and all."

"What kind of olives?" Miguel asked as he inhaled. "Mmm. . . . garlic and jalapeño. My favorite."

I found myself beaming at him. Yes, I had shot

my zombie mother, been infected with lycanthropy and electrocuted, but we had olives and new friends, even if one or both of these was a vampire. Maybe everything was going to be okay after all.

Satire, *n.* An obsolete kind of literary composition in which the vices and follies of the author's enemies were expounded with imperfect tenderness.
　　　　—Ambrose Bierce, *The Devil's Dictionary*

"As to me, I leave here tomorrow for an unknown destination."
　　　　—The last line of the last letter from
　　　　Ambrose Bierce, December 26, 1913

Chapter Eighteen

Ambrose scrambled the eggs in butter. I insisted. Have you ever cooked eggs in a cast-iron skillet without lubrication? Ever tried cleaning up afterward?

While he cooked, Ninon and Miguel told us what they knew of the Dark Man and Saint Germain. The good news was that the original Dark Man was dead and his son probably was as well. The bad news was that there were a number of Saint Germain clones running loose, and that one of the clones had gotten enough DNA from the Dark Man to begin cloning another of his parent. Ninon's group had been steadily sabotaging Saint Germain's "clinics" in the third world where he carried on his genetic experiments, but there was always a new one springing up. Though reluctant to embrace the idea, they had begun to wonder if there was some new supernatural agency at work.

When we were done eating, which was quickly, we shared our story and I got out my vacation photos. We were all careful with the computer, and only Miguel and I touched it. Ninon and Miguel seemed to especially enjoy the photos of Saint Germain in the crocodile's stomach. Miguel asked if I would mail him an attachment so he could use it for wallpaper on his laptop.

Perhaps it was that Miguel had the gift of putting me at ease, or maybe my recent transformation had disabled old conversational boundaries, but I found myself talking easily about what I had seen and experienced.

When we finished looking at the photos, Ambrose suggested that I do the dishes while he and the others took care of the bodies out in the road. A braver woman would have insisted on helping, but I simply couldn't face seeing my parents or the sheriff again. It wasn't just that I was suddenly thanatophobic. Truth to be told, I was worried that I would look at the corpses and feel nothing at all.

Then I would know for sure that I really had become a monster.

I got dressed. I didn't have a lot of options. Zombies had taken their toll on my limited wardrobe, so I was wearing my teen jeans and a cropped sweater that was a decade out of style.

The kitchen sink had a faucet but also an old-fashioned hand pump that worked fine when the power went out. I took my time drawing water, and when I had finished with the plates, I got out the hand-crank coffee grinder and ground up some beans. The old tin coffeepot was still in the cupboard, so I filled it with water and grounds and took it into the living room where I once again built up the fire. I thought that the others would probably want something hot to drink when they were done. Also, it kept me busy so I couldn't think.

This time I was listening hard and I heard them approaching the house. I was waiting by the back door with coffee boiling in the fireplace. We still had no power, but it didn't really matter because none of us felt the cold or had trouble seeing in the dim light.

". . . still has facilities in Somalia, North Korea and Iran." Ninon's voice was light but I could tell she was annoyed. "Reaching them has proved difficult."

"So you think he's after the lycanthropy virus now?" Miguel asked. He set a knife on the table by the door. I recognized it as the one I had driven into that sinister shadow. "Did you catch Pan's shadow?" he asked me softly.

"I caught someone's," I answered, telling the truth without thinking.

"I believe so. He tried for you too, didn't he?" Ambrose asked Miguel. "That was what I read about in Mexico."

"Yes—the bastard tried again after he found out that the female vampires can't reproduce and are basically brain-dead besides. Since only the males can create other vampires, he needed either my father or me, and Smoking Mirror wisely did a disappearing act."

Smoking Mirror. I knew that name. He was supposed to be some kind of Aztec death god. This made Miguel even more of an enigma. Probably I should have been afraid, but somehow I just couldn't manage it. We had werewolves and Frankenstein and a whole raft of zombies—what was an Aztecan god to that?

I could suddenly smell ozone on Ambrose and knew he had been starting fires. The door opened a second time, letting in a gust of air. No one was on the other side and I told myself that it was only the wind and a latch that hadn't closed properly. It was not a ghost that had followed him home.

"I find it interesting that he sent a golem instead of a clone. Perhaps we have pressed him harder than we thought and he hasn't had time to resume cloning. We need to take some time to compare notes and strategize." Miguel shut the door firmly. I liked his voice. It didn't make me shivery the way Ambrose's did, but I found it almost hypnotically relaxing. That was probably useful when he was lulling prey.

"I have another cabin in Alaska. I couldn't take Joyous there before because of the altitude," Ambrose was saying as he stopped to wipe his shoes on the mat by the stove. "It is deep in a valley and can only be reached by air. As the Realtor put it: It's inaccessible from without and not to be left from within. It's a ghastly and lonely place in winter but very private. And none of us has to worry about being affected by the cold—unlike the zombies." He kissed me absentmindedly as he brushed by. "We could meet up there and start working on a plan. I've got enough arms stashed there to hold off Armageddon."

"*Bien.* It would be best if you left here at once. Does anyone know that you're in town?" Ninon asked. *Anyone.* That was code for *anyone human.* I noticed that she didn't have snow on her boots, perhaps because they were stilettos.

"No, no one knows. Except Saint Germain, I guess. There's no sign that any of the next-door neighbors are in residence," I answered before Ambrose could. "Anybody want coffee?"

"Yes, please," Miguel answered, taking a turn at politely stomping his ice-covered boots on the mat so he wouldn't muddy the kitchen. He closed the door softly. "I know it's all in my head, but that snow looks damned cold."

I glanced out the window. The sun was up, but only barely, and the snow did indeed look very cold. It was strange to think that I would never have to worry about cold or my heart again.

"We need to turn in our rental car and get tickets." Ambrose started for the living room. "And I'll have to arrange for new IDs for Joyous and I."

"I can help with that," Miguel said, following down the hall. "Faking IDs has become a sort of hobby. Dumas's wife has been teaching me. Harmony is an ecoterrorist. Have you heard of The Spider?"

"I have indeed," Ambrose answered, clearly impressed.

"Do we have to fly?" I asked, coming into the room behind them and pushing by. They turned and looked at me as I bent to pick up the tin coffeepot. The bottom was scorched but the coffee smelled good. I hoped the boiled grounds hadn't made it too strong. I had never fixed it this way before, and was guessing about proportions.

"What did you have in mind?" Ambrose asked. There was no hint of condescension in his voice. No one was treating me like the new kid on the block, even though I was.

"We are going to leave this place, right? I'll probably have to sell it since we can never safely stay here again." I began pouring coffee into the tin cups. There were porcelain teacups in the cupboard, but that just wouldn't have felt right under the circumstances.

For a long moment no one answered.

"I'm sorry. I know this is your family home, but that would be wisest," Ninon said gently. I don't think she knew what to make of me, and I didn't feel like explaining that the family home didn't mean all that much because I had never been part of the family. Keeping it had just been my defense mechanism, a way of pretending to myself that I had some connection with my parents.

"I don't mind that, but there is something of my father's that I want to bring with me and we can't fly with it."

"What is it?" Ambrose asked. I knew he was

thinking about weaponry, and I was suddenly worried about disappointing him with my whimsy.

"It's out in the shed," I said. As one they put down their coffee cups and waited for me to show them.

"Can I see it?" Ambrose asked.

"Now?"

"If you don't mind. Haste is the order of the day. The sooner we leave Bar Harbor, the safer it will be for everyone else."

Everyone else. That was code for *humans.* I doubted zombies could do much to anyone in the living room. Not anymore.

Shrugging, I put down the pot and headed for the back door. I stopped at the telephone table and opened the tiny drawer in the desk and removed a set of keys.

We all crunched through the ice in silence. I opened the old padlock and pulled open the shed door. It took some effort because the snow had drifted against it during the night, but I was a lot stronger now and I didn't need any help from Ambrose.

"This is it," I said proudly, and everyone looked intently at the green shroud that covered the treasured contents. Realizing that they didn't recognize it just from the shape I added: "My father was a huge fan of the movie *Vanishing Point* and he kept this 1970 white supercharged Dodge Challenger here at the house. My mother didn't approve, but she let him have his toys." Just not his damaged daughter.

I pulled the tarp off the car and smiled at the gleaming paint. The hood was cracked open because of the cables running to an outside battery. The car had been left on a trickle charge while the caretaker was away for the holidays. "It gets lousy gas mileage, but the son of a bitch can go. It's like riding a rocket."

"Holy shit," Miguel said, and gave a soft laugh.

Ninon didn't react beyond a small smile that said she appreciated the need for pretty toys. But Ambrose ran an appreciative hand over the hood, stepping back as I pulled the top back and removed the cables from the battery.

"Beautiful," Ambrose said, though I had a feeling he preferred horses.

The car wasn't dusty. Part of the caretaker's job was to see to the maintenance of Dad's automobile, and he obviously had put a lot of care and attention into it. He was especially willing because I let him drive it in town when the weather was good. This kept the battery charged, and the gas didn't go bad in the tank.

"Let me start it. You have to hear the engine." Eagerly, I got in the car and jammed the key home. In spite of the cold, the car started right away and screamed like an angry beast.

"Wow." Miguel laughed again.

I smiled at him. "I know."

"Ninon has a Cobra," he volunteered, and we began talking cars.

Even in the cold, the shed was a bit odoriferous, and with the engine running it was like standing in the bell of a trumpet played by a halitosis sufferer who never changed the spit valve. I also knew from experience that where Ninon stood near the door, there was every chance the vibrations from the car's engine would eventually send the snow off the pitched tin roof right onto the top of her head. I reached out a reluctant hand and switched off the engine. Playtime was over.

"Okay," Ambrose said. "It's crazy, but we'll drive as far as we can and then we'll put her in storage. I'm not sure how far that will be. We are going to Alaska. In January. This isn't exactly an all-terrain vehicle."

"But you can control the weather," I pointed out.

"So can you now," he answered with a small smile. "But only to a limited degree and for a short period of time. We can call storms if they get within range and make small bubbles of calm around us, but we won't be diverting any blizzards or tornados."

"We'll manage." I nodded to myself. Feeling happier, I pulled the shed door back into place. I didn't bother locking it this time.

I knew there were some bad times ahead, and I doubted very much that I was going to like turning into a wolf whenever the moon was full, but I couldn't help but marvel that I was standing in freezing snow, manhandling heavy frozen doors without aid, and not worrying about my stupid heart giving out on me.

Ambrose waited for me while I fussed needlessly with the door.

"How soon can you be ready to leave?" he asked me, sensing my reluctance to actually depart. I wasn't sentimental, but I was sure this would be the last time I saw the place and touched the things my father had.

I forced myself to stop being maudlin and just say good-bye to the old life I hadn't liked anyway.

"We can leave as soon as I pack up some clothes and that Bacchus china piece in the dining room. I have some other arrangements to make if we are going to sell the house, but I can take care of them on the road." I reviewed my mental checklist. "The lawyer for the trust can manage most things for a while, but some of it I'll have to hire others to deal with."

"Like?" Ambrose asked. This was simple curiosity. I realized that he didn't know very much about the nuts and bolts of my daily life, nor I about his.

"My rent is paid through the trust but eventually I'll have to close up the apartment in Munich. And sooner is probably better than later. It isn't like I'll ever go back there to live," I added. "And I am taking a long break from writing biographies. I think I'm more of an action-adventure kind of girl now, and I am going to have to break this news to my editor. He isn't going to like that, and I'm thinking the Band-Aid approach is best." He cocked a brow. "You know, best to just rip it off quickly."

Ambrose grinned. "I suspect I will end up thanking God daily that you aren't a ditherer. Many other women would be whining and crying."

"You might want to add a prayer of thanks that

I like perverts while you're at it," I muttered, my eyes flicking downward and catching the slight tenting in his jeans. "Is that erection ever going to go away?"

"Yes. Eventually. It's a side effect of the shifting and calling up lightning. Up until now, I've considered it damned inconvenient, but I can think of occasions when it might be handy."

"At any other time I'd probably be happy about this."

"There's a first time for everything," he agreed. "And I'm looking forward to 'any other time.'"

"Really. You have more stamina than I. This has already been a long day and the sun is barely up."

Scribbler, *n.* A professional writer whose views are antagonistic to one's own.

Ink, *n.* A villainous compound of tanno-gallate of iron, gum arabic and water, chiefly used to facilitate the infection of idiocy and promote intellectual crime.

—Ambrose Bierce, *The Devil's Dictionary*

Chapter Nineteen

We closed up the house, setting everything back in order and wiping the place for fingerprints. It didn't matter if mine were there, but the others' prints, I was told—especially Miguel's—might set off some alarms if they were discovered by law enforcement. Do I sound paranoid? I didn't feel paranoid after Miguel and Ninon filled us in on how many low friends in high places were willing to help Saint Germain. And the mess in the graveyard might well attract attention from the wrong people, even if a coroner officially found that the bodies had been incinerated by lightning.

We'd burned some firewood, but the woodpile was large and I doubted that the house's caretaker would notice anything. Especially not after he saw that the car was gone. We considered letting him report it stolen, but decided that could complicate things down the road if we were ever stopped by the police. Instead, I left a short and breezy note saying that I had taken the car for a road trip to Savannah. No one was happy about leaving this note as proof that I had been in Maine, but it seemed the lesser of evils, given that Saint Germain already knew about me.

I had thought the violence in Fiji bad, though at that point it had been impersonal, but his using my parents against me had given me a whole new appreciation of just how awful things could be. He'd miscalculated there. I think maybe the experience had been supposed to break me, to scare me away from Ambrose. But it had had the opposite effect. My hatred of Saint Germain was now soul deep.

Ninon took their rental and Miguel drove ours back to the airport. They were going to fly to Quebec and then meet us in Alaska with—are you ready?—Lord Byron and Alexandre Dumas. Who knew both these men were alive and well?

Our road trip was largely uneventful. We avoided bad weather all the way to Washington and made excellent time since we were able to spell each other while taking turns sleeping. We didn't need to be in Alaska until the next full moon, but somehow settling in one place and staying for a while seemed wonderful.

We met Alexandre's wife, The Spider, in Seattle and she gave us new IDs. Again, as with the others of our kind, I found that I liked this woman a lot. Harmony was quiet and competent. She told us where to shop for colored contacts to disguise our

275

strange eyes. It was in a nice area where they had several boutiques, and I treated myself to some new clothes.

We had no trouble with our new passports crossing into Canada, so Miguel had obviously done his work well.

Not feeling the cold as I used to was a huge bonus, but the physical change did mean that both Ambrose and I had enormous appetites and needed to eat often. He told me I would never get fat and needn't worry about cholesterol, so I let myself go wild and had hot cinnamon rolls drowning in melted butter with a side of strawberry waffles with whipped cream every morning. Ambrose shuddered at my choices, but I think he got a kick out of watching me enjoy myself.

As I promised, I did buy a cell phone for us to use. Actually, two, since I burned out the first one when I got annoyed. They were throwaway types where you bought your minutes as needed. I used the second phone to call my attorney and to let him know that I wanted to sell the Maine house and that I was closing up the apartment in Germany. I told him that all correspondence should be sent to my publisher for the time being as I would be traveling, doing book research for several weeks and would be unavailable by mail or phone. Mr. Fiske wanted a better explanation for my sudden decision to sell the family home, but I put him off. I think perhaps the changes in me go deeper than either Ambrose or I expected, because the attorney backed off the moment I willed him to. Maybe it's that my voice is still a bit raspy and deeper than before.

We put the car in storage in Juneau and retrieved a small plane out of a private hangar at the airport to take us to the valley where Ambrose's cabin was located. You understand why I can't be precise about this, yes? Saint Germain hasn't found the cabin yet and it's nice to have a bolt-hole that no one knows about.

Okay, this is where the story gets even weirder.

We set down about two miles from the cabin on a narrow ice field that looked too short to be safe, but somehow Ambrose managed to put the plane down with room to spare. We had a great many supplies onboard and knew we would have to make a couple of trips to retrieve everything. We can see well in the dark and can survive intense cold, but I was feeling very small and vulnerable out in the white wilderness and not looking forward to making any trips after dark, so we hurried to unload.

Perhaps it was foolish, but I was so confident that the zombies couldn't follow us into this ice chest of a place that I wasn't really looking for anyone to be there when we landed. After all, the others weren't coming for a couple days yet. It was supposed to be just us and the polar bears. But as I pulled on a new green parka and fished out my gloves, I caught movement out of the corner of my eye near a giant black upthrust of stone.

I spun quickly, slipping on the ice and almost falling. "Look." I didn't point at the three males exiting the plane a hundred yards away from us. I recognized the airplane. It was a Feisler Storch, a remarkable bi-wing that is very rare. The antique plane was second place on the list of unusual things, though. The three creatures climbing out of her were far more extraordinary.

Since the change I had been seeing auras around people and animals. They came in many colors and I was beginning to be able to read them, kind of like a mood ring. But these three men had coronas like nothing I had ever seen. The power in them was enough to make my eyes ache.

Ambrose stopped beside me. His eyes narrowed and I saw him sniff at the freezing air. Belatedly, I did this too. I was still not used to having these advanced senses of hearing, sight, smell and taste at my disposal. The wind was eddying our way, and I was able to make out their personal smells. The two with silver coronas, one with red spikes, smelled of hot earth, rocks baking in the sun in the middle of a desert. The third man, with an iridescent green aura tinged with the colors of a stormy sunset, smelled oddly of chocolate. None of them were human.

They weren't like us, either.

Only seconds after I pointed, the three men became aware of us. They turned as one to stare in our direction. It was then that I noticed their eyes. If I had thought them human before I would have been disabused of the idea as soon as our gazes met. Their eyes glowed with a powerful phosphorescence that made me think of aliens—and I don't mean third-world refugees.

Without hesitation they crossed the snow field to join us. They made no sound and left no tracks on the ice. The hair on my arms began to rise but it wasn't with fear. I guess it was a kind of supernatural dread and awe of being in the presence of men so obviously nonhuman.

For a moment I thought about suggesting to Ambrose that we run. But where? I had the distinct feeling that anywhere we went they could follow.

"Hello," one of the silver-shrouded beings said, coming to a halt about ten feet away.

"What are you?" I asked without thinking.

The beautiful being smiled, looking almost angelic.

"I was about to ask you the same question. My name is Jack Frost and I am . . ." He paused, selecting his words carefully. "I am fae."

"Fae? Like, *faerie* fae?" I probably sounded stupid, but he didn't seem annoyed with the question.

"Yes. Faerie. Death fae to be precise."

"I thought your kind had perished," Ambrose said. He came up behind me and put a hand on my waist. I could feel the heat of his body through my parka and knew that he was planning to toss me aside if the men made any sort of an aggressive move. In theory, I could change into a wolf and protect myself, but we hadn't tried it yet.

"Most of us have. We are the most endangered of species." Jack smiled. "These are my friends, Thomas Marrowbone and Abrial Nightdemon."

"So you are Unseelie?" Ambrose asked. There

was no judgment in his voice, which was reassuring. I had only the haziest of notions about faerie species from my Celtic mythology class in college, but I seemed to recall the Unseelies were the bad ones. The name Nightdemon was also unpleasantly suggestive. I wondered, without realizing then how unusual the thought was, if he were an incubus.

"They were," the one called Thomas answered. "That distinction means nothing now, as the faerie courts are gone." This was said to me, and I realized that he was probably able to read my thoughts. I tried very hard to think politely.

"But what are *you*?" I asked, sniffing again. I might be superhuman but the sudden temperature shift still made my nose run. "Your aura is very beautiful," I added.

"My aura?"

"You look like an electric margarita at sunset."

Thomas laughed. I liked the sound, and I could feel Ambrose relax.

"I am part fae, part wizard and part dragon. The sunset would be the dragon part, I imagine."

"Oh. I didn't know there were any dragons left." It was all I could think to say. Dragons, faeries—it was all too weird. "You aren't from around here, are you?"

"Just one is left . . . that we know of. And that is plenty," Abrial Nightdemon said. His voice was deep and a little scary. I was suddenly certain that, of the three, this man was the most dangerous. "And what are you, if I may ask without causing offense? We haven't met anyone like you before."

"Well, I don't know if there's a name for us. I recently heard someone refer to Amb—us—as the Dark Man's get, but I am strictly second-generation and had nothing to do with that whacko." They waited politely for more explanation, so I went on: "We're battery-drainers, I guess. Storm-callers. In fact, if you have any cell phones or watches, you may want to stay back. I'm still having trouble controlling things, and I sometimes short electronics out. I already ruined a cell phone."

"But you are something else as well," Abrial said, and he also took in a deep breath and I knew he was tasting us. "Something with fur. Not selkie." It didn't sound like he thought this was necessarily a bad thing.

"We're lycanthropes. Shape-shifters," I said cheerfully. "Wolves, I guess. I haven't changed yet, though, so I don't know for sure. My name is . . . What *is* my new name?" I asked, turning my head to look up at Ambrose. "I keep forgetting."

He answered me. I could hear amusement in his voice. Then Ambrose introduced himself, using his real name.

"Sorry to sound so stupid," I said, turning back to the others who were showing signs of shock at Ambrose's announcement. That meant they were literate, at least by human standards. I found myself liking them. "I used to be Audrey. And Joyous. I just changed again. We're hiding out from a very bad wizard who raises zombies while we wait for our friends. We have to decide what to do about the prick."

I never—not in a million years—thought I would be saying things like this. But in some ways it was wonderful.

"Saint Germain?" Jack asked. His voice was serious.

"Yes. Do you know him?" I could feel Ambrose tense again, and he began to draw power out of the air. Unable to help myself, I began pulling in power too. Saint Germain's name has that affect on us.

"We know of him," Jack answered carefully. His eyes had shifted to Ambrose, and I knew he felt the gathering power and wanted to reassure us. "Our paths had never crossed until recently. But we have reason to believe that he may have discovered the body of a hobgoblin and may be trying to clone it. We were obliged to destroy one of his clinics in North Korea. He has also been using our . . . transportation system to travel places he shouldn't go."

A destroyed clinic in North Korea would make Miguel and Ninon very happy.

"Cloning hobgoblins would be very bad?" I guessed, relieved as Ambrose slowed in gathering energy. Calling storms gave me a headache, though I'd practiced every day with him, just in case I ever needed to do it on my own.

"Very bad," Thomas agreed. "We have come to investigate the . . . grave site where the hobgoblin's body was originally interred."

Ambrose looked around. "That might be difficult at full dark. It's nearly that now. Would you like to join us at my cabin for the night?" I could feel his power dissipating into the air as he spoke. This reminded me that at this time of year there was barely two hours of sun each day this far north. "It's about two miles up that ravine."

I looked where he pointed. Pre-change I would never have considered trying to hike such rough terrain. Now I was looking forward to it. I thought it might even be fun to be a wolf here. There were a lot more dangerous places to go furry, that's for sure.

"That would be very nice, since it is on the way to the site we must investigate," Jack said. "May we help you carry supplies?"

"Thank you," Ambrose answered.

I suddenly realized that the whole conversation had been exquisitely polite and almost Victorian in tone. I wondered how old these fae were. At least as old as Ambrose; of that I was sure.

"Are there more of you?" Jack asked as we all turned toward Ambrose's plane.

"Yes and no. There are no more lycanthropes, but the Dark Man had other . . . patients. There are at least six others who survived the purge. Perhaps more. Some of them will be joining us in a day or so." Ambrose paused as he got out a tarp. The plane would have to be covered both to keep off snow and also to hide it from other planes or helicopters. Maybe even from satellites. "And you?"

"Only a dozen or so," Jack answered. "But those of us who survived are . . . strong. I think we can make a go of it. We may also be able to help you with your travels. We have an extensive underground network."

I was almost certain that he meant this literally.

Ambrose nodded. "That's good. I have the feeling this world is going to need as many strong people as it can get."

"Sadly, I fear you are right."

Hobgoblin, *n.* A creature that inhabits small minds and also rural Alaska.

—Ambrose Bierce, *The New Devil's Dictionary*

Chapter Twenty

Though we had company, Ambrose and I curled up together when we slept. Perhaps the timing wasn't the best, but I felt the need to say some words that were long overdue, even if we had an audience.

"I know I am messed up and miles from knowing what is normal," I whispered into the curve of his neck. "But I just wanted you to know that I love you and I'm grateful for everything you've done for me."

Ambrose's arms tightened briefly around me, and he kissed the top of my head. "I'm no more an expert on what is normal than you, but I love you too. And I am every day grateful that God finally took pity on me and sent you my way."

"He—or she—works in mysterious ways," I agreed.

"Now go to sleep. Tomorrow we start building a new life."

"Okay. There was just one other thing . . ."

"Yes?"

"I'm pregnant."

I felt Ambrose stiffen.

"Are you sure?"

I glanced down at my stomach where a tiny aura glowed. The color was a match for Ambrose and I was sure it was a boy.

"Yes."

I looked up at Ambrose and saw a smile as bright as the sun. Then, just as quickly worry replaced it with a frown and drawn brows.

"Joyous—"

"Don't worry about the child." Thomas's soft voice spoke from across the room, confirming that he could hear our unspoken thoughts. "There is a place we can take you where the full moon will have no effect."

We looked at each other. We had no reason to believe this stranger, but we did. Ambrose and I settled in once more, his hand over my abdomen, and this time surrendered to sleep.

Author's Note

Hello again! Thank you for choosing to visit with Ambrose and Joyous—and Ninon and Miguel. And Jack and Thomas and Abrial. We've all missed you.

Don't gasp, but I don't have any books to recommend for research this time beyond pointing you at Bierce's own works. He can tell you more about himself than I can, and in a lot more pithy style. Poor, brilliant Ambrose. I don't think anyone would argue about his being a deeply troubled man, and it has given me great pleasure in being able to imagine for him a happier end. Peace upon him wherever he may be.

As always, it's great to hear from you. Please write when you have time or inclination. You can find me at either *melaniejaxn@hotmail.com* or PO Box 574, Sonora, CA 95370-0574.

Health, wealth and happiness to you all,

Melanie

USA Today Bestselling Author of *Dragonborn*

Jade Lee

Horrific are a dragon's claws, its fiery breath and buffeting wings. Potent is its body, fraught with magic down to the very last glistening scale. But most fearsome of all is a dragon's cunning—and the soul that allows it to bond with humans.

"Exotic and unique!"
—*Romantic Times BOOKreviews* on *Dragonborn*

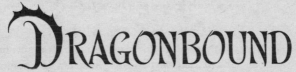

DRAGONBOUND

Sabina was the one girl of her generation chosen as Dragonmaid, friend and caregiver to the copper dragon of her nation's tyrant king. There she witnessed the greed, lust and rage such a beast could incite—and acquired her own very dark secret.

Handsome of face and mighty of sword, Dag Racho ruled Ragona with an iron fist and the help of his wyrm. But the line between man and beast has blurred, and a woman has come for them. Revenge, salvation and three kingdoms hang in the balance—and the fate of two hearts.

ISBN 13: 978-0-8439-6047-1

Winner of American Title IV

Helen Scott Taylor

HE'S A BIKER WITH AN ATTITUDE

What woman wouldn't be attracted to Niall O'Connor's soft Irish brogue and dark good looks? But Rosenwyn Tremain must find her father, and she isn't going to let a sexy, stubborn Irishman and his motorcycle distract her. Rose's intuition tells her he's hiding something, a secret even the cards cannot divine. Her tarot deck always reads true, but how can one man represent both Justice and Betrayal?

SHE'S A WOMAN ON A MISSION

Magic. Niall's body tingles with it when he finds the woman snooping in his room. Rosenwyn might believe she's a no-nonsense accountant, but her essence whispers to him of ancient fairy magic that enslaves even as it seduces. Her heritage could endanger those he'd die to protect, but her powers and her passion, if properly awakened, might be the only thing that can save both their families, vanquish a fairy queen bent on revenge, and fulfill a prophecy that will bind their hearts together with . . .

THE MAGIC KNOT

ISBN 13: 978-0-505-52796-7

Natale Stenzel

Author of *Pandora's Box* and
The Druid Made Me Do It

Daphne Forbes always knew the world was an odd place. Unlike most CPAs, she grew up the daughter of a druid. Unlike her father, she eschewed the supernatural. But magic was coming to trip her up. In the form of an enchanted cornerstone, it was set to knock Daphne's socks off—or at least one of her shoes—and the rest of her clothes were soon to follow.

Magic filled Daphne, empowered her, shifted her shape and raged wild as a summer storm. Enter Tremayne. Whether the tormented newcomer was truly her guardian or something more sinister, one thing he wanted was clear. Daphne wanted him, too. She had spent her whole life with control but little power; this was just the opposite. She was suddenly between a magic stone and…someplace harder. And we're not (just) talking about Tremayne's abs.

BETWEEN a ROCK AND A Heart Place

ISBN 13: 978-0-505-52783-7

JENNIFER ASHLEY
JOY NASH
ROBIN T. POPP

A lone werewolf defies his entire pack and everything he's ever known to protect a demon woman from the "Wolf Hunt." ♠ A vengeful vampire thirsts to claim a "Blood Debt" from the two beings responsible for his eternal nightmare: the Old One who turned him—and the beautiful Sidhe muse who killed him. ♠ Haunted by her past and reeling from her sister's murder, one woman turns to a sexy spirit-walker on a ghostly cruise ship that takes them "Beyond the Mist." ♠ Together, three *USA Today* bestselling authors pool their vast talents and fantastic world-building to bring you...

IMMORTALS:
THE RECKONING

ISBN 13: 978-0-505-52768-4

☐ **YES!**

Sign me up for the Love Spell Book Club and send my FREE BOOKS! If I choose to stay in the club, I will pay only $8.50* each month, a savings of $6.48!

NAME: _____

ADDRESS: _____

TELEPHONE: _____

EMAIL: _____

☐ I want to pay by credit card.

☐ **VISA**   ☐ **MasterCard**   ☐ **DISCOVER**

ACCOUNT #: _____

EXPIRATION DATE: _____

SIGNATURE: _____

Mail this page along with $2.00 shipping and handling to:
Love Spell Book Club
PO Box 6640
Wayne, PA 19087
Or fax (must include credit card information) to:
610-995-9274
You can also sign up online at **www.dorchesterpub.com**.
*Plus $2.00 for shipping. Offer open to residents of the U.S. and Canada only.
Canadian residents please call 1-800-481-9191 for pricing information.
If under 18, a parent or guardian must sign. Terms, prices and conditions subject to change. Subscription subject to acceptance. Dorchester Publishing reserves the right to reject any order or cancel any subscription.